A Lingering Shadow
An Arabella Stewart
Historical Mystery
Book Two
D.S. Lang

Also by D.S. Lang

Arabella Stewart Historical Mysteries
A Precarious Homecoming
A Lingering Shadow
A Lethal Arrogance
A Baffling Absence
A Fatal Reunion
A Surreptitious Undertaking
A Treacherous Accusation
An Uncertain Ceremony
Arabella Stewart Historical Mysteries Boxed Set 1
Arabella Stewart Historical Mysteries-Books 5-8

Doro Banyon Historical Mysteries
The Catalogued Corpse

Watch for more at https://www.dslangbooks.com.

In loving memory of my mother, who taught me to love books long before I could read.

Prologue

Ohio—April 1920

Arabella Stewart gazed into the vanity's mahogany framed mirror. Her face, although still unlined, appeared pale and her brown eyes had dark circles beneath them. Were the smudges now permanent? In France, Bella had thought coming home would return her to normalcy. Now, after being back for several months, normal life seemed like a distant illusion. During her almost two-year absence, so much had changed. Yet, as she looked into the mirror, she could still see traces of the girl who had left home in January 1918 before sailing for France three months later.

Her attention moved to one of the silver frames on her vanity. A sixteen-year-old version of herself smiled back. So did the two young men standing on either side of her—her brother Matt and his best friend Jax. All of them looked so happy and so hopeful. In their youthful innocence, they had looked forward to wonderful futures.

A momentary smile touched her lips but faded as she looked at the next photo. All three of them were in that one, too, but they wore uniforms and the smiles didn't quite touch their eyes. In retrospect, Bella realized each of them had tried to keep up a good front during that one shared weekend in Paris.

In some ways, she was still keeping up a front. The past two years had stolen her parents and her brother. Would Ballantyne, her family's resort, be lost, too? She and her business partner, Mac MacLendon, were working hard to avoid that end, but they needed luck, as well as determination, to succeed in their quest.

Bella turned her attention away from the photos and from the past. Today, the first guests of the season would arrive. Both anticipation and excitement filled her. Everything was riding on a successful year—her family's legacy and her own future. If Ballantyne was lost, where would she go? What would she do? Bella couldn't even imagine answers.

She crossed the room and gazed through the window, which looked out over the front porch roof on the south side of the inn. If she glanced to the east, the drive to the cottages was visible, although the structures themselves were not. But she could see the lawn sweeping down to the wide creek, the dock, and the golf course. The tennis courts, now overgrown, were not clearly discernable. A sigh escaped her. Would they be able to re-open them this season? And what about the dock? Mac said it was safe for fishing, but the boats had been stored for almost three years. Since the wide creek emptied into a nearby river that ran north to Lake Erie, boating had been a popular pursuit prior to the Great War. Few guests had ventured farther than the river, but some had enjoyed traveling the few miles to the lake. Would that happen again? This season, she and Mac were focusing on the golf course. Perhaps next year, things would be back to normal.

After a deep breath, Bella took one last look at the photographs that had, for months, been in her travel bag. Only yesterday had she dug them out and placed the two, along with a photograph of her parents, on her vanity table. Looking at them evoked happy, but bittersweet, memories.

As much as they sometimes sustained her, Bella couldn't live on recollection. She had decided as much before returning home in December. Brief reminiscences, like a crackling fire on a winter day, brought warmth to heart and soul. Lengthy musings were more hazardous because, like quicksand, they could exert a dangerous pull that was hard to escape. The Great War cast a long, dark shadow over many lives—Bella's included.

With a last glance in the mirror, Bella put a smile on her face, and headed out of her suite.

While the past was very much with her, she had resolved to focus on the future.

Chapter One

Later that day, Bella was at work when a guest arrived. "Good afternoon, sir. I'm Arabella Stewart. Welcome to Ballantyne." Excitement grew as she said those words for the first time in over three years. "Good afternoon," the tall, trim man said as he approached the front desk.

When he didn't offer his name, Bella glanced at the reservation list. Two guests, both male, were expected to check in between noon and three o'clock, so she tried the first name on her notepad. "Are you Mr. Monticello?"

A scowl immediately formed on the man's narrow face. "Monticello? Is he here already?" His hostile reaction surprised Bella. For a moment, all she could do was look back at him. Finally, she gathered her wits and answered the question. "Not yet. He and three others have reserved a cottage for a long weekend. Do you know him?"

The man's nostrils flared with a sharp intake of breath. "I know him. I'm sure I know all four, and I'd rather not cross paths with any of them."

His tone and expression, as much as his words, telegraphed deep dislike. Uneasiness sapped some of her enthusiasm. This wasn't how Bella had hoped to begin the season. "We only have three cottages ready right now, and they are grouped together," she replied. Placating the man seemed wise. "We could get another one closer to the inn prepared in a couple of hours."

"I want to get settled as soon as possible and play a round this afternoon, so I'll take what is available." His displeasure remained obvious despite the concession.

Bella cleared her throat. The man still hadn't identified himself, but only one other name was listed as checking in during this time period. "Of course, Mr. Neece." When he didn't correct her, she hurried on. "I'll have someone help you get settled." Bella rang the bell on the counter and one of the Ironton twins, their newly hired helpers, emerged from the kitchen. "Dick, please see that Mr. Neece has everything he needs? He will be in cottage three." She handed their guest a key as she spoke.

"Yes, Miss Bella," the sixteen-year-old boy replied with a bright smile. He turned to Neece. "I can help with your bags and all, sir."

The guest merely nodded. "Fine. Let's get going." He turned on his heel and headed toward the door.

"Mr. Neece, should we expect you for dinner?" Bella called to his retreating back.

He glanced over his shoulder at her. "No, I'll be visiting my son after golf," he replied before continuing toward the door. Neece nearly ran into Mac, Bella's partner and honorary grandfather.

"Good day, sir," Mac said to the taller man. "Mr. Neece, isn't it? We have nay seen ye for a long time. Tis glad we be to have ye back at Ballantyne." He extended his hand.

Neece paused for a moment before engaging in a handshake. His expression didn't lighten as he said, "The past two years have been difficult for all of us. If you'll excuse me, I want to get situated, so I can play this afternoon."

"Of course," Mac said as he stepped aside and let their guest pass.

"You know that man?" Bella asked.

"Aye," Mac replied as he crossed to stand in front of the counter. "He used to come with seven friends several times a year. The eight of them usually arrived on a Wednesday or Thursday for a long weekend."

"Was a Mr. Monticello one of his group?" Bella inquired.

Mac's gray gaze narrowed. "That he was. What makes ye ask, lass?"

Briefly, Bella reviewed her exchange with Neece. "He didn't seem very happy," she said in summary.

"Mr. Neece was always reserved, but ye be right that he seems rather brusque now. I don't recall him being like that." A frown creased the older man's weathered features.

Bella chewed on her lower lip. "I don't want any of our first guests of the season to be displeased. We need to get off to a good start."

Mac's expression relaxed as he offered a smile. Despite his lined face and silver hair, his eyes glittered with youthful optimism. "Ah, lass, try not to worry so much." He patted her hand.

"Neece may have had a falling out with his friends, but that dinna reflect on Ballantyne. Remember, ye Grandfather Stew and I took a very big chance when we originally built the resort. We took more risks along the way and, with good planning and hard work, they paid off. Ye and I have already agreed to do what's necessary to save Ballantyne. We may have some challenges as we go, but we can handle them."

Despite lingering anxiety, Bella smiled in return. "I'm sure you're right. It's just that so much is riding on us having a good season. Every time I go into Moreley, people mention hoping that if Ballantyne gets back to normal, the town will, too."

"It will take time," he advised, "and the path may nay be smooth, but I think both will happen, eventually."

Eventually could mean a few months, a few years, or longer. Mac, nearing seventy, shouldn't have to rebuild what he and her grandfather had—more than three decades earlier—struggled to start and maintain, but he was willing and so was she. "You're right, Mac." She certainly hoped so. "Minnie has lunch ready, so you should eat something."

"Aye, or she'll be chastising me for being late." Mac's silver-gray eyes again sparkled with mirth.

"She is a curmudgeon, but she's an excellent cook and housekeeper. I hoped she would be friendlier once she got settled," Bella admitted. "It's been almost a month, and she's as dour as ever. I can certainly understand why her sister- and brother-in-law couldn't let her work in their mercantile. I wouldn't put her at our front desk, either."

"I agree. Working with the public tis nay her strength, but she be an excellent cook and housekeeper," he said before disappearing into the kitchen.

Bella couldn't argue with his observation in any way. Minnie Mars had worked hard to help them prepare for the inn's reopening. Not only that, she was a marvel in the kitchen. If only she was more congenial.

***

After that, Bella focused on answering the phone. When the sound of a car pulling up outside drew her from her tasks, she glanced at the clock. Mr. Monticello must be arriving. With luck, Neece was on the golf course and far from the inn and cottages.

Moments later, the door swept open and a short, plump man of about fifty stepped into the foyer. "Good afternoon," Bella said immediately. "Welcome to Ballantyne."

He doffed his bowler to reveal a bald head. "Good afternoon," he replied, heading to the front desk. A wide smile brightened his round face. "I'm Malcolm Monticello. My friends and I have rented one of your cottages for the next few days." His cheerfulness was at odds with Neece's severe attitude. Bella wondered if he would become equally stern if he knew the other man was on the premises. Not that she planned to blurt out the information before offering a warm welcome.

As Bella started to reply, her attention was drawn to footsteps descending the staircase. A pair of women's shoes came into view. Minnie had been upstairs cleaning. Did she have to come down right now? Her surly attitude wasn't helpful, especially when a guest had just arrived. Bella found her own smile faltering, but when Minnie retreated, she breathed a sigh of relief and looked back at the well-dressed man in front of her. "We put you in cottage four. It's the last one on the right side of the drive, and it has a lovely view of the course. I think you will enjoy it." Briefly, she wondered about mentioning Mr. Neece, but thought better of it as she realized she hadn't introduced herself. "I'm Arabella Stewart. We spoke on the phone last week."

"Lovely to meet you in person, Miss Stewart. I'm sure you don't remember me, but I recall you and your brother and parents, of course." His good humor faded. "I was so sorry to hear about you losing them."

"Thank you," Bella replied. Over the past few months, she had heard many condolences and, while she appreciated the kindness, each one was a reminder of loss and grief. With effort, she kept her own smile in place. "We're glad you and your friends have decided to return to Ballantyne."

"We haven't had the opportunity to get back here since before the war, but your cottages are lovely," he replied. "I am looking forward to a peaceful weekend with friends and golf. I've had a tedious—although short—week, so I'm hoping I can get settled soon. One friend, a Mr. Abbott, will be here later this evening. Until then, I'll enjoy some quiet time. After I change, I may walk the course, if that's all right."

"Certainly." Anxiety bubbled up. What if he and Neece crossed paths? Her mind scrambled to assess the logistics. Neece should already be playing the inward nine, so if Monticello started walking the outward one, the two men should not see one another. Bella cleared her throat. "If you start your walk on the first hole, you should have the front nine all to yourself."

"An excellent idea," Monticello said. His smile returned.

Relief spread through Bella. The pair wouldn't meet yet, which would give her a chance to ask Mac more about the men and about whether or not to reveal Neece's presence to Monticello and his group. Perhaps, Mr. Neece was the only one holding a grudge and the other men might not be upset.

"We can provide dinner for you, sir."

He smiled again. "Not necessary, my dear. My wife packed a picnic basket, so I'll partake of that."

"As you wish, Mr. Monticello. I'll get someone to show you to the cottage and help you get settled." She rang the bell, and Dale Ironton emerged from the kitchen where Bella had left him to scrub the floor. "Would you be kind enough to take Mr. Monticello to cottage four and help him with his bags?"

"Yes, miss," the boy readily agreed.

Bella looked back at their guest. "The cottage doesn't have a phone, but I can send someone to check on you later."

"I'll be fine. No need to check on me. I can walk back here if I require something."

She nodded. "We serve breakfast in the dining room. If you and your friend plan to play early, I can have it ready at seven o'clock."

"That sounds perfect."

"Here is your key," she said and handed it to the man. "Dale will help you, sir."

Monticello nodded to Bella and turned to the boy. "I'm grateful, son." He glanced back at her. "And to you, too. My friend and I will see you in the morning for breakfast. The others should arrive around noon, so no need to worry about them."

"Wonderful. I'll look forward to seeing you tomorrow morning, and please let us know if we can do anything to make your stay more comfortable."

Monticello turned away. As Bella watched him go, she smiled again. He seemed like such a nice man, much kinder than Mr. Neece. If his friends were the same, they would make wonderful guests. And hopefully, they'd be regular visitors again.

The sound of Monticello's car had barely faded away when Bella once again heard footsteps on the stairs. This time, Minnie came all the way down. One look at the older woman's severe expression was enough to make Bella's smile wane. If anything, Minnie looked more unpleasant than usual. "Why is that man here?" Minnie asked in a harsh tone.

Bella's gaze narrowed in surprise. "He's a guest. Mr. Monticello and his friends are renting a cottage for the weekend."

"Where are the friends?" Again, the housekeeper-cook's tone was harsh. Combined with her hard expression and rigid stance, she offered a formidable presence. Although Bella was not petite, Minnie had at least three inches and twenty pounds on her. The woman's size and strength didn't intimidate Bella, but what about their guests? Would any be put off by a woman of hefty stature and surly manner? Again, Bella knew she had to deal with the housekeeper-cook more effectively. And keep her away from the front desk.

"Mr. Abbott will be here this evening after six o'clock. The others won't come until tomorrow." Bella took a deep breath to calm herself. Why did Minnie have to be so disagreeable? She needed to speak with Mac about how to better handle the woman. After all, Bella was her boss. Not vice-versa.

Minnie's severe features took on a contemplative look. "Is he coming back here for dinner?" Evidently, the woman hadn't eavesdropped. "No. He said his wife fixed a basket for him.

He'd just like to be alone and enjoy the solitude until his friend arrives."

"At least he won't cause no more work," Minnie muttered.

Bella felt her patience slipping away until the last shred was gone. "He's a guest, and I expect you to treat him with courtesy and respect." Her own voice held an unusual firmness, but Bella wanted to get her point across. Perhaps, she'd been too tolerant with the older woman.

Minnie glared at Bella. "You don't really know him."

Bella stared at the housekeeper in consternation. What was wrong with the woman? "No, I don't, but our guests deserve to be treated with proper consideration. He and his friends will join us for meals over the weekend. You may see him then, so I expect you'll be genial and accommodating. Ballantyne has always been known for its hospitality, and we plan to keep it that way." "I know how to treat people like him," Minnie said, her voice still hard and harsh.

The cryptic reply was typical of the woman, but she was being downright nasty now. Why?

She had barely caught a glimpse of Mr. Monticello. Would she be the same with all their guests? Some people wrongly assumed that visitors to the resort were wealthy, demanding, and pretentious, but that was not the case. For many years, middle-class families had enjoyed trips to Ballantyne. The golf course, tennis courts, boat dock, and walking paths had been popular pursuits. Many also enjoyed spending Christmas or Easter at the inn. Besides, whether guests were rich or middle class, they deserved to be treated well. Minnie needed to understand that.

Bella had no yardstick to gauge the housekeeper-cook's reaction because Monticello was the first visitor that Minnie had seen. She needed to stay in the background away from people, Bella thought. Rudeness would not be tolerated from any employee. "Mac and I expect you to adhere to our standards with our guests. If you cannot do that, we will have to look elsewhere for a cook-housekeeper. Do you understand?"

For several moments, the older woman simply looked at Bella. Finally, she gave a single nod of her gray head. "I understand," she replied, turning toward the kitchen, and disappearing inside it.

Relief filled Bella as she watched the woman retreat. Minnie's response to Monticello seemed strange but, perhaps she was just quick to judge, along with being prickly. As long as the woman acted appropriately toward guests and co-workers, they should get along well enough.

***

Once Minnie was gone, Bella returned to her paperwork. About an hour after Monticello's arrival, she became aware of rain splashing against the windows. Dark clouds had rolled in and a drizzle had come with them. In a short time, the light drizzle turned to steady rain. Not many players were on the course, but some would finish their rounds. With luck, conditions would improve by the next day when more guests were expected. Complications like bad weather were not a good way to get back on track, she thought with anxiety.

Minnie's voice interrupted her reverie. "I have supper in the oven. The roast will be ready in a couple of hours. Now, I'll get on home." The older woman stopped a few feet from the counter. As usual, her features were set in a seemingly perpetual frown.

Evidently, their discussion hadn't changed her general attitude. Bella still hoped it would alter Minnie's way of handling guests. Otherwise, she would have to pursue her threat of hiring someone else, which would add another complication. "One of the twins could drive you. I hate for you to walk in the heavy rain. You'll be soaked before you get to the main road." The boys were both good drivers, and Bella didn't mind letting them borrow the Model-T. Besides, she knew they considered getting behind the steering wheel to be a treat.

The other woman shrugged. "I have my sister- and brother-in-law's Packard. Took the side way in, so it's closer to the cottages than the inn."

Alarm flickered through Bella. "You came across the old wooden bridge on the east side of the property?"

Minnie nodded.

"It needs repair work, so Mac and my dad roped it off more than two years ago."

"No ropes now," the other woman said. "If you excuse me, I'll be on my way."

"Don't use it going home. Like I said, it's not safe."

Minnie gave a brief nod before she turned and disappeared into the kitchen.

***

The downpour became a drizzle before going back to steady rain, so players left the course to take refuge in the large foyer, or they headed straight to their automobiles. Shortly after Minnie left, Dale lit a fire in the grate while his twin dutifully lit the lamps. With the early onset of darkness, the big room became a haven of cozy comfort. Bella served coffee and cookies to their guests. Despite the inclement weather, the small group was cheerful. As she observed them, relief filled Bella and happy memories returned.

How many days had she come home from school to find golfers gathered around the massive stone fireplace as they took shelter from rain? More than she could count. On those occasions, her mother had always asked their then-housekeeper, Julia, to serve refreshments. That was if Julia didn't take it upon herself to do so. What a charming, cheerful woman she had been. Her wedding had been both a joyous and a sad event. Although she hadn't moved far, Julia was occupied with her new home. Even so, she had worked at Ballantyne when Bella was in France. Now, the former housekeeper was with child and unable to help. Bella certainly missed her.

At least Minnie Mars had left before many golfers gathered at the inn. Bella worried about how to handle the new cook-housekeeper. Somehow, she needed to exert her authority without being too bossy. Mac was running the golf part of the resort while Bella had taken charge of the inn and cottages. Looking back, she realized that her mother had made a challenging task look very easy. Surely, not every employee had been as pleasant and pleasing as Julia. How had her mother dealt with difficult workers? Bella wished she knew.

After a time, the guests began to leave until the foyer was empty. The twins returned as the last of the players departed. They appeared to be damp around the edges, so Bella suggested they sit by the still-blazing fire. "There are cookies left, and I'll fix hot cocoa. You two look like you could use something to warm you up."

They nodded as they took seats near the fireplace. Both were of medium height and medium build with light brown hair and hazel eyes, mirror images of each other. Telling the pair apart had taken Bella more than a week. Even now, she had to look twice to be sure which one was which. Within minutes, she had the hot drinks and cookies for them. "Here you go."

"Thank you," they chorused.

"Did Mr. Monticello seem happy with the cottage?" Bella asked as she put a tray with treats on the table in front of the fireplace.

"Yep, he said he and his friends had stayed in that one back before the war," Dale replied. "He must have a lot of money," Dick observed.

"He must be rich," his twin asserted. "He gave me a big tip. His wallet was full of bills, and he has a gold watch."

His brother frowned. "I woulda helped if I had knowed. Maybe you should split the tip with me. Mr. Neece didn't give me no money."

"No, Dick. You didn't do nothing. You don't deserve none of my tip."

"You know I'm saving for a new bike. My old one is a wreck. I can't even keep up with you when we go to town and back. You get any place five or ten minutes ahead of me because mine is in such terrible shape." Dick took a long drink of cocoa. "C'mon, Dale. We're brothers, twins, so we should share."

Dale shook his head. "Nope. I earned it, so I keep it."

"Well, I'll go see if he needs anything," Dick said. "I'd like a tip, too."

The exchange disturbed Bella, who wasn't sure whether or not to intercede. On occasion, the boys had uttered similar sentiments. They were clearly jealous of those with more, and that was most people. Since the pair had been orphaned a year earlier, they had fended for themselves. Even before then, the Ironton family had struggled to survive on their small farm. Bella understood their neediness, but she didn't want them to become bitter. "Dick," she put in, "Mr. Monticello doesn't want to be bothered. He's tired, and he wants to enjoy some quiet time until his friend gets here, which should be soon. If he walked the course, as he planned, he may be enjoying a hot bath or taking a nap."

The boy's features grew solemn. "I won't bother him none. I'll just see if I can help. Maybe he'll want a snack or something."

"His wife sent a picnic basket with him. He said that would be sufficient," Bella said, her tone slightly sterner.

An expression akin to belligerence crossed his boyish face. "When is his friend coming?"

"Any time now," Bella replied, "but mind my words. I don't want you bothering him. Do you understand me?"

A moment passed before Dick spoke again. "Yes, ma'am." Although his words indicated agreement, his rebellious expression did not.

It wasn't until after the pair left that Bella realized she didn't know if he'd meant *yes* to not bothering Monticello or *yes* that he understood. Obviously, she wasn't adept at dealing with young boys, a thought that troubled her. They were relying heavily on the twins, as well as Carl and Curt Molitor, their greenskeeper and his younger brother. Carl was more than willing to shoulder additional chores and do it with good cheer, but any task that required reading, writing, or ciphering was hard for him. Although Curt was diligent and kind, he was battling demons both from the Great War and from an incident in December. At times, he still retreated into himself and, on occasion, he went off for an entire day. Curt had assured Bella that wouldn't happen once the season started, and she wanted to believe him.

A lump of sorrow rose in Bella's throat. Because Curt Molitor had held her brother as he lay dying on a French battlefield, the former sergeant would always have a place at Ballantyne. Bella would make sure of that. As for the twins and Minnie, she needed to watch all three and get some pointers from Mac about handling employees more adeptly.

***

About an hour after the last golfers of the day left, a Ford touring car roared up to the inn.

Dick, who was putting fresh wood in the fireplace, immediately rose and went to the front door.

"What a beauty," he cried, his attention on the vehicle.

From her post at the desk, Bella laughed. The boy's reaction was typical for one of his age. Of course, automobiles were still new enough to fascinate many folks. She glanced out the window and better understood the response. The large car was impressive. "That should be Mr. Abbott, Dick. He will join Mr. Monticello. Since your brother just gathered some supplies to take to cottage three for Mr. Neece, he can help Mr. Abbott with his valise and golf clubs. After you finish with the fireplace, will you run over and see if Mac needs anything? I thought he would close the shop before now, but he may require help with something."

The boy's face fell in obvious disappointment. For a moment, Bella thought he would object.

Instead, he nodded and said, "Yes, miss."

Even so, Bella noted he was in no hurry as he tinkered with the wood. When the front door opened, her attention moved from Dick to the tall, muscular man entering the lobby. He doffed his flat driving cap as he strode across the front hall. His almost black hair gleamed in the light, and his equally black mustache did as well. A dapper gentleman, Bella thought, as he nodded to her. "Good evening. I'm Charles Abbott. I believe my friend Malcolm Monticello arrived earlier in the day. We've engaged one of your charming cottages for a long weekend."

Bella smiled in return. "Yes, Mr. Monticello arrived several hours ago. He was tired, but planned to walk the course before taking a nap. I haven't seen him since then.

Rain set in a bit ago, so he may have gone straight back to the cottage. His wife provided a picnic for him.

However, we can offer you dinner. It should be ready shortly."

"No, thank you," Abbott replied with a smile, "my wife did the same. Now, if you can let me know which cottage, I'll get settled myself."

Since Dick was hovering near the front desk, Bella relented. Besides, it was only fair that both twins had the chance to earn a tip. "Dick can show you the way to the cottage and carry your bags in."

"Yes, sir," the boy readily agreed.

Abbott nodded. "Thank you, son. My things are in my car parked in the side lot."

"Mr. Monticello has a key, but I'll also give one to you," Bella said. "I imagine he's been back in the cottage for a while."

The man inclined his head. "I'm sure Malcolm went out for a walk. Only torrential rain would keep him from taking his daily constitutional."

"If he walked, he probably got damp, but a fire was laid in the cottage's small sitting room earlier today. He may be there, cozy and comfortable," Bella observed.

"Sounds wonderful to me," the man said. "The long drive in a steady downpour was a bit frazzling. It finally changed to drizzle about a half-hour from here."

"We had the same weather, but it should be pleasant tomorrow." Bella certainly hoped the sun would appear. "If you need anything else, please let me know."

"I'm sure we'll be fine. We've always enjoyed our visits here. I have every confidence that this trip will be no different."

After Abbott and Dick headed to the parking area, Bella returned to her desk with the goal of completing paperwork before dinner. About ten minutes later, Dick returned.

"He must be rich like Mr. Monticello," the boy observed in awe. "He gave me a big tip like Dale got, and I only had to put his bags inside the front door. He said he'd carry them to his room."

The two men had to seem rich to boys like Dick and Dale. Although the townspeople were kind, most of them were also struggling in the war's aftermath and pandemic. Business had plummeted when the Spanish flu hit the area hard. In the aftermath, a post-war downturn caused recession throughout the country. When most areas started to rebound, Moreley had experienced a crime wave that culminated in a murder only the day after Bella's arrival home. A sigh escaped her at the memory. The killing had been solved in short order, which boded well for the future.

Now, nothing stood in the way of rebuilding both town and resort.

Unfortunately, at this point, few locals could offer two orphaned twins much more than the occasional meal or odd job. Only the Downings, who owned the mercantile, had provided steady, albeit part-time, work and the most basic of housing—the attic of their store. Once again, Bella was glad she and Mac could proffer more. Since starting at Ballantyne, the twins had been ensconced in the suite once occupied by Julia—a much more pleasant living situation than a drafty, dusty attic. Bella just wished their envy didn't show quite so often or so much. "I believe both Mr. Abbott and Mr. Monticello are successful businessmen," she observed. "They're lucky," he said in an odd tone.

Her gaze narrowed on him. Jealousy did no good for anyone, so she said, "I'm sure they work very hard for their money."

A moment of silence passed. "Sometimes, hard work don't help," he muttered. "I'll tend to the fire now."

Before he got away, Bella spoke again. "I know you and your brother worked very hard to save your family farm. I'm sorry you lost your parents and your home."

The boy's eyes glistened before he turned away. "We're lucky you and Mac hired us and gave us a place to live. I don't know why Curt and Carl went back to the cabin when the suite is much nicer."

The Ballantyne greenskeeper and his brother had spent the winter living in the inn. "They get up before dawn to take care of the golf course. If we reopen the tennis courts, they'll care for them, too. Because they're early risers, they also go to bed long before the kitchen quiets down." Bella hoped they'd have enough guests for activity to take place after the evening meal. "The cabin is isolated and peaceful, so they like that."

He glanced back at her. "Good. Now, I'll see if Mac needs anything."

Bella watched him go with mixed feelings. The twins' expressions of envy troubled her, but perhaps such feelings were to be expected. The boys had worked hard to save the family farm. Despite their diligence, the bank had taken it in the end, which left the pair homeless. Again, she worried about their attitudes. She'd ask Mac for advice because he'd had more experience with young boys than she had. With that thought in mind, she headed to the kitchen.

Bella checked the roast, prepared the rest of the meal, and set the table. The twins and Mac should be ready to eat within the hour. Carl and Curt had likely returned to their cabin once the rain began and would, as was their custom, fix dinner themselves. Before she accomplished her tasks, she heard shouting in the foyer. Immediately, Bella dashed out to see what was wrong.

A frantic Abbott was yelling, "Help! I need help right now! Malcolm is dead!"

Chapter Two

Bella rushed to the front desk where Abbott, his face pale and eyes wide, stood gasping for breath. "What?" Surely, she had misunderstood him. He couldn't have just said his friend was dead. Monticello had been very much alive only a few hours earlier. "Malcolm is dead. I found him on the floor in the cottage parlor."

"Are you sure? Maybe he's just unconscious." Bella's mind reeled as she tried to grapple with his assertion. Perhaps, the man had suffered a heart attack.

Abbott's expression hardened. "He isn't unconscious. He's been murdered, and you need to call for help right now."

Shock held her in place for a suspended moment. "Murdered. That's not possible," she murmured. In late December, the area's first-ever murder had taken place on a farm outside town. A second one in such a short time seemed unlikely.

"It is possible. I fought in the Spanish-American War, Miss Stewart, and I know the difference between a natural death and a violent one, especially when the murder weapon is by his body."

Abbott's voice trembled as he spoke. Whether it was from rage or shock, Bella didn't know. All she knew for sure was that they had to check on Mr. Monticello. "I'll call Doc Smedlay and then go back to the cottage with you. He can meet us there." As Bella picked up the telephone's earpiece, Abbott spoke again.

"It's too late for a doctor, but we need a constable here right away. I want Malcolm's killer caught as soon as possible."

Slowly, Bella absorbed the information. "Please sit down, Mr. Abbott. I'll contact our town physician and the constable right away."

"I told you. Malcolm is beyond help." His voice was strained and harsh, and his gaze was filled with emotion.

Mac, who was just coming in, looked from Abbott to Bella. "What be wrong, lass?"

Abbott answered quickly. "My friend has been murdered, and you need to send for the constable immediately."

Mac froze in place. When he spoke, his voice was soft with reassurance, "Lass, call Jax and Doc."

The tall man's nostrils flared with a sharp intake of breath. "Malcolm doesn't need a physician," he practically shouted.

"Yes, but Dr. Smedlay also serves as the coroner," Bella replied, picking up the phone. Once she had reached the operator and explained the situation, Bella turned back to the guest. "They'll be here as soon as possible."

"I'll wait at the cottage," Abbott said before dashing out the front door.

Bella turned to Mac and briefly repeated what Abbott had told her. "I think we should go to the cottage, too."

"Aye, we should be with him," Mac, his ruddy face now ashen, agreed.

***

When they arrived at the cottage, Bella and Mac went inside to find Abbott in the parlor with his friend's body. Abbott's face was a study in anguish as he kneeled at Monticello's side.

Fresh shock hit Bella as she took in the scene. Blood matted the sparse hair on one side of the dead man's head while a dark bruise was visible on his cheek. Laying only a few feet away was a broken club, a mashie. The heavy iron head, attached to the lower half of the wooden shaft, bore crimson smears. Bile rose in Bella's throat, and she wondered if she'd always think of this scene when looking at a middle iron. She stepped back. When she glanced at Mac, she saw his silver eyes were wide with shock. He looked as dazed as she felt.

"Let's wait on the porch," the old pro suggested after several moments of silence had passed.

"Ye, too, Mr. Abbott. We can do nay more for ye friend here."

Their guest slowly nodded and rose to his feet. The trio—shaken and silent—went outside. Mac took a seat in one chair and urged Abbott to do the same. The other man shook the idea off and paced the length of the porch repeatedly.

Since she felt weak at the knees after noting Monticello's wounds, Bella sat down. The wait for Jax and Doc seemed interminable, but when she checked the watch pinned to her blouse, she saw that less than fifteen minutes had elapsed between the time Abbott had rushed back into the inn and when Jackson Hastings pulled his Chevrolet Chummy to a stop in front of the cottage. The young constable quickly climbed out and mounted the porch stairs two at a time. Doc Smedlay, a robust man in his late fifties, followed at a slower pace.

Jax nodded to Bella before going to Mac and Abbott. The old pro immediately introduced their guest to the newcomers, while Bella looked on. Despite her lingering shock, she studied the constable. Her brother's best friend.

Clad in his uniform, Jax looked every inch the lawman. The image remained hard for Bella to absorb, almost as hard to absorb as the changes in him. Not exterior changes as much as interior ones. He was still tall, lean, blonde, green-eyed, and handsome. New lines fanned out from tired eyes that had seen too much, but it was his demeanor that was often different.

When she had arrived home in December, Bella had helped him investigate another murder case. Although Jax had objected to her assistance at first, they had managed camaraderie while working together. However, once the case was solved, Jax stayed away from the resort, which had once been a second home to him. Bella understood why. War wounds had put an end to Jax's dreams of being a golf professional, and he'd admitted that being at Ballantyne made accepting the fact difficult.

Would she ever stop thinking of him as tied to Ballantyne? For years and years, he'd spent every spare hour at the resort. Jax had first come as her brother's friend. Soon, he'd become her friend. Eventually, he'd been her girlhood crush and, later, her occasional escort. For a time, it seemed like the future held more for them. Then, war had interceded and their relationship had changed along with almost everything else in her life. Bella fought back the bittersweet memories rising to the surface and focused on the matter at hand.

As Jax moved toward the cottage door, he swept off his constable's cap to reveal blonde waves that appeared unrulier than ever. "Doc and I will take a look." He started forward but stopped when Abbott spoke.

"Jackson Hastings. They call you Jax."

Confusion filled Bella. Why did that matter? Only a bit earlier, Abbott had been eager for the constable to arrive. Now, he cared about what people called Jax?

Jax looked as puzzled as she felt. "Yes, people usually call me Jax," he replied in a baffled tone.

The older man's gaze narrowed on him. "I played in the four-ball one year that you and your friend Matt won."

Bella saw a dark flush rise in Jax's lean cheeks. His reaction to hearing her brother's name was always the same—uneasiness and silence. That puzzled her. He and Matt had been best friends for almost twenty years, but Jax never spoke about her brother now. Although grief affected people differently, his response always seemed odd and off-key.

In the lengthening silence, awkwardness grew. Finally, Mac spoke. "Jax and Matt won several times before they went to France. Now, Jax has taken his father's old job as constable." Abbott's gaze went from Jax to Mac and back. "I see." His tone and expression clearly indicated disbelief and displeasure, but he said nothing more.

Jax's jaw tightening was his only outward reaction. "I'd like to look at the scene with

Doc. Mr. Forrester should be here soon."

"Our local mortician," Bella supplied for Abbott.

Abbott nodded at Bella before turning to Jax. "I'll go in with you."

"I'd rather you stay here, sir. I don't want the area disturbed any more than it already is," Jax said before disappearing into the cottage.

Abbott's expression turned mutinous, but he said nothing more as Jax strode into the cottage with the physician close behind him.

***

About fifteen minutes later, George Forrester arrived at the cottage. Tall and rangy, he exuded a calm and subdued manner that served him well in his chosen profession. "Good evening," he said to Mac and Bella. "I assume Jackson and Doc are inside."

"Aye," Mac replied, "and the deceased's friend. He went back inside, although Jax asked him to stay out here."

"I'll go in then," Forrester said.

Wanting to hear what was said, Bella moved to the open front door and listened. "How long ago did you find him, Mr. Abbott?" Jax asked.

"It's been about thirty minutes. He was lying here when I came in." The man's voice was still rough and raspy, as if he were choking back tears.

"He's been gone longer than that," Jax said. "Don't you think so, gentlemen?"

Bella realized he must be addressing Smedlay and Forrester since both said *yes* almost simultaneously.

When Abbott spoke again, anger had replaced sorrow. "Of course, he was. I certainly didn't kill him. He was one of my best friends."

Jax's reply wasn't audible, but Bella knew he must be trying to placate Abbott. She certainly hoped so, because the man had been honest in his assertion about only arriving a half-hour earlier.

The murmuring continued, and after a few minutes, a scowling Abbott emerged. "Your so-called constable insists I stay away from the crime scene. I do not wish to spend the night in this cottage, and he told me I cannot go home, either. I hope you have a room for me," he stated. His displeasure was as clear in his voice as it was on his face.

Bella immediately replied, "Of course."

Mac agreed. "We would be more than happy to have ye spend the night in the inn at no cost to you, sir."

Abbott's expression didn't lighten, but he gave a terse nod. "The constable says I can go there now."

"I'll run ahead and see about a room," Bella said. "I can also fix dinner for you."

Abbott grunted. "After this, I'm hardly hungry. Since I'm not needed here, I'll wait for you at the inn." He immediately went to his automobile, got in, and drove down the lane leading back to the inn.

Bella turned to Mac, who said, "Go ahead. Jax can come to the inn when he's finished here. Since I'm guessing he also missed his dinner, why don't ye see what ye can salvage? We can all have a bite later, and I'll get Mr. Abbott's bags before I come to the inn myself."

With a sigh, Bella nodded. "I won't reheat the roast, but I could make sandwiches. They'll be ready whenever you come in."

"Good idea, lass."

With that, Bella hurried to the inn. Abbott had roared off in his roadster without a thought for her, so he was waiting on the porch when she walked up. Of course, she could hardly blame him. After all, he had just found the dead body of his friend. That had to be a horrible shock to him, because it certainly was to her. The image of Mr. Monticello with the broken mashie next to his wounded head refused to ebb. Why would someone attack him? Who would attack him? The questions reverberated in her mind.

Bella forced her thoughts away from the ugly images and scrambled to consider which room would be best for Abbott. All of them were ready, but some were smaller than others. Due to his shock and anger, she wanted to provide a pleasant space since the man deserved peace and comfort.

By the time she and their guest were inside the lobby, Bella had made up her mind. One of the inn's second floor suites would give him privacy and luxury. Neither would lessen the horror of finding his friend's dead body, of course. Nothing could accomplish that.

She hurried to the front desk and grabbed a key. "Our best suite is ready. It's comfortable and secluded." After a moment's hesitation, she went on, "It's just up the stairs and all the way to the back. Neither of our helpers seems to be here now. Mac will bring your bags with him, and we'll get them to you right away."

"That's not a big concern at the moment," he barked as his gaze narrowed on her. "Where are those helpers of yours? The one who took my bags into the cottage disappeared immediately. He said he has a twin brother. Where is he? Is anyone talking to them?"

The accusation in his voice made Bella cringe, and uneasiness filled her. "No one has looked for them, sir. Jax...er, the constable, can speak with them tonight." Bella bit her tongue. Abbott had already indicated his doubt about Jax's ability to solve the case. She surely didn't need to add to his skepticism by not using Jax's title. *So-called constable* was hardly a sign of respect.

"Just show me to my room. I'd like to be alone." His tone was disgusted and dismissive.

Since she could think of nothing to say, Bella led the man to the suite. After telling him to ring if he needed anything, she went back to the main floor. Abbott's question about the twins was troubling because they should be getting ready for dinner, as they had every evening since their arrival at Ballantyne. The two growing boys never needed to be called; they were always early...except tonight. Dinner was already more than an hour late, and neither one was around. Bella's thoughts went back to the twins' interest in Monticello's money and watch, and she tried—but failed—to remember if the timepiece and chain had still been on him.

A long sigh escaped her. She had begun the day feeling excitement and anticipation. Now, fear and worry replaced those emotions. Bella headed to the kitchen. While she waited for Mac, and hopefully the twins, Bella prepared sandwiches and made coffee. She also got out the pound cake Minnie had made earlier in the day. After she finished the preparations, Bella thought about the murder again.

Who had killed Monticello and why? Her mind immediately went to who had motive, means, and opportunity. As a child, she had been fascinated by her maternal grandfather's stories about his cases. A retired lawman, George Moore had often told tales of crimes that he and his men had solved. Bella, Matt, and Jax had spent many a winter evening listening raptly to him. When Bella was recuperating from rheumatic fever, her grandfather had not only regaled her with reminiscences, the two of them had put together albums with newspaper clippings and notes with more details. He had said she had a flair for investigations, and so had Senior Constable Richard Jenkins, who had also helped Jax with the murder case last December. Even Jax had admitted that Bella had been instrumental in helping to catch the killer.

Ernest Neece's reaction when he learned Monticello was also a guest entered her mind. So did Dick's and Dale's focus on the man being rich. And there was Minnie Mars' odd reaction. What about the day's golfers, but why would one of them murder Monticello? Had a stranger slipped in and killed him?

Bella's reverie was interrupted when Jax and Mac walked into the kitchen. Both men looked weary, so Bella quickly said, "Sit down. I made sandwiches, and there's pound cake and coffee." Mac immediately did as she suggested, but Jax hesitated. Finally, he replied, "I need to ask the two of you a few questions. Then, I'll be on my way."

"Nonsense, lad. Ye said ye hadn't eaten," Mac put in. "Ye might as well join us. Besides, looks like ye could use a good meal."

Bella studied Jax. He'd lost weight in France and gained none back. "There's plenty of food." For a moment, Bella thought he'd refuse again. Instead, he nodded.

"All right," Jax replied as he finally joined Mac at the table. "I won't talk to Doc and

Forrester until tomorrow. Tonight, they wanted to get back to town and deal with Monticello." Another lump formed in Bella's throat. "That poor man." She hurriedly put the tray of sandwiches on the table before fetching coffee and cake. Once she sat down, she glanced from Mac to Jax. "Have you seen the twins?"

"No, aren't they back here in their rooms?" Mac replied.

Bella shook her head. "No, I haven't seen either of them since about four-thirty, but I thought they'd be here to eat." She glanced at the table where she had laid out enough place settings for the boys.

Jax's brow furrowed. "Is it common for them to not eat dinner with you?"

Apprehension gripped Bella. After her earlier exchange with the twins, she was concerned about their attitudes. "It's possible they went to town." But neither had mentioned being away this evening.

"Do they go often?" Jax asked, his gaze narrowing on her.

The additional question and his scrutiny further annoyed Bella. Why was Jax so suspicious?

The twins were still young, barely sixteen. He certainly didn't see them as suspects, did he? "Occasionally." She felt Mac's steady gaze on her and shifted restlessly. "They got substantial tips from Mr. Abbott and Mr. Monticello, so they may have gone to the café for supper." "I'll look into that," Jax replied. He took one sandwich from the tray and began to eat.

Bella wanted to know more, but wondered if Jax would answer any questions. In December, he had wanted to keep her out of the case, citing worry for her safety. Richard Jenkins' intervention had mollified Jax, and he had thanked her for helping in the end. Now, a murder had taken place at Ballantyne, and she wanted to help solve it as soon as possible. "I'm sure you will," she observed. "I know my Grandfather Moore always said getting the important details was crucial to solving any case. How do you plan to proceed?" The query should be a benign inroad, but she held her breath as she waited for a reply.

Chapter Three

Jax laid down his sandwich, and for a long moment, stared at her. "It's a bit early to have a detailed plan since I've only just started to gather information." Even as he replied in an even tone, dismay gripped Jax. He remembered her grandfather's tales about police work and her fascination when she had been sick with rheumatic fever. He and Matt had laughed at her desire to become a detective. How ludicrous, they had both said. Once she was well, her interest had disappeared almost as quickly as it had arisen, but Bella had cited it during his last—his only, until now—murder case. Her current enthusiasm did little to quell his concern. He couldn't deny she had been helpful in the Schwarz case. However, she had ignored a directive and put herself in danger. That moment, when she had been a viable target for the killer, still haunted his dreams. Or more accurately, his nightmares. Jax realized the tension filling him must be obvious to Mac when the older man spoke again.

"It's only been a short time since Mr. Monticello was found. I'm sure it will take a lot longer to get all the necessary information," Mac put in.

His tone and expression were conciliatory, and Jax recognized both as an effort to ease any tension growing between Bella and himself. The old pro didn't understand that Jax and Bella had no future together. Mac had brought the idea up in December, and Jax had fobbed him off. Any possibility of a relationship had died with Matt in France.

Not that Bella wanted anything more than casual friendship from him. Her future was Ballantyne. It could never be his.

Jax's attention went to Bella. Her dark hair, much like her brother's, was cut in a bob that framed her lovely face. She was still one of the prettiest girls he'd ever known. Prettiest, smartest, kindest, and—unfortunately—bravest. The last concerned him most.

At that point, Abbott tapped on the kitchen door before opening it. "Excuse me. I wonder if I might use the phone on the counter out here. I want to call Malcolm's wife."

"Of course," Bella replied. "Is there anything else you need?"

"Nothing," he replied before stepping away from the door and letting it close behind him. Briefly, Jax thought about telling the man that he would call the widow, which was what he'd planned to do. He released a pent-up breath. Perhaps letting the man do it was better.

For a moment, all of them were silent before Bella spoke again. "I don't envy him having to tell her the bad news."

"Nor do I," Mac said. "'Tis a terrible thing to carry such devastating information."

Jax swallowed hard. The task of writing to Bella about the deaths of her parents, lost during the influenza pandemic, had fallen on the other man's shoulders. Tragically, they had died within weeks of each other, and only a short time after Matt.

Bella laid one slender hand over Mac's broad one. "Grief is less of an ordeal when it's shared."

Fresh consternation hit Jax, and he flinched. Her words were true, but they cut him to the quick. After Matt's death,

Bella had wanted to share her grief with him, and he'd turned away. He realized how that must have appeared, but it had been guilt, not indifference, driving his response. Guilt still shaped his actions around her. Guilt and fear. He'd promised her to look out for Matt, and he'd failed miserably.

Suddenly, his appetite gone, Jax laid the rest of his sandwich aside. For a moment, he sat still and quiet. Once Bella and Mac went back to their meals, he pulled a pad out of his front jacket pocket. "I'd like to ask the two of you a few questions now, while everything is fresh in your minds. We can go into more detail tomorrow."

Bella said nothing, but Mac readily agreed, "Of course."

"What time did Mr. Monticello arrive?" Jax asked.

"Right around three o'clock," Bella replied.

Jax turned to the older man. "Did you see him?"

"Nay, not right then. But perhaps thirty minutes later, he stopped at the shop to ask about walking the course. He planned to go around all eighteen. I dinna know if he did. Heavy rain hit shortly after four o'clock. He had an umbrella, so he may have continued around both nines. Most golfers left the course, though."

Jax asked a few other questions, but Mac knew little about the hours preceding Monticello's murder since he'd been in the shop all afternoon. However, he was able to tell Jax that Dale had joined him there after three o'clock. Jax dutifully scribbled the information down before turning to Bella. With effort, he schooled his features. Jax didn't want to be at loggerheads with her. He wanted to get the information and leave before she further inserted herself into the case, which seemed all too likely.

"And you sent Dale to the shop about that same time, so he didn't make any other stops," he said, looking directly at Bella.

"Yes. He was finished here, and I thought Mac might need his help. I'm sure he didn't dawdle on the way," Bella replied.

"I see. But he and his brother both saw Monticello arrive?"

"They had been helping me. After the drizzle started, some players came in here, and I served refreshments."

"Did either of the twins have any reaction to Monticello? Say anything about him?" Jax asked as he continued to write. When she didn't immediately reply, he glanced up and saw her lick her lips in a gesture that could have indicated nervousness. But why would she be uneasy?

"They admired his car, of course." She offered a smile. "And his clothes."

"Anything else?" Jax asked as his gaze narrowed on her. Her brief replies increased his suspicion. Was she withholding information to protect the boys? Would she do that?

"They admired his watch, and Dick mentioned the big tip."

He paused in taking notes. "But you can't be sure if either of them, or both, went to the cottage later?" Something akin to alarm rounded her dark eyes before she looked down at her plate.

"No, I can't."

"Neither can I," Mac agreed. "I dinna need the lad to stay at the shop."

Both answers bothered Jax. Could the twins have killed Monticello? He didn't know the boys well. They seemed polite, but they were dirt poor and struggling without their folks. Had they robbed Monticello while he was on the golf course only to find him in the cottage? Jax tucked the idea in the back of his mind and went on to another question. "What about Mrs. Mars? Was she still here when Monticello arrived?" Jax's gaze narrowed on Bella.

"Yes. She was finishing upstairs before getting the roast ready. She had an odd reaction to him." Bella revealed Minnie's tirade about Monticello. "She's not a sweet soul, but her dislike was all out of proportion."

Jax frowned. "That seems strange. I've only seen Mrs. Mars in passing when she worked in the mercantile. She wasn't friendly, but she wasn't openly critical of anyone, as far as I know."

"No, she isn't friendly, which is why we aren't having her work at the front desk despite being shorthanded." If the season went well, they could employ more people and not ask their current staff to handle multiple jobs.

"Has she berated anyone else?" Jax asked, going back to the part that most interested him.

A half-shrug lifted one of Bella's slender shoulders. "She hasn't worked here very long. Only a few weeks. We spent that time getting the inn and cottages ready for guests. Today is the first that we've had people come into the inn. But she is critical of the twins at times." Bella hesitated before continuing. "She said they'd stolen money from the Downings when they worked in the store." Jax stopped writing and looked at Bella. "I never got a report about that."

"No, I don't imagine the Downings would have reported it. When I talked to them about hiring the boys here and giving them a place to live, Mr. and Mrs. Downing were very enthusiastic and had only good things to say about Dick and Dale. After we hired Minnie, and she accused them of stealing, I called Mrs. Downing, who said her sister was confused and hadn't counted the money right that day. She also said Minnie hasn't been the same since her husband and son died in France."

"That would be hard for anyone," Jax observed. Heaven knew, he was still coping with the aftermath of war himself.

"Aye," Mac put in. "She has reason to be difficult, but we spoke with her about criticizing the twins and let her know they report to Bella."

"Did she have a problem with that?" Jax asked.

"She rarely has much of a reaction to anything. That's why her remarks about Mr. Monticello were so stunning," Bella replied. "Typically, she is dour but not nasty. I've tried to be understanding due to her losses. After the incident with him today, I had to repeat that we expect her to treat all guests with respect and kindness." She glanced at Mac. "I was planning to tell you about the incident this evening."

The older man smiled. "It sounds like ye handled it well, lass."

Bella offered a weak smile. "I hope so."

Jax continued. "What about Curt and Carl? Where were they this afternoon?"

Bella and Jax exchanged a glance before Mac spoke. "They end their workday around three o'clock. If we dinna have extra chores, they head to their cabin. As ye know, they rise early to work on the course, so they settle in for the night early, too."

"What motive would Minnie have to kill Mr. Monticello? What motive would Curt or Carl have? Or the twins, for that matter?" Bella asked.

Bella's consternation didn't surprise Jax. Having her employees under suspicion wasn't apt to sit well with her. "I don't know that any of them do, but I can't overlook people who were here this afternoon. Especially not anyone who expressed an immediate dislike of the victim. There could be more to Mrs. Mars' reaction than meets the eye. Or there could be nothing at all. I won't have any idea unless I talk to her and the others. As for the twins, they seemed envious of Mr. Monticello. It is possible they robbed him while he was out walking, and he returned while they were in the cottage. That could have caused panic. Carl and Curt don't seem like strong suspects to me." He exhaled sharply. "I have to interview them all, Bella. It isn't a choice. It's my duty."

"Of course," she said after a prolonged silence.

Jax pressed one finger to his temple before going on. "I can wait until tomorrow. I know the twins and the Molitor brothers will be here. Will Mrs. Mars?"

"Yes, she expects to work. I don't know how busy we'll be after word of the murder spreads, but she is supposed to be here in the afternoon. She can get the baking done for the weekend. If we don't have cancelations, we'll need refreshments."

"Try not to fret so much, lass. Jax will get this case solved as soon as he can."

Frustration hit Jax again. "I want to solve it as much as you two do, and I will do everything I can to wrap the case up quickly." "We know, lad," Mac assured him, but Bella merely nodded.

"I have a few more questions," Jax continued. "Exactly when did you see Carl and Curt today?" he asked as he glanced from Bella to Mac.

"They came into the shop shortly after three to see if I needed them for anything. When I said I didn't, we chatted a while before they planned to head to the cabin," Mac replied.

"Did you see either of them after that?" Jax asked Bella.

She shook her head. "No, I haven't seen them since lunch. They either eat with us or pick up sandwiches then, but they almost always have dinner at the cabin."

"No one saw Carl or Curt after four o'clock," Jax said, more to himself than to anyone else.

His observation increased Bella's anxiety. He had asked as much already. Why was he repeating the questions? At present, only their employees were suspects. That disturbed her more than she wanted to admit. She and Mac were struggling to restore Ballantyne to its former glory. The resort's future, and perhaps the future of Moreley, depended on that. What would happen if a member of their staff was the killer? The question kept resurfacing. She had been concerned last winter when a murder had taken place nearby and Carl and Curtis had been questioned, but this was worse. Much worse.

"No, but they go to bed very early because they get up before dawn to work on the course," Bella pointed out. "Unless there's a specific task around the inn, we seldom see either one of them after three-thirty. As I said, they rarely join us for dinner." "What about other guests? How many are here now?" Jax asked.

"We have a gentleman in cottage three," Bella replied.

"He's by himself?" Jax looked up from his notepad.

"Yes, he is," she told him. "He arrived around noon, played a round, and planned to visit his son afterward. His car wasn't in front of the cottage when we were at number four, so that must be what he did."

"I dinna see him after he went off number one," Mac added. "He may not have played the entire course since rain set in."

"Do you think he might have given the twins a ride into town?" Jax continued to scribble in his notepad as he spoke.

"It's possible," Bella replied. "If he left the course early due to the rain, they might have seen him then and asked for a lift."

"Where does his son live?" Jax asked. "I don't know. I didn't ask." Bella sighed. At the time, it hadn't occurred to her to inquire. Now, she wished she had.

Jax turned to Mac. "Who did this man play with?"

"He was a lonesome," the old pro said. "His name is Ernest Neece. He's from Toledo, the same as Abbott and Monticello. All of them have been here in the past."

Jax's green gaze narrowed on the older man. "Do you know if they're acquainted?"

"Aye," Mac replied. "They used to come with some others. Eight of them, so two foursomes. I have nay seen any of the group for a couple of years until today."

Bella hesitated briefly before adding her own knowledge. "Mr. Neece wasn't especially happy to hear that Mr. Monticello was here this weekend." "Did he give a reason?" Jax paused his writing to look at Bella.

"No, he just looked and sounded upset." She chewed on her lower lip. "I didn't mention him to Mr. Monticello." Maybe she should have done so. Maybe she would have learned something important. Maybe she could have prevented a murder. Once again, her mind whirled with possibilities. Had Neece killed Monticello? Bella tried to recall Neece's exact words, but her mind was clouded with anxiety.

"I'll need to speak with Neece, too. I'll drive by the cottage before I leave. If he isn't back yet, I can interview him tomorrow." Jax jotted down more information as he spoke.

One of their guests being responsible wasn't much better than one of their employees being the guilty party. At least it wasn't to Bella. The last thing they needed was bad word of mouth. "We're right on the main road," she replied. "Someone could have driven back to the cottage or used the east side road. It goes between cottages three and four."

Surprise flickered in Jax's gaze. "The road is in pretty rough shape from what I could tell," he replied, but he stored the fact in the back of his mind. "Did either of you see or hear a car between three o'clock and six o'clock? There's a good view of the main parking area from both the shop and the inn."

Jax's observations were accurate since the entrance to the resort led to a car lot between the two buildings. Bella looked at Mac, who was shaking his head. "The only vehicles

I saw or heard during that time were players leaving. I dinna see Monticello arrive. I only saw him a bit later, as I said."

When Bella said nothing, Jax looked at her. "Did you see anything or anyone suspicious?"

"Minnie Mars said she came in the side way this morning and parked over there near the cottages. I didn't see the Packard, so I didn't know she had driven here until she told me just before going home."

Jax's eyes widened as he looked back at Bella. "Does she usually come that way?"

"She might. As I said, she rarely drives, but she borrowed the Downings' Packard today. She often walks. Anyhow, I told her not to use the bridge again because it needs repair," Bella said.

"Aye, it does," Mac put in. "Archer and I roped it off nearly two years ago."

Bella frowned. "Minnie said the rope was down."

"Twas nay down when I was out that way a month ago," Mac said. "Rope was still across both ends of the bridge."

"The Bunny Bridge?" Jax asked.

"Aye," Mac replied. "I had forgotten ye kids called it that when ye were small."

The exchange made Bella smile as she was briefly swept back in time. "I'd forgotten, too." A wry grin curved Jax's lips. "You're the one who named it since a mother rabbit had young ones under it one year."

"I remember," she said. "I suppose rabbits still nest out there since there are quite a few on the property.

"You haven't been out that way lately?" Jax inquired.

"No, not since I got home, actually. Mac told me about the bridge being unsafe, and I don't have a reason to go that far."

Jax nodded. "I'll look at it. Not sure I'll find anything, but you never know." He flipped the notepad shut and put it in his jacket.

The gesture surprised Bella, who had been waiting for more direct questioning. "Don't you want to know what Mac and I were doing, and if anyone saw us?"

Jax's features softened and, for a moment, Bella was swept back in time to when they'd been friends, and he'd been a fixture at Ballantyne. "Mac said he was in the shop all afternoon, and he already made a list of today's players, so I can easily check with them. You have people who say you were in the inn, and I can contact them, if needed. I'm not putting either of you on my suspects' list, if that's a concern to you."

The note of amusement in his voice made Bella laugh with relief. "I wasn't actually concerned," Bella replied, and she hadn't been. But she had wondered, and being able to chuckle over something, anything, felt good.

"I think that's about all I need for tonight," Jax said. "Thanks for talking with me."

"Of course, lad," Mac was quick to say. "If either of us can be of any help at any time, ye need only let us know."

"Thanks, Mac. I appreciated you helping look around the cottage to see if the other part of the club shaft was tossed aside there."

A sick, sinking sensation assailed Bella as she took in the information. Using a golf club to kill someone was appalling. Clubs were to be used for fun, not evil. "You didn't find it."

Jax shook his head. "No, but the gathering darkness made it difficult to see far. If it had been within a few feet of the cottage, we might have seen it. Not that the killer tossed it away here. After all, he took the grip along for a reason. A wise move, since that's where any fingerprints would be. I already looked in Abbott's vehicle. Nothing there. Before I go, I'd like to search the twins' room, too, and Neece's cottage."

"Of course," Bella agreed. "I'll go with you."

For a moment, she thought he would object. Instead, he gave her a quick nod.

Chapter Four

Jax didn't want Bella accompanying him, but he had no good excuse to keep her away. After all, she was a partner in the resort, so she had every right and reason to show him her property.

What bothered him was the more she knew, the likelier it was that she'd involve herself in the case. And possibly put herself in harm's way. Her courage in serving as a Signal Corps operator was admirable, but she didn't need to take more chances, especially not with a killer on the loose.

After bidding Mac goodnight, Jax followed Bella down the short hall to what was once the housekeeper's suite. Despite two sixteen-year-old boys occupying the rooms, the area was relatively neat. Jax carefully searched under the beds, in the cupboards, and through the drawers to no avail while Bella stood in the doorway with her arms around her waist. Although she said nothing, her disapproval was palpable. Jax wanted to offer more excuses. Only grim determination kept him silent until he finished his task. He was the constable. He didn't need to explain his actions to Bella.

"There's nothing here that offers any clues."

"I didn't think there would be," Bella replied. "I can't imagine either Dale or Dick committing such a violent crime."

For a moment, he studied her troubled expression. "I don't think either of them would have gone to the cottage planning to kill the man. It's more likely they went to steal his pocketbook or watch or something else of value. If he left the course early due to the rain, he might have interrupted them and one grabbed the club without thinking."

Bella chewed on her lower lip. "I suppose that could have happened. But using a mashie. It really bothers me."

"I understand," Jax said. "We both know a club can be dangerous. How many times did Mac, your Grandfather Stew, or your dad warn us about being very careful with them when we were kids?"

"Many times," Bella murmured, "especially after Don March wasn't paying attention and walked up behind Tom Hartz when he was taking his backswing. When Don collapsed into a heap on the ground, I thought he was dead." A slight shiver rippled through her. "So did I," Jax agreed. "Luckily, he only had a bad concussion."

"And a huge bruise."

Jax nodded. "Monticello was hit at least twice, maybe three or four times, once on the back of the head. If that was the first blow, the intention could have been only to keep him from seeing them. The twins—or one of them, at least—might not have realized that a club could be lethal."

He wasn't sure why he revealed so much to her. To offer reassurance? To elicit her viewpoint? Or because he still had trouble keeping his distance? Staying away was the only surefire way to do that.

"Good points," she replied. "I just don't want to believe either of the twins would rob the man, let alone attack him."

"I know. But they aren't the only suspects. You mentioned the side road going between the cottages to the east end of the property. It's possible Abbott came early and entered there. After all, he's been here in the past, so he must have known about that entrance. It hasn't been used recently, but his vehicle could get through. With the rain, it's hard to say, but it is splattered with mud," Jax observed. "And you said Mrs. Mars used the Bunny Bridge today."

Bella couldn't help but smile at the reference to her childhood name for the crossing. "Yes, but there's also Mr. Neece. He definitely dislikes Monticello, and he had to know the side way, too."

"Let's go to his cottage. If he isn't there, can you get us in?"

"I have an extra key."

As the pair stepped out of the inn and into the dark night, Jax pulled a flashlight from his pocket. "The gas lights help, but this will make it easier to see."

When they got to the cottage, Bella sighed. "Mr. Neece isn't back." She pulled the key out of her pocket. While Jax held the light on the lock, Bella opened the door. Once inside, she flipped on the switch and an overhead light came on. "My dad was certainly wise in running electricity to the cottages. He wanted to replace the outside post lights, but my mother thought the gas ones offered more charm. Of course, she thought the same thing about the inn."

A low chuckle escaped Jax. "They do, but electricity would make it easier to search the area after dark."

"I doubt if she ever thought a crime would take place here," Bella said with a trace of asperity. "I certainly didn't."

"Neither did I," he admitted before beginning the search. After a thorough inspection, his shoulders slumped. "Nothing here, either."

"But you didn't expect there to be, did you?"

"No, I didn't. It was wishful thinking because fingerprints would be such a big help." "You can look outside more tomorrow," she suggested.

"Nolen and I can search along the road tomorrow but, with the creek running into the river only a mile from here, I'm not optimistic. With all the rain we've had, both are high. If the shaft didn't get caught on something, it could be in Lake Erie, since it's only miles to the north." The last was likely an exaggeration. Even so, finding the club was unlikely.

"Maybe so, but it probably got hung up in debris. I'd be happy to help you look."

Dismay filled Jax. Her offer came as no surprise, but he resisted. "That's not necessary, Bella, and it's probably futile to spend a lot of time looking." Before she spoke again, he hurried on. "Let me walk you back to the inn. Then, I need to go." She opened her mouth, but quickly shut it. Jax didn't imagine she was giving up. But he'd fight her involvement. She didn't need to put herself in danger. Neither spoke again until they reached his Chummy. "Thank you for letting me look in the suite and cottage. As I said, I'll be back tomorrow to speak with Carl, Curt, Neece, and the twins. Of course, I want to talk with Mr. Abbott again, too. Have a good evening."

"Good night," she replied with a sigh.

Jax didn't say more or look back. Instead, he got in his car and drove away.

***

When Bella went back inside, she found Mac sitting in a chair by the stone fireplace in the entry hall. "I am guessing ye dinna find the other part of the mashie."

"No, we didn't. We found nothing else of use, either." As she sank into the chair across from him, Bella briefly reviewed for Mac what Jax had said about the twins possibly being caught while attempting theft.

"Aye, it is possible. And they might nay know a golf club can be deadly."

"But the same isn't likely to be true for Neece or Abbott, and Jax suspects them almost as much as he does the twins. Or so it seems." Actually, Bella wasn't sure what he thought. He had not been very forthcoming.

Mac's gaze narrowed on her. "Let's nay worry about it tonight. Jax will investigate, and I know he will find the killer." The older man paused for a moment. "I suppose ye want to help again."

Bella smiled. "Of course, but Jax didn't seem eager for my help."

For several moments, the old pro looked pensive. "The war took a toll on him, lass, and Jax was always reserved. Nay with ye and Matthew, but he took a long while to become easy with ye grandparents, ye parents, and me."

Briefly, Bella considered Mac's observations. "Yes, I remember, and you're right about the war changing Jax. He's said as much more than once. This evening, for a little while, he almost seemed like his old self, though." He'd seemed like the old Jax at times during the last murder case, too, but that never lasted. How could it be when the war had forced him to give up his dreams? "Aye, but Abbott made it clear that he finds Jax lacking as a constable. Some in town still do, too. With only one murder investigation and less than a year on the job, the lad is inexperienced, to be sure, but he'll bring in help."

Her brow furrowed. "What kind of help?"

"After we left the cottage, Jax mentioned Constable Jenkins from Karston."

A smile touched Bella's lips. "He and his wife were instrumental in solving the Schwarz case last December, and I'm sure he'd be a big help now. He has a lot of experience, since he was a city police detective before spending years as a town constable." She had faith in Jax, but she wanted the case solved as soon as possible. If outside help accomplished that goal, she favored it.

Although, she also favored being involved, she doubted Jax would invite her input. Not that Bella would be deterred by his reluctance. Senior Constable Jenkins had welcomed her involvement in December. Perhaps he would do so again. She planned to find out as soon as possible.

***

Jax returned to the office to find his young deputy, Nolen Rogers, still working. A smile brightened the younger man's freckled face. "I'm doing paperwork," he said as he gestured to the neat stacks of paper on the counter.

"Great," Jax replied as he crossed the room. His gaze narrowed on his former platoon sergeant. At twenty-one, Nolen still looked boyish, but Jax knew his youthful innocence had been ripped away in the trenches. "I'm sorry you had to stay late, Nolen. I'll make sure you get paid for the extra hours."

"Thanks, Jax," Nolen replied. His smile faltered. "I still hope I'll get hired full-time soon. It's been almost four months since Senior Constable Jenkins talked to the mayor about it."

Jax nodded as he swept off his cap and put it on a hook by the door. "I know, and I've talked to the mayor myself, more than once. The town council is supposed to discuss it again at the next meeting. I'll need you to work more until we solve this murder, and I'm sure, Mayor."

Cawlings will agree to that." Nolen was the sole support of himself and his mother, a responsibility the younger man took seriously. But, after serving in France, the boy took most things seriously. He had been a good platoon sergeant, and he was a good deputy. Getting him hired on a full-time basis was one of Jax's top priorities.

"So, it was a murder." Nolen's expression grew solemn.

"I'm afraid so," Jax replied before summarizing what he had learned while at Ballantyne.

When Jax wrapped up, Nolen said, "I saw the Ironton twins go into the café earlier, but I didn't notice when they left."

The information immediately engaged Jax's interest. "Did they ride their bikes?"

"No, two men in a Winton touring car dropped them off. I didn't get a good look at them, but the car wasn't familiar."

"Did you see if they stopped in town?"

Nolen shook his head. "No, they just let the boys out, turned around, and headed back toward the main highway. Why?"

"Talking to the men probably wouldn't add much even if we could find out who they were, but it gives us a time for the twins leaving Ballantyne." Jax paused for a moment. "I'm going to call the mayor and get approval for you to work full-time until we solve this case. Even with you being here extra hours, I'm also going to see if we can get Richard Jenkins to help us out. You know how it was with the Schwarz case. All hands on deck."

"I don't mind. I can work as many hours as you need me."

"Good," Jax replied. "You've put in a long day, so head home but be here first thing in the morning. I'll need you to make some calls while I go back to Ballantyne for interviews. We may search along the road to see if the other half of the mashie was tossed out there. I doubt it, but we can try. As high as both the creek and river are, it's most likely gone." Jax sighed. "I hope

Richard can come tomorrow. After I talk to Mayor Cawlings, I'll call Jenkins tonight."

"Yes, sir. I'll be here first thing tomorrow."

After putting the papers away, Nolen left while Jax went into his office. Once there, he slumped back in his chair. Being at Ballantyne and hearing Abbott refer to the four-ball took Jax back, back to an event that now seemed like he'd read about it instead of experiencing it himself. At one time in his life, it had been the highlight of his year. As a young boy, he had caddied.

When he turned eighteen, he'd partnered with Matt, and excitement had kept them from sleeping for a week ahead of the event.

The memory made Jax open the middle desk drawer. All the way in the back were two photos. He reached in and retrieved one. The edges were frayed, and the paper was crinkled. For a year and a half, he'd kept it in his uniform pocket. How many times had he pulled it out? Dozens, to be sure. For weeks and months, the photograph had kept him sane, had kept him going. Even when he'd been shivering with cold or sweltering from heat, covered in mud and lice, exhausted and hurting, he'd looked at the three smiling faces and he'd smiled back.

Emotion clogged his throat. The picture had been taken on the starting day of their first try at the Ballantyne Four-ball Championship. He and Matt had been so thrilled, so proud, so young. Between them stood an even younger Bella who looked equally buoyant. She'd only been sixteen, two years younger than Matt and himself. Even so, they'd all thought they were very grown-up.

A raw, rasping sigh left him as he reached back into the drawer and pulled out another photo. It was also of the three of them, but it had been taken five years later in France. He hadn't looked at it in almost that long because the memory was more bittersweet than pleasant, more poignant than healing.

Neither he nor Matt were smiling. By then, they'd already been in the trenches for several weeks. By then, they'd lost fellow officers. By then, they'd lost men. By then, they'd realized there was no guarantee that either of them would ever leave France.

Jax's heart clenched painfully as he studied his best friend's face. Matt had put on a happy façade for his sister, but the camera revealed the weariness in his body and soul. As Jax moved on to his own image, he realized he looked as hollowed out as Matt. Jax had thought he had maintained a bright exterior for both his buddy and Bella. Had he really, or had he only fooled himself? His smile seemed phony now. Fatigue and worry had consumed him. Every loss of a platoon member or a fellow officer had taken a toll. Every tale from a British or French officer had made him wonder how they'd survived for four awful years. The American Expeditionary Force had only been in the fight for months, and Jax had found the death and destruction appalling.

His attention went to Bella's image. Once again, he was surprised. Her wide smile, he realized, didn't quite reach her eyes. He was very aware that she had presented a more convincing front than either he or Matt had. Notwithstanding long hours and difficult conditions as a phone operator, she had maintained her good humor and bright outlook—for them.

The trio had never been in the same place at the same time after the photograph. Somehow, they'd all managed to be in Paris for that one long weekend. Mostly Matt's doing, Jax remembered. The pair had crossed paths when their platoons were relieved for a few days. Both had leave, and Matt convinced Jax to go along. And convincing had been needed since Jax and Bella hadn't been in touch for months. The breach was mostly his fault for suggesting, in multiple letters, that she stay home instead of joining the Signal Corps. Finally, she'd told him to stop writing. Once Matt found out, he was even more insistent that Jax go to Paris and see Bella.

Those three days had been a brief reprieve from the fighting for Matt and himself. They had talked and laughed about the past. They had dreamed about the future. All references to the war had been assiduously avoided. Just as importantly, Jax had apologized to Bella—and she'd accepted. They'd agreed to correspond again, and he'd felt relieved.

Following those few days, Jax had seen Bella only once...his mind skittered away from the memory. It was still too raw, too painful. He hastily shoved both photos back into the drawer and slammed it shut. No good could come of getting lost in the past. No good at all. Heaven knew, he had enough to consider in the present. Contacting the mayor was at the top of his list.

***

Jax didn't have a chance to call the mayor. Instead, Carlton Cawlings showed up shortly after Nolen left the constable's office.

"I just saw Forrester, and he told me about a murder at Ballantyne." Cawlings' narrow lips were set in a grim line.

"Please sit down, sir," Jax said, gesturing to the chair across from his desk.

Cawlings took a seat, but his expression didn't soften. "Do you have any suspects?" The man's dark gaze remained steady.

"The body was found shortly after six o'clock, Mayor. I gathered a fair amount of information while I was at the resort, but I can't say we actually have viable suspects yet." Jax outlined the main points before saying, "I planned to call you this evening because I'd like your approval for Nolen to work full-time until we solve the case, and I'd also like to invite Richard Jenkins to help again."

The older man nodded. "Both are good ideas." With one hand, he smoothed back his hair, although the gesture was hardly necessary. As usual, the mayor had used Brilliantine, a cream that held his black locks back from his angular face. "I know you're aware of how much the town is depending on Ballantyne's success. Without it, I'm afraid Moreley will never get back to normal."

The admission surprised Jax. Cawlings usually expressed nothing other than complete optimism about the future. To say he was the town's biggest supporter would be an understatement. "Yes, I understand how important finding the killer is to Ballantyne and to Moreley." And to Jax himself. More than once, Cawlings had pointed out that not everyone on the council supported the young constable. As a youngster, Jax had vowed never to follow in his father's footsteps as constable, and everyone in town knew it.

Cawlings thrust his long legs out in front of him. "Mac and Bella are working hard to get the resort back on track. I feel they can. After all, Ballantyne has a wonderful reputation." The mayor ran one hand over his face. "We've been through a lot around here. Now this. We don't need another murder getting into the news and keeping people away. On top of all that, once word gets out, townsfolk will be worried about a killer on the loose."

Jax gritted his teeth. The older man's tone indicated Jax might not realize all the facts, but he did. A lecture from the mayor was neither necessary nor welcome. With supreme effort, he kept sarcasm out of his voice. "All I can do is solve the case as soon as possible, and that's my aim." The older man inclined his head. "That should go a long way in easing people's minds." Cawlings leaned forward and braced his elbows on his knees. "The world is changing, and crime is going up everywhere. Since last winter's killer also committed the other crimes, Moreley has gone back to being a peaceful place. Until now. I know you are doing your best. Tomorrow night, the council will discuss hiring Nolen full-time on a permanent basis. I'm going to make a strong pitch because you need more help."

"I appreciate that, Mayor, and Nolen will, too."

Cawlings gave a slight nod. "If Mac and Bella run big golf tournaments again, more visitors should come as spectators. At least, they will if the past is any indicator. There was always a spillover of resort guests coming into town for other activities and shopping. If that happens, I know you and Nolen will have your hands full at times."

"I'll look forward to that, sir." Jax would be just as happy to have his young deputy employed on more than a part-time basis since Nolen and his mother barely made ends meet.

Cawlings finally smiled. "Mac said they might even open for Christmas this year. Of course, that will depend on how the summer season goes. It would be good for the town if they can.

Perhaps train service would improve, too."

"Indeed, it would," Jax agreed, but the mayor's hopes seemed rather high. As he had observed, the area had been racked by problems and losses. In their wake, empty storefronts littered Main Street and vacant houses dotted the town. A lot was riding on Ballantyne, the area's main draw, flourishing. Jax didn't need anyone to tell him that solving the murder was crucial.

The mayor, his smile still in place, got to his feet. "Getting back to normal will be a great thing for all of us."

"Of course." After Jax bid farewell to Cawlings, he slumped back in his chair. As far as he was concerned, nothing would ever be normal again. How could it be when so many people had died? Influenza had taken a few townspeople, but the Great War had also stolen sons, fathers, brothers, and friends. Sometimes when he encountered grieving neighbors, guilt threatened to choke him. Several men in his platoon, some only boys, had died in France. Like Jax, most had been members of the local National Guard unit and, like him, they had been called up in the summer of 1917. More than one parent, sibling or spouse had asked Jax to look after a loved one.

And he had tried. But he had failed too often. Now, looking into the faces of the survivors was often more than he could bear.

Jax closed his eyes, but images from his months in the trenches failed to disappear. Not only had he lost his best friend, he had lost the best part of himself, and that was something he feared would never return. That knowledge stayed with him long into a restless night.

Chapter Five

When she woke the next morning, Bella yearned to stay in bed, pull the covers over her head, and go back to sleep. She wanted to pretend it was yesterday morning and that last night had never happened. Impossible, of course. One of their guests had been murdered, and the sooner the killer was found, the better for everyone. Having a murderer at large was frightening.

As she stared at the ceiling, fresh anxiety swirled through her. The troubling truth was, not all murders were solved. If this one wasn't...she let the thought die away. Only the previous morning, Bella had resolved to focus on the future. Doing so was arduous when the past had left gaping holes in her heart. Four holes, if she was honest. Her parents and brother hadn't wanted to leave her. They'd been snatched away. But Jax seemed just as unreachable as they were. Not that he was really gone, at least not in a physical sense, but he wasn't part of her life since they were no longer on similar paths.

Bella yearned to help with the case, but she had been afraid to ask him outright. *Afraid.* That was not a word usually used to describe her—not by others and not by herself. Why was she afraid to ask Jax, not only about helping with the investigation but about why he had walked away from her that day in France? Away from her and to a pretty, young French nurse. Partly because she feared what he might say, but also because Ballantyne was her primary concern now. It couldn't be for Jax. Not when his war wounds had ended his golf career. Even being at the resort was hard for him, as he'd admitted last winter. Bella didn't want to add to his pain, so she didn't renew their relationship. He didn't try, either, since moving on was the only option for both of them.

With effort, Bella pushed the troubled thoughts out of her mind, hurriedly got up, and dressed for the day. After a late and restless night, she'd overslept. Mulling over painful memories was not a productive use of time. Finding Mr. Monticello's killer and saving Ballantyne should be at the forefront of her thoughts.

Mac and the twins were probably waiting for breakfast, so she scurried down to the kitchen. Once there, Bella found the three of them already eating. A plate, piled high with toast, sat in the middle of the big table and a bowl of oatmeal was in front of each of them.

"Good morning, lass." Mac spoke first.

"Good morning," Bella replied. "I'm sorry I overslept. I can fix bacon and eggs, though."

"Nay," the older man said. "We're fine. I made coffee and cocoa. There's oatmeal still in the pot on the stove. Get some and join us, lass."

Bella poured a cup of coffee and took a small portion of oatmeal before joining the group at the table. All three looked as grim as she felt. Could the twins be responsible for Mr. Monticello's death? The possibility threatened to destroy her appetite.

After Bella got settled, Mac said, "I told the lads what happened last evening while they were in town and that we expect Jax will be back early today."

When neither of the boys spoke, Bella turned to them. "I was surprised you didn't come to dinner last night."

The two exchanged a long look before Dale spoke. "We shoulda told you, but two golfers was leaving when we was. They offered a ride." "Did they give you a ride back here?" she asked.

The boy shook his head. "No, they was headed home. In the café, we met up with a couple of buddies, and one brung us home." The boy paused for a moment. "Mac said Jax wants to talk with us, but we didn't know nothing about Mr. Monticello being killed until this morning."

"Tell Jax that," Bella advised. "He's speaking with anyone who was here yesterday afternoon. It doesn't mean he suspects you." Bella tried to sound reassuring, but she knew Jax would create a list of those with no alibi. And she knew the twins were on it. She was tempted to quiz Dale and Dick about exactly when they had left Ballantyne. Only knowing Jax was likely to ask the same questions, and possibly accuse her of rehearsing the boys, kept Bella from pursuing that idea.

"Just answer his questions, lads," Mac advised. "That's what Arabella, and I did. If Jax has more questions for us, we'll answer those, too."

Dick spoke up then. "We didn't do nothing wrong."

Bella and Mac exchanged glances. "We know that, but everyone who was here yesterday is a suspect," she said even though that was not the complete truth, since she and Mac weren't. She couldn't believe, didn't want to believe, that either boy had been responsible for the murder, but their jealousy of the dead man bothered her. Could one, or both, of them have gone to the cottage to steal his watch and money and, when discovered, kill Monticello? Jax's theory was never far from her mind, and it was quite unnerving.

The pair went back to eating, which Bella took as a sign that they were mollified. Could they be so calm if they were guilty of murder? She hoped not.

When they quickly finished their meals, the twins thanked Mac and left the table. Once they were gone, Bella laid her spoon down and turned to her partner. "I hope Jax finds some other suspects. I hate having the boys under suspicion, and I'm afraid how Curt will react when he finds out there was another murder. He still blames himself for what happened in December." Curt had come upon the scene when Jax and Richard were attempting to arrest a killer who held a gun on them. Curt had been trying to get the weapon when it discharged, accidentally killing the murderer.

"I know, lass, but Jax will go easy with Curt, and the twins and Carl, for that matter. He's a good man. He won't be harsh."

Bella weighed the words. Jax had changed, but not so much that he would grill anyone, and certainly not people who were fragile like Curt Molitor. "I'm sure you're right. Jax said he'd talk to Minnie, too. Maybe she saw or heard something that will help." Fresh anxiety gripped her as she recalled Jax asking about Minnie's reaction to Monticello. It was odd, but surely it wasn't significant. "Perhaps. Try not to worry, lass. Jax will get to the bottom of the crime, and we'll move ahead with our plans."

Because she didn't want to upset Mac, Bella forced a smile and replied with as much optimism as she could muster. "You're right, Mac. I'll put my worries aside and focus on what needs to be done right now."

"A wise plan, lass." Mac got to his feet. "With the steady drizzle, I dinna think we'll have many golfers, but I'll open the shop anyhow."

"Hopefully, the weather will clear up soon," Bella said. And hopefully, the murder case would also be cleared up soon. Everyone in the area would rest easier when it was.

***

After Mac left, Bella went about cleaning the kitchen. She was almost finished when a tap sounded at the interior door, and she turned to see Mr. Abbott. "Good morning, sir," Bella said in a cheerful, welcoming voice. Although Jax considered him a suspect, she didn't, and Abbott was still a guest. His initial shock and grief had been obvious. She wasn't surprised when the man continued to scowl.

"It might be good for you," he observed in a cold, hard tone. "But I've lost one of my oldest and dearest friends, so good is hardly the right word as far as I'm concerned."

Didn't the man know she had meant it as a simple greeting, not a statement on the reality of the day? With effort, Bella reminded herself that he deserved her sympathy. "I'm so very sorry, sir. I know you've suffered a terrible loss."

A half-shrug lifted one of his broad shoulders. "Thank you," he said, but the chill didn't leave his tone. "It would help if I could leave. I don't see why your constable insists

I stay. He asked a lot of questions last night. Foolish questions."

"Constable Hastings wants to speak with you again." Bella was proud of herself for not using Jax's first name. Abbott already harbored enough doubts about him. "He wants to speak with all of us. I believe he'll be coming later this morning."

"I didn't get here until after Malcolm had been...after he died. I don't see what I can add that would help. Of course, I will if I can. Then, I'd like to get on the road. If your coroner, such as he is, releases Malcolm's body, I'll accompany him. His family wants him home as soon as possible."

"That's very understandable," Bella murmured. This was clearly not the time to pose intrusive questions. Instead, she gestured toward the dining room. "If you have a seat at the table, I'll bring your breakfast as soon as possible. Would you like sausage, eggs, and toast? Or I can make pancakes."

"Eggs, toast, and sausage are fine."

"I'll bring a basket of muffins and a cup of coffee right away. That will give you a start while you're waiting for the rest," Bella suggested.

The man merely nodded before turning toward the dining room.

A sigh left Bella as she headed back to the kitchen. How was she going to get any extra information out of him? Maybe she should let Jax handle this man, but the idea didn't appeal to her. Jax's dismissive attitude rankled quite badly. She had been a big help on the Schwarz case, and he'd admitted as much at the time. Despite that, he was clearly trying to keep her out of this case, and it struck much closer to home than the Schwarz murder had. Why couldn't he understand her need to help? She was no longer a little girl tagging along after her big brother and his best friend. She was an adult. Jax might not want her assistance, but he was getting it, even if she had to act independently. As Bella had learned from her maternal grandfather, murders were not always solved quickly—or even at all. She had to make sure this case was wrapped up soon or risk losing more guests and, in the end, Ballantyne.

***

When Bella took coffee and muffins, Abbott thanked her with a nod and, within minutes, she went back with the rest of his meal and the coffeepot. She laid his plate in front of him before asking if she could refill his cup. When he nodded, she poured more coffee for him before asking, "Is there anything else I can do for you, Mr. Abbott?"

"Can you call that constable and see when he's coming back? I'd also like to know if your doctor and part-time coroner will release Malcolm's body today."

This could be the opening she wanted, Bella decided. "This is a small town, sir, but Doc Smedlay has handled autopsies for years. He has a lot of experience."

"With murder victims?"

"No, of course not. We've only had one murder in the county, as far as anyone can remember."

His gaze narrowed on her. "When was that?"

"Last Christmas."

Dismay flashed across his broad face. "You've had two murders in four months?"

A flush rose in her cheeks. "Yes, but none before that, and the last case was solved within a few days."

"Your constable solved it alone?"

Bella hesitated before replying. "No, several of us worked on the case." After all, that was the truth.

"Are you saying *you* worked on it?" Surprise underlined each word.

Bella's chin lifted a fraction. "I helped, yes."

His gaze narrowed on her. "I suppose an inexperienced constable needs all the help he can get," Abbott muttered. "I know Hastings didn't have the job before the war. How long has he had it now?"

"About ten months. He only came home from France last spring, but his father was the town constable for over twenty years."

A grunt left Abbott. "What did the boy do before he went into the army? I know he was an avid amateur golfer. Did he work with his father?"

Her gaze skittered away. At twenty-six, Jax was hardly a boy. "No, he worked as an assistant professional at a golf course nearby."

"My heavens," Abbott said. "It's worse than I thought. Malcolm didn't deserve to die like he did. He was a good man, a family man, a church-going man. When he wasn't working, he was with his wife and children or serving our community in some capacity. This crime needs to be solved, Miss Stewart, and I'm not sure anyone here understands the urgency in that. Or, despite the success last winter, that anyone has the skills to do it unless the same team is assembled." "I understand the urgency, sir. All of us do, especially Jax. The murder will be solved, and as quickly as possible if I have anything to say about it. My grandfather was our town constable before Jax's father, so I'm aware of how important it is to solve any crime expeditiously," she hurried to assure him. "Grandfather was a police detective in Toledo before he moved to Moreley, so he had solved murder cases. Many of them. He told me about some. In fact, I had rheumatic fever when I was young, and he spent a lot of time sharing the stories. Once I was strong enough, we wrote them down. He wanted to have a memoir." She wasn't sure why she had said so much. Babbling wouldn't help. "I also helped solved the Schwarz murder last December."

His gaze narrowed. "Hm," he began thoughtfully. "Perhaps you have some insight that would help Constable Hastings again."

Sudden optimism spread through Bella. That was exactly her thought. "I think I might," she readily agreed. "I don't want to spoil your breakfast, but maybe I could ask you some questions later."

Abbott gestured to the empty chair nearest him. "There is no time like the present.

"Just let me put the coffeepot back on the stove." The man nodded. She hurried off and quickly returned with a pad of paper. "I hope you don't mind if I take some notes."

"Of course not."

She was surprised by his willingness to work with her. Many men—most men—would have laughed at a woman trying to solve a crime. Or maybe he was guilty and thought he could bamboozle her. With that thought in mind, she planned to be careful. Getting information was important. Being swayed was to be avoided. "Thank you," she said, returning to the table. "I appreciate your cooperation."

"Miss Stewart, my own sister served as a constable during the war. My family is from England. I emigrated here with my younger brother, but the rest of my relatives are still in our village. Almost all British men of a certain age went to France. That left many jobs open, including posts as town constables. My youngest sister served our hometown for the entire war and stayed on until a veteran was hired in her place. I don't doubt the man needed a job to support his family, but I don't know that he was more qualified than my sister. She certainly didn't think so."

His revelations explained why he had a slight accent, although Bella hadn't identified it as British. "I know many English women took jobs that traditionally went to men, and it was true here to a lesser extent," Bella observed. "In fact, I served in the Army Signal Corps as a telephone operator."

Surprise flashed in the man's eyes before he smiled. "You're a brave young woman, Miss Stewart. You operators were instrumental in helping us win the war."

His praise made her smile. The female operators had connected calls much more quickly than their male predecessors had. However, she pushed that thought aside. "What is your sister doing now?"

His smile widened. "She started a detective agency with a friend who also lost her job as a constable—to a veteran, of course." His expression grew solemn once again. "So, Miss

Abbott, I know women can be as good as, and even better than, men as detectives."

"Her own detective agency with a female partner. Very impressive," Bella observed as she took a chair across from Abbott and laid her notepad on the table. "You said Mr. Monticello had a family. A wife and children?"

"Yes. He and Lucy have been married for more than twenty years. I stood up with him. They have two boys, eighteen and nineteen." Sadness darkened his gaze. "And his mother lives with them. A sweet lady. This will hit the whole family very hard."

The man's obvious grief made Bella realize again that, despite his brusque tone and stiff demeanor, he was mourning the loss of a close friend. To her way of thinking, that made him an unlikely suspect, and she found herself less and less convinced of the likelihood. "You say he was involved in the community and at church."

"Malcolm was a deacon at his church, and he served the community in various ways. He was a Scout leader when his boys were younger. He spent a lot of time with them. His boys, his wife, and his mother always came first. Of course, he was busy with work."

Bella began making notes as she listened. "He sounds like an outstanding man," she observed.

"He was. One of the best I've ever known."

A moment passed before Bella asked the question that had been nagging at her. "Then, you don't think someone might have followed him here. Someone with a grudge?" Or preceded him, she thought as an image of Ernest Neece came to mind.

Abbott quickly shook his head. "Absolutely not. You could ask anyone who knew him—relatives, neighbors, co-workers, friends. Malcolm didn't have an enemy in the world." A harsh breath left him. "No one would have followed him to settle a score. His gold watch and chain, a gift from his father, and his money were missing. Robbery seems like the only motive to me."

Unfortunately, it seemed like the only motive to Bella, too, but that meant someone here, someone she knew, might be the killer. The idea sickened her. As much as she wanted the murder solved, she didn't want the killer to be a local, much less a resort employee. "Yes, well, we'll have to see. It's still too soon to know much for certain."

A frown creased his brow. "You agree that robbery is the clearest motive."

A good investigator follows the clues where they lead, not where he wishes they would go.

Her grandfather's admonition, made more than once, echoed in her mind. If she really wanted to help solve the murder, she had to keep that idea foremost in her thoughts. "Yes, it would seem to be."

"I hope your constable is up to the job."

Since she had already indicated Jax was inexperienced, Bella felt uneasy—and guilty. "I'm sure Jax will do a good job."

"I believe I can rely on you to make certain he does."

Bella simply nodded. She wasn't sure why Abbott had taken such a strong dislike to Jax, but she could hardly complain. After all, that was the reason Abbott was willing to talk with her. That, along with his own sister being a detective in England.

Anxiety played along her nerve ends. Jax would be furious when he found out that she'd discussed the case with Abbott, but maybe he wouldn't have to know. She could at least wait to reveal anything important until Richard Jenkins arrived later in the day. Jenkins, she was sure, would once again be open to her help. Perhaps, his wife Jenny would be part of the team again.

Those thoughts buoyed Bella's spirits. "Do you know a Mr. Ernest Neece?"

Abbott's dark brows rose a fraction. "Yes, why do you ask?"

"He is also a guest here. In fact, he's in cottage three. When he arrived early yesterday afternoon, I thought he was Mr. Monticello coming a bit early." She considered how to reveal Neece's reaction. "When I called Mr. Neece by the wrong name, he got very upset...not so much about the mistake on my part, but because Mr. Monticello was coming."

A heavy sigh left the man. "Ernest used to come here with us. Unfortunately, he became quite hostile toward Malcolm and dropped out of our group." His voice was almost a monotone and his expression was equally blank.

The man's revelation meshed with Neece's words, but Mr. Abbott didn't seem upset upon hearing about Neece. Bella wondered why, so she asked, "What caused the problem?"

Abbott leaned back in the chair. "Ernest blamed Malcolm for something far beyond his control," he replied in a clipped tone. "Now, if you'll excuse me..."

The statements were at odds with Abbott's earlier assertion that Monticello had no enemies. Even so, Bella realized the man would not reveal the crux of the problem. Still, she needed to convey one more point. "Sir," she began, "I don't know how Constable Hastings would feel if he knew you and I talked. He may see it as me interfering." *May* was not the right word because Jax would surely construe her talk with Abbott as meddling.

For a long moment, Abbott studied her expression. "I can see how that might ruffle his feathers," he observed. "I agree there's no sense in upsetting him. It's been my experience that police don't like to be mistrusted or doubted."

Guilt stabbed her. She didn't really mistrust or doubt Jax. She simply didn't like his unwillingness to include her in the investigation. "I have had little experience with the police, other than knowing my grandfather."

A low laugh left the man. "I should probably explain that remark. I'm an attorney, and I often defend people in court. My experience has been that the police don't like to be second-guessed when they're doing an investigation, not even when they're bungling it. Although I'm sure Constance—my sister—would object to my observation."

Part of Bella wanted to defend Jax, but another part resented his dismissal of her. That part won out. Abbott had talked with her and might again. If Jax didn't find out right away, no harm was done. She could reveal the information to Jenkins. That would ease her guilty conscience without the added complication of letting Jax know she had gone behind his back.

***

The morning after the murder, duty led Jax back to Ballantyne, but hesitation gripped him once he stopped in the parking lot. For most of his life, being at the resort had evoked pleasure and excitement. Before the war, he hadn't had a single second of doubt about his dream of being a golf professional. Not even his father's dismissal of the goal as *darn foolish* had swayed Jax.

A shattered wish was only part of his need to stay away from Ballantyne and Bella. His guilt was just as much a barrier.

Finally, he threw the car door open and climbed out. In December, he'd spent little time at the resort during the murder case. This time was different. Repeated visits to the scene of a crime taxed him, but in the war Jax had led his men over the top and across No Man's Land more times than he could count. He could certainly face his past in order to do his job.

As Jax approached the pro shop, he glanced at the golf course. A light drizzle made the tall oaks, maples, pines, and birches appear hazy and faded. But his memories were crystal clear. How many mornings like this one had he and Matt slung their bags over their shoulders and headed to the first hole? Dozens, certainly. Hundreds, probably. A smile played across his lips.

Matt's dad had sometimes joined them. Other times, Bella had begged and pleaded to play along. Most of the time, they had let her. Those days seemed very distant now, but they had ended less than three years ago when he and Matt had left for the army.

His good mood fled as quickly as it had come. He and Matt had known they might not make it back home, but why did Matt have to die? The question had plagued Jax for nineteen months, and it would undoubtedly plague him for the rest of his life. How could it not, when he was responsible for his friend's death?

He pushed the memories away and hurried toward the shop. Some nights, the war returned to him, although not as often as when he'd first gotten home. Most days, Jax could do his job and not think about the past or his dreams for the future. A rueful smile touched his lips. More than once, Matt had said the two of them could be co-professionals at Ballantyne when Mac and Archer retired. Bella's father had seconded the idea, and the Scot had agreed. Only weeks before America joined the war, Jax had mentioned it to Bella, who had been all smiles. Had that been only three years ago? Sometimes, it seemed like a lifetime.

As he followed the well-worn path to the shop, Jax was reminded of his first visit to Ballantyne. One autumn day, Matt had invited Jax to come home with him after school. Although the resort was only a few miles out of town, Jax—at age six—had never been there. While his father occasionally checked on the place in his role as constable, Hannibal Hastings never took his young son along.

Jax had been agog as soon as he set foot on the property. The inn, once the sprawling retreat of an industrialist, had amazed him, but it was his first sight of the little golf shop that stayed in his mind.

Bella, then four, had insisted on tagging after Matt and Jax. All the way from the inn to the shop, she'd chattered about the *elf cottage*, as she called it. Matt's gentle teasing had made the close bond between the siblings immediately clear to Jax. Once they had gotten within sight of the shop, it was also clear why Bella had her own name for the structure.

Made of river rocks, the story-and-a-half building had a small stoop, an arched front door, and large mullioned windows facing the golf course. Jax easily recalled Matt teasing Bella about the wooden golf bag rack sitting on one side of the entrance. *What do your elves use that for? They sure don't play golf.* Bella had giggled at her brother and retorted that they might.

Jax's pleasure at the memory faded, and he took a deep breath before stepping inside. Mac greeted him immediately.

"Good morning, lad."

"Good morning."

A welcoming smile formed on the older man's lined face. "Come sit by the fire. It's a chilly, damp morning and the warmth will do ye good."

Jax took a seat by the old stone fireplace. "It's a good day to be inside." The warmth of the blaze was as welcoming as Mac's expression, and some of Jax's tension melted away.

"Aye, that it is." The older man leaned back in his chair. "What do ye have this morning? Mostly questions or some answers?" Mac's voice—with its Scottish lilt—was calm, but anxiety shadowed his lined face.

"I'm afraid I don't have any answers yet," Jax admitted with reluctance. Solving the case quickly was important, and he was frustrated at not having a clear path forward.

"It's still early in the investigation," Mac observed, but his expression remained solemn.

Jax nodded before looking around the shop. Once, it had been as familiar to him as his own bedroom. Maybe even more so, since he'd spent all of his free time at the resort, especially after his mother died.

His gaze moved on. The wall across from the fireplace held a few golf clubs and bags—for golfers to purchase, if they hadn't brought their own. Another wall anchored the counter, and the third boasted an array of photographs. Jax's attention came to rest on one of himself and Matt. Two young, smiling faces looked back at him. Between them was a large sterling silver loving cup. Conflicting emotions gathered to form a hard lump in his throat as Jax recalled the day it had been taken. When Mac spoke again, Jax knew he was thinking about the same day. "That was a wonderful event," the old pro observed, his own voice rough and ragged. "We were all so proud of ye and Matthew for winning the four-ball on ye first attempt."

Jax swallowed hard over the regret threatening to choke him. "We were pretty excited ourselves." In those days, he and Matt talked about playing in the four-ball every year and going to other tournaments as well. But war had come and stolen those dreams, just as it had stolen Matt's life. As the familiar regret gripped him, Jax stared into the flickering flames, but he no longer felt their warmth.

Several moments of silence passed before Mac spoke again. "I know the shrapnel in ye arm and shoulder are problems. Is there nay anything to be done?"

The old pro's sincere concern put a chink in Jax's emotional armor, and he made a major admission. "Doc has a surgeon friend in Toledo who thinks he might be able to help. I haven't gone to see him yet."

"Why not, lad?" When Jax didn't immediately reply, Mac went on. "I'm sorry, I dinna mean to pry. But the game was ye life, ye passion. Why aren't ye eager to see if surgery would help?"

"You're not prying, Mac," Jax responded. "Even with surgery, there is no guarantee I could play competitively again." He was surprised at the deep regret he heard in his voice. Jax had faced facts long ago. Long before he had left France and every day since then, he'd known his dreams were dead. "In fact, it's highly unlikely."

"And because ye can't pursue that dream, ye gave up the game entirely." It was a statement, not a question.

They'd had a similar, but briefer, talk last winter. Then, Jax hadn't mentioned the possibility of surgery. "I don't know that I've decided I'll never play again. I just haven't thought about it much." That wasn't the whole truth because Jax did, far too often. Twenty years of hopes and wishes died hard.

Mac studied Jax for several moments. "We've missed ye here, and ye must know the welcome mat is always out. I thought after the holidays that ye might come more often, but I suppose ye are busy."

The use of *we* pricked Jax's conscience, and it concerned him. Had Bella and Mac discussed him? If so, what had they said? Evidently, nothing about that day in France and his hasty dismissal of her. Mac would not approve of his behavior, he was sure. Jax didn't approve of it himself. If only he could go back in time and fix his mistake. Jax brushed aside his errant thoughts. "Thank you, Mac. I appreciate that." He reached into his pocket and pulled out a small pad and pencil. "I wondered if I could go over a few more facts with you."

"Of course. I don't know how much help I'll be. I told ye all I knew yesterday. Have ye uncovered anything that will help solve this awful crime?" Anxiety once again shadowed the older man's lined face.

"Not yet. I'll talk to the twins, Curt, and Carl while I'm here. And again with Mr. Abbott. I'm also hoping to speak with the other two men, the friends who were coming today, and with Neece, too. He wasn't back at the cottage when I left here last night." "The two friends canceled," Mac told him with a troubled look on his face.

Jax frowned. "But Abbott should still be here. I asked him to stay, so we could follow-up this morning."

"He's made no secret of the fact that he wants to leave as soon as possible. He and the other two feel it isn't safe here."

Now, Jax clearly understood the other man's anxiety. "They were planning to participate in the four-ball, weren't they?"

"Aye, but they aren't any longer. Neither are some of their friends. Abbott called the other two men last night, of course. Evidently, they immediately contacted several others." Mac paused for a moment. "We really hope ye can solve this murder quickly, Jax. I know it's asking a lot of a two-man department, but we spruced up the cottages and prepared the inn with the idea that the four-ball would attract a sizeable crowd and that would lead to the place getting back to normal. Now, with this murder, I don't mind saying I'm concerned, and I know the lass is, too." The older man's observations didn't surprise Jax, but they loaded a heavier burden on his shoulders. Ballantyne had been his second home; he loved this place almost as much as Mac did, almost as much as Bella, and he couldn't bear to think about them losing it. "It's very early in the investigation," Jax pointed out in what he hoped was a reassuring tone. "We solved the Schwarz murder fairly quickly. I talked to Senior Constable Jenkins in Karston. He'll be here this afternoon. I'll go over all the current information with him."

Some of the tension left Mac's expression. "He's a good man." Then, he smiled. "And so are ye."

The praise wasn't deserved, Jax thought, but he appreciated it. "Thank you, sir." He put pencil to paper. "Have you spoken with Curt or Carl this morning?"

"No, due to the weather, they most likely stayed at the cabin today. Carl knows when conditions will keep golfers off the course, so he decides whether or not to mow himself. If the rain looks to be lifting, he and Curt will head out then." Jax nodded. "And the twins?"

"Dale and Dick were at breakfast. They said a couple of golfers gave them a ride to town. The two of them had a bite at the café. They ran into a couple of friends, and one of the other lads drove them home."

That coincided with Nolen's observations, so Jax replied, "Good." Perhaps, he could eliminate them as suspects. Narrowing the field would lead to a faster conclusion.

"We said you'd want to talk with them this morning. They're probably working around the inn, but Bella can tell you where."

When Jax wrapped up with Mac, he stood and shook the older man's hand. "Thank you for going over these points with me. It's very helpful, Mac."

"I'll help in any way I can, lad, and so will Bella. I suppose ye'll be wanting to speak with her next."

Wanting was not really the word that Jax would have used in this context. What he wanted to do was get as far away from Bella as possible. But what he needed to do was something else entirely. Somehow, he needed to keep her out of the case. Surely, she was too busy today to do much. "Yes, I should go over a few points with her, too." "She's at the inn. You'll probably find her in the kitchen."

Jax bade Mac farewell and headed out. The footsteps taking him to the inn faltered more than once. He'd known being constable wouldn't be a dream come true, but Jax hadn't figured it would be this onerous. His father's biggest case had been an attempted bank robbery. After less than a year on the job, Jax had already had two murders to investigate. It was not how he'd planned to spend his time after the war. Far from it.

Slowly, Jax made his way from the shop to the inn. The old Georgian mansion had been built over forty years earlier by an industrialist who later fell on hard times, which enabled Mac and Stew Stewart, Bella's grandfather, to buy the place and pursue their own dreams.

Climbing to three stories, the white clapboard with its impressive pillars and black shutters was imposing. The expansive porch was vacant, but the Adirondack chairs were freshly painted and gathered in their usual arrangement. From them, he knew, occupants had a clear view of the eighteenth green. Jax resisted the urge to turn and take in that view himself. He needed to get information and go, not dawdle, ruminating on the past and all that had been lost. After a deep breath, Jax went to the door and stepped inside. Unfortunately, Jax didn't have more time to regroup because Bella wasn't in the kitchen; she was behind the front desk.

"I just spoke with Mac. We went over some of the information that I already gathered. I wondered if you might have a few minutes to do the same." Jax approached the counter as he spoke.

"Yes, of course," she replied. "I have a fire going in the kitchen. Why don't we talk there?"

He followed her into the familiar room. Again, Jax fought the memories that were never far from his mind when he was at Ballantyne or near Bella. Yet, even in old surroundings, he felt torn between the past and the future.

"Please sit down." Bella gestured toward the big round table. "I have coffee. Would you like some? I also made cookies this morning. They go well with coffee." "You don't need to go to any trouble," he said.

"It's no trouble. Like I said, the coffee is made and the cookies are baked." She poured two cups of coffee, put a half-dozen cookies on a plate, loaded everything on a tray, and carried it to the table.

Jax remained standing until she joined him. Once she sat down, he followed suit.

"How can I help?" Bella asked.

Jax removed the pad and pencil from his pocket. He placed the pad on the table and looked down at it, studying his notes. "When I spoke with Mac, he mentioned that the victim's two other friends canceled."

She sighed. "Yes, they did. They think it's too dangerous to come here."

He looked up at her then. "I see. But Abbott is still here, isn't he?"

Bella nodded. "Only because you insisted he stay. He came down for breakfast. Afterward, he went to the library to read. I haven't seen him since then." "Did he say anything about his friend Monticello at breakfast?"

A moment passed before she answered. "We all ate in the dining room together. About all he said was could he have more jam and what time would lunch be."

"A man of few words."

The jangling of the telephone interrupted, and Bella hurriedly stood up. "I'll be right back."

***

The reason for the call didn't surprise Bella, but it upset her. Another guest had canceled. Feeling weighted down by anxiety, she slowly returned to the kitchen to find Jax, still looking amused after his last comment and munching on a cookie. He seemed very much like his old self at the moment, but guilt pricked her conscience. She had gone behind his back, and she hadn't shared what Abbott had told her. Maybe she should. But if she told him, he'd undoubtedly lecture her about staying out of the case.

His smile faltered when their gazes met. "Is something wrong?"

"The call was another cancellation."

A grim expression came over his face. "I'll get the case solved as soon as possible. Richard Jenkins will be here this afternoon. Nolen and I will go over everything with him. I think his help will be invaluable."

"I'm sure it will. He's a very good detective." Jax had given no sign he would welcome her help again, which wasn't surprising. It was only because of the senior constable's intervention that Jax had allowed Bella to take part in the last murder investigation. Evidently, she would need to appeal to Richard again. Even so, she gave Jax another chance. If he responded positively, she could provide the information gleaned from Abbott. "I learned a lot from him. I remember him saying we had a good team, so maybe I can help again."

Jax's stern expression intensified. "As I told you last night, that's not necessary."

Irritation resurfaced, but Bella clung to patience as she formulated a response. "You thought the same thing last December, but I was a big help. Richard said so, and you finally admitted it, too. Remember?" Continuing to remind wasn't working, yet she persisted.

He ground his teeth until a muscle jumped in his jaw. "Nolen is working full-time during the investigation. He may even get a regular schedule on a permanent basis. With Richard here, we'll have a strong team."

Bella hesitated for a moment. "I still think I would be a big help. I'm the one who first spoke with Abbott. And I'm the only one who spoke with Mr. Monticello at length."

"Yes, I know, but I have your statements." He lifted his notepad. "You don't need to get involved any further."

Fresh frustration filled her, and Bella took a long, deep breath. "The future of this place," she said, lifting one hand and gesturing around the room, "this entire place. The inn, the cottages, the course—everything—are at stake. Mac might not have told you, but we have already lost other guests, not only for this weekend, but we've had players pull out of the four-ball. We need that event to be successful, Jax." She was admitting far more to him than she had planned, but desperation and fear drove her. Ballantyne and Mac were her last ties to her past and to the only future she could imagine. "You know I'm able to help."

"Yes, you mentioned that already and more than once." An edge crept into his voice.

Bella frowned. "Is Jenny coming with Richard?

"No, she isn't," Jax replied, paused briefly, and hurried on. "That is, I don't know if she is or not. We don't need anyone else right now. Besides, you're one of the owners, and your involvement could be taken as a conflict of interest, especially since I'm interviewing your employees."

Heat flamed in her cheeks. "I wouldn't try to influence your investigation, and I'm already involved."

"Only peripherally."

"I'm the one who first spoke with him and with Abbott," she repeated.

"Yes, and, everything considered, I'd think that is more than enough involvement," he said in a terse tone.

Bella scowled at him. "You and Nolen have to protect the town, not just deal with a murder."

He inhaled and exhaled slowly. "As I said, Jenkins will assist us. I'm sure we can handle things."

Although Jax was clearly losing patience, Bella was not deterred. "I could help you. I've already compiled a list of suspects."

His jaw dropped. "Do you think I'm so incompetent that I didn't make a list of suspects myself?"

"I'm just trying to help like I did with the Schwarz case."

"Yes, you helped. The problem is, you don't follow orders."

Her brow furrowed in confusion. "What are you talking about?"

Jax pinched the bridge of his nose. "When we caught up with Gus Schwarz's killer, I told you to stay in the car because he was armed and unpredictable."

"I did."

"No, you did not," he asserted. "You got out and hurried over to where you could have easily gotten caught in crossfire if Richard or I had needed to fire back at the killer."

For several moments, Bella mulled over his words and mentally reviewed the scene. Finally, she shrugged. "I didn't get out of the car until his gun went off. He fell to the ground almost immediately, so I wasn't in any danger at that point."

His green gaze filled with some inexplicable emotion. "You couldn't have known he shot himself, Bella. He could have shot Curt. And he could have shot you when you ran willy-nilly into the fray."

"You and Richard had your guns on him so, even if he hadn't shot himself, I was safe," she protested.

At least ten seconds passed before Jax responded. "You were not safe. You were foolish and headstrong. I told you to stay in the car, and you didn't. I don't need to worry about you doing the same thing again. Next time, someone could get seriously hurt." Her gaze narrowed and her jaw tightened. "You're being ridiculous, Jax." His words seemed more like criticism than concern, which only annoyed Bella more.

"Stay out of this, Bella," he said in a hard tone.

"Or what?"

This time, he didn't pause before replying. "Or I'll arrest you for interfering with a police investigation."

Dismay hit her like a brick. "You wouldn't dare."

"Oh, yes, I would and don't think I won't. I am the town constable, and you are a private citizen. We have different roles. Mine is to find the killer, and yours is to stay out of the way."

For long moments, she stared at him in disbelief. "Why are you being so high-handed? Why are you still making weak excuses to keep me from assisting? You know I helped last time, and I didn't put myself or anyone else in danger at any point in the investigation. Why won't you admit that?"

"Because it isn't what happened. You can reframe it any way you want, but that doesn't make your perspective true. I neither want nor need your assistance with this case. Concentrate on the resort and let me do my job without constant interference."

An uncomfortable silence ensued before Bella responded. "Interference? I'm not interfering.

I'm trying to help like I did in December."

He exhaled slowly. "I agree you contributed in the last case, but I have to weigh that against your foolhardiness at the end."

"I was not foolhardy," she shot back.

"I'm sure you don't see it that way."

Anger simmered inside Bella. "Mr. Abbott wants to leave, and you refuse to let him. We can't afford to have people spread negative gossip about this place. You know that, Jax."

He drove his fingers through his hair in a gesture that telegraphed exasperation. "Bella, I told you I understand, but my first concern has to be solving the murder, not catering to anyone's personal wishes."

"Personal wishes? My personal wishes have nothing to do with it."

"I was referring to Abbott, not you. Why do you have to take everything so much to heart?"

"I take the possibility of losing Ballantyne very much to heart. It's my legacy from my family.

Do you really not care if Mac and I can keep it?"

"You ought to know the answer without asking," he replied before turning on his heel and leaving the room.

Bella watched him go with mixed emotions. Jax's assertion that she had put herself in danger during the Schwarz case was simply ridiculous. Yet, she couldn't help recalling his concern for her. Genuine, if unnecessary, concern. Even worse, his last question made her ache. Of course, he knew how much the resort meant to her and Mac, so why didn't he understand her need to solve the murder quickly? Although she didn't enjoy being at odds with Jax, he refused to give an inch, so she wasn't giving one, either.

Chapter Six

Jax stopped in the empty foyer and tried to regain some semblance of control. Bella had made similar accusations last December when he'd told her not to get in his way. His warnings arose from worry. Why couldn't she understand his position? Why had she asked such a careless question? *Do you really not care whether or not Mac and I can keep it?* Of course, he cared. Probably far too much.

Once he felt more composed, Jax continued to the library, where he found Abbott sitting with a book in his lap. The man wasn't reading. Instead, he was staring into the fireplace, but he turned at the sound of Jax's approach. Immediately, he scowled. "Can I leave now, constable?"

Jax took the chair across from the older man. "Not yet, I'm afraid. I need to ask you some questions."

To that, Abbott said nothing. Instead, he continued to stare at Jax.

Undeterred, Jax pulled out his notepad and reviewed what he now knew about the crime scene. The man, still tight-lipped, clearly disliked answering repeated questions, but Jax persisted.

After a half-hour, he gave up on the interview but continued to deny approval for the man's departure. Jax wanted Jenkins' opinion on that, although he didn't admit it to the guest. During the interview, Abbott had once again intimated he found Jax to be both incompetent and unprepared. That didn't sit well. Not well at all, especially since he'd still been smarting from Bella's accusations. Tired and dispirited, he went to Neece's cottage next, but found no trace of the man. Fresh frustration filled him. Where was he? Although Jax didn't want to question Bella again, he saw no alternative.

On his way back to the inn, he ran into Carl and Curt going to lunch, so he followed them into the kitchen. Bella smiled at the brothers and ignored Jax. Not that he'd expected a warm welcome from her. "Is there something you need?" she asked him in a brusque tone without looking his way.

While Curt and Carl—who carefully averted their gazes—took seats at the table, Jax paused in the kitchen's doorway. "I've only spoken with you, Mac, and Abbott. I'd like to interview everyone else before I leave."

"We can talk after lunch," Carl offered. His narrow face softened into a shy smile. "We'll be happy to help, if we can."

"Thank you," Jax replied. "I'll wait for you in the foyer." He paused briefly. "Will it be all right if I use the library for the interviews?" The question was posed to Bella.

When she didn't reply immediately, Jax shifted restlessly from one foot to the other. Since he probably deserved the cold shoulder, he simply waited.

"Yes, of course," Bella finally replied. Her gaze briefly met his before moving away. "You might as well join us for lunch."

The invitation was grudging, but Jax accepted it with as much equanimity as he could muster. "Thank you."

Mac, Dick, and Dale arrived moments later. "The rain doesn't look to be letting up, so I closed the shop," the old pro said once everyone was at the table. He smiled at Jax.

"Nice to have ye join us, lad. Were you able to speak with Mr. Abbott again?"

"Yes, and I looked for Mr. Neece, but he wasn't at the cottage, and his car was still gone. Do you know if he went into town?" Jax asked. He was glad Mac gave him an opening to inquire about the other man, because asking Bella anything was fraught with difficulty.

"I have nay seen the man since he finished his round yesterday," Mac replied. He glanced at Bella. "Have ye seen him, lass?"

A frown furrowed her brow. "No, I thought he was still in the cottage, since the weather isn't good." Bella's gaze went around the table. "Have any of you seen him today?" Each one responded negatively. "He must have gone elsewhere to eat or maybe to see his son again."

Both ideas seemed reasonable, so Jax went about eating the soup and sandwich that Bella had provided. Mac continued to chat with him and the others at the table, but Jax couldn't help noticing that the twins never looked his way. Their behavior wasn't necessarily a sign of guilt, although it was unusual. Dale was typically talkative and open, while Dick followed his brother's lead. The same was not true for either Curt or Carl, so their intermittent comments didn't surprise Jax. Carl had always been shy, but Curt had only become reserved in recent times. Since Jax understood and respected both brothers, he didn't press them.

When the twins finished first and excused themselves, Jax hurriedly spoke up. "I'd like to speak with both of you. Separately."

Dick and Dale looked at each other before acknowledging Jax.

"All right." Jax wasn't sure which twin had replied since he hadn't yet learned to tell them apart.

"Perhaps I could take notes for you like I did in December," Bella said.

The statement, more challenge than overture, wasn't a surprise, and his arm and shoulder were no better now than they had been last winter. That made his handwriting hard to read. Even so, part of Jax wanted to refuse, but another part knew help was a good idea. Not only would Bella neatly record everything, her presence would mollify the twins, and probably Curt and Carl. In addition, she might stop pressing him for further involvement. These interviews wouldn't put her in danger, so why not agree?

"Thank you," he said at last, before glancing from twin to twin. "Whichever of you wants to be first is fine. It won't take long."

"I'll go first."

Although the boys were identical twins, this one had a cocky attitude that showed in his quick reply and slight smirk. Jax had dealt with a few young, brash army privates, and he could deal with this kid. Even so, Bella being present might evoke more information.

When they all got to the library, Bella smiled at the boy and said, "Sit down, Dale."

He said nothing but took the seat indicated by Bella. Dale folded his hands in his lap as his hazel gaze flitted to Jax. "I don't know nothing, constable."

The boy's words and tone held a note of rebelliousness, but that wasn't unusual with one his age, so Jax let it go. "It's standard procedure for us to interview anyone who interacted with a victim or who was in the proximity of the crime. Often people have helpful information even though they may not realize it."

Dale said nothing, but Bella added, "That's very true, and I know you want to help Constable Hastings catch the killer. We all do."

"Of course," the twin said as he relaxed back into the chair and again looked at Jax.

The boy was clearly placated by her presence. Letting Bella participate had been a wise idea, Jax decided, before focusing back on matters at hand. "You helped Mr. Monticello with his bags when he arrived. Is that right?" Although he already knew that was the case, Jax wanted to start with the most benign questions, to give the boy the chance to tell his side. "Yep, I went with him to the cottage and carried his things in." "Did you speak to him for long?"

Dale shook his head. "Only for a few minutes."

"Was there anything in particular that you noticed about Mr. Monticello?" Jax asked.

The twin's attention went to Bella, but she was looking down at the notepad. Briefly, Dale glanced at Jax before focusing on his clasped hands. "No, nothing."

"You didn't admire his car or clothes or watch?"

Dale's eyes, wide with alarm or surprise, returned to Jax. For several moments, he didn't speak. When he finally replied, his voice was low and hushed. "He had a nice car and watch, but so do a lot of people."

The disclaimer bothered Jax, but he moved forward without comment. "My understanding is that both you and your brother were in the inn or the pro shop afterward, but I wonder if you might have seen anyone else near the cottage."

"I didn't see nothing at all." This answer came quickly.

"I see," Jax said, maintaining his casual tone and relaxed posture. "I suppose you already heard that he was killed with a golf club."

Dale's eye grew wide once again. "A golf club wouldn't kill no one."

The statement gave Jax pause. As he had told Bella, the twins might not know how lethal the equipment could be. As he studied Dale's pale face, Jax felt uneasiness stab him. The twin, he noted, had again looked away from him. In addition, Dale was shifting restlessly in the chair. His uneasiness was a palpable force, and Jax felt it resonate within him. "A golf club can be a deadly weapon. It certainly was in this case."

The color drained from the boy's face. "But we didn't kill that man."

"Constable Hastings isn't accusing you, Dale. Give him a chance to ask his questions," Bella put in.

Once again, Jax was glad Bella was involved in the interview, because Dale nodded and relaxed. "Miss Stewart is right. I simply need to gather information."

Dale chewed on his lower lip. "We wouldn't steal nothing, either. I know Mrs. Mars accused us of robbing money from the mercantile. We didn't, though. Our ma and pa taught us not to take what don't belong to us."

"Very good advice," Jax replied. "That's all I have for you right now, so if you'll send your brother in, I'll talk to him and the two of you can get back to work after that," Jax told him.

Dale nodded and hurried out of the room. When he was gone, Jax turned to Bella. "What do you think?"

Surprise flashed in her dark eyes before she looked at the pad of paper in her lap. Bella rolled the pencil between her fingers. "He was nervous, but that means nothing. He's young and, except for his twin, alone in the world." Bella met Jax's gaze. "You were very good with him, kind and patient. I don't think he knows much, though. I hope he doesn't."

Her praise indicated a softening, something he welcomed. Jax didn't express his own hope that the twins knew nothing, but he wanted that to be true. Even if the case was a robbery gone wrong, murder was a capital crime. A seventeen-year-old had been the first Ohioan to be electrocuted. That knowledge provoked additional anxiety. If the boys had killed Monticello, even accidentally, news of the crime would spread far and wide, which could be the death knell for both the resort and town. And what would happen to the twins? The entrance of Dick Ironton ended his reverie. "Come in and have a seat." Jax gestured to the chair where the other twin had sat.

Dick sat down, but didn't look at either Bella or Jax. Instead, he focused on the floor in front of his chair. Jax glanced at Bella and gave her a slight nod.

"Dick, Constable Hastings only wants to ask you a few questions. It won't take long. Just answer honestly."

The boy glanced at her. "I don't know nothing, Miss Bella."

Bella offered a reassuring smile. "That's fine. You may know nothing that's helpful, but that's all right."

Dick gave one nod of his head before looking at Jax.

"Did you see Mr. Monticello at all?"

"Not more than a glance. I was mostly in the kitchen. Dale went with him to unload the car.

When I helped Mr. Abbott later, he had me put his bags inside the door." "What did your brother tell you about Mr. Monticello?" Jax asked.

Something akin to alarm flashed in Dick's hazel gaze. For several moments, the boy said nothing. "Not much. Just that the man gave him a big tip."

"I see." Jax paused briefly. "I understand you were working here and that you also went to the pro shop to see if Mac needed help."

"Yes, sir."

"While you were going back and forth, did you hear or see anything unusual?" Jax inquired.

Dick shook his head. "No, sir, nothing."

Jax took a slightly different approach with Dick. "Do you know how Mr. Monticello was killed?" If his brother was aware, this twin must be, too. Still, Jax wanted to see the boy's reaction.

The boy nodded. "I heard he got hit with his own golf club," he replied in a tentative tone.

"That's right." Jax paused before taking another avenue, one he hadn't pursued with the brother. "Do you and Dale play golf?"

"No, sir. We grew up on a farm. We didn't have no money to come to Ballantyne."

"And you never caddied here, either?"

"No. We always had chores to do. My pa said the farm had to come first."

"Your father was a smart man," Jax replied, although some boys from nearby farms caddied to make extra money. "Did you see or hear something out of the ordinary yesterday?"

"No, sir. Nothing at all."

Jax nodded in response. "That's all I have for you, Dick. I appreciate your cooperation." "Yes, sir." Dick rose, nodded to Bella, and hurried out of the library.

Once the boy was gone, Jax perched on the edge of his chair and looked at Bella. "He seemed more cooperative than his brother."

"Dale is more forward and confident, while Dick is shy, but earnest. Usually, Dale takes the lead, and Dick lets him."

"Like yesterday when Dale helped Monticello?"

She nodded. "Yes. Both were in the kitchen when I rang the bell, but Dale is the one who came out. I'm sure it's because he stepped forward first. Even if Dick objected, Dale persists until he gets his way." "They probably discussed how to answer my questions." Frustration filled Jax.

"I'm not sure they would have anticipated your queries, though. As they said, they spent most of their time on the family farm. They quit school even before their parents died. I'm not saying they aren't bright, but they aren't very experienced in the ways of the world."

"You're probably right about that," he agreed, "but neither of them has a strong alibi." "The twins are still suspects."

Bella's voice was flat, and her expression was grim. Didn't she understand his position? Or did she not want to understand? Jax wasn't needlessly singling out her employees. "I can't take them off the list, but I'm not done investigating. Far from it."

"I know," she admitted. "It would be a big help if we could find the rest of the mashie."

"It sure would. I haven't looked yet, not that I think we'll find it." Jax slumped back in the leather chair. "Neither Dick nor Dale added much else that was helpful," he observed.

"I don't think they know anything that might be helpful."

Her words repeated what she had said earlier, and he couldn't deny the possibility. "That may be true, but they don't have ironclad alibis," he replied, "and I was hoping they did."

Bella's expression softened. "I wish they did, too, but I can't believe either of them or, heaven forbid, both of them, were involved in killing Mr. Monticello."

"I know you don't want to consider it being a botched robbery," he said, "but it is possible." Bella chewed on her lower lip. "Yes, I suppose it is." Her reply was barely audible.

Chapter Seven

Their exchange was interrupted by a rap at the door. Curt Molitor, tall and lean, stepped into the library. "You wanted to talk with me, lieutenant."

"Yes, please have a seat," Jax said, indicating the chair next to him. Once Curt was settled, he continued. "This is the same procedure as the Schwarz case. I have to talk to everyone who might have seen or heard anything that would help solve the murder."

Curt's solemn expression didn't change, but he nodded in acquiescence. "I understand." "You and your brother went back to the cabin yesterday after three o'clock. Is that right?" Jax asked.

"Yes, that's our usual time to quit work, and we always check with Mac before we finish for the day," Curt replied. "Sometimes, he has something for us to do around the inn or cottages." "And you usually eat dinner and go to bed early," Jax said.

"Yep. We get up before dawn, so it's early to bed."

Jax nodded. "Did you see Mr. Monticello at all? I understand he planned to walk the course before getting settled for the evening."

Curt nodded. "Yep, when we were walking home. He stopped for a few minutes to tell us that the course looked good and he was eager to play today. After that, he went on and so did we."

"That was shortly after you left, Mac?

The former sergeant's brow furrowed as if in concentration. "Right after that. Maybe three-thirty."

"Was there anything unusual about Mr. Monticello or the way he acted? Did he seem nervous or anxious in any way?" "No, not at all."

Jax cleared his throat. Curt's restrained manner and short answers were typical of him; at least, they were since he'd come home from France. "You and Carl were together after you left

Mac and until this morning."

"Yes, we've been together since we left Mac yesterday until now," Curt clarified. "The rain kept us from our usual work today. Otherwise, I'd be working on one part of the course, and he'd be working on another."

"I see," Jax said. Curt seemed to relax. "Did you talk with anyone else on your way to the house yesterday?"

"We didn't see no one else," Curt said. "Most of the players were already on the back nine, and that's not on our way home. Mr. Monticello said he wasn't following the holes. Just walking here and there. Wherever no one was playing."

"I hoped one of you might have seen something or someone," Jax murmured.

"Am I a suspect?"

The blunt question didn't surprise Jax, but Curt's troubled expression did. "You're not even actually a witness, but you've narrowed the time frame for the murder a bit, and that's helpful. I may need to speak with you again, but probably not." Curt didn't need any additional stress, and his alibi seemed solid. Not to mention, he had no motive.

Curt paused for a moment before responding. "Glad to help."

"Thanks again for talking with us, Curt. I appreciate it." Jax offered what he hoped was a reassuring smile.

"Of course," Curt replied before nodding at Bella and leaving the room.

His brother appeared only moments after Curt left. The interview with Carl only confirmed what Curt had said. Once the greenskeeper left, Jax turned to Bella. "What did you think?"

"Neither of them knows much that's helpful." Bella chewed on her lower lip. "But Curt still seems very uneasy. I worry about him."

"So do I. After we get this murder solved, I'll talk with Curt more often. I should have been doing that, especially since the Schwarz case. Curt took that so hard." Jax laid his head against the chair and closed his eyes. "I should talk more with all the men."

The utter weariness emanating from Jax troubled Bella as much as Curt's continuing uneasiness. That made her respond without considering her words or their earlier impasse. "Jax, you can't take everything on yourself. You have your hands full with your job."

He opened his eyes. "I can do more to help them once this is case is solved," he repeated. "I need to do more."

Bella was about to argue when Mac entered the library.

"Mr. Neece still isn't back, and there's not much to do in town, so I called the café to see if he was there. Sam Push said he had nay seen him."

"Do you think he would have driven to Boxwood to eat?" Bella asked. "The weather isn't good for golf, but where has he been?"

"I dinna know, lass. I just wanted to tell ye two that he was nay here or anywhere I could find."

"Thanks, Mac," Jax said. The old pro nodded and exited the room. Jax turned back to Bella. "I'd like to go out to cottage three and see if there's any sign of foul play."

"Foul play," Bella echoed. "Mr. Neece's car is gone. He probably went to see his son again, or something." The possibility that another guest might have been killed was alarming.

"I know," Jax told her, "but that's not a guarantee he's gone, too. He might have come back late last night and not left again. I don't want to miss something important, even though it's not likely he's in the cottage when his automobile isn't here. I can't be sure that he isn't a victim, too."

His words increased her apprehension. A host of possibilities—all bad—filled Bella's mind, but she did not voice any of them. Instead, she said, "All right." She led the way into the foyer and retrieved the extra key. However, instead of handing it to Jax, she said, "I'll go with you."

"That's not necessary," he told her.

Once again, her dark gaze grew stormy. "It's our cottage and our guest," she pointed out. "Just let me get a rain slicker." Bella swept out of the room before he could offer further argument.

When she returned, the two of them made their way through the light drizzle. Although it was probably unnecessary, Bella knocked on the door before inserting the key. As she stepped inside, Jax laid one hand on her arm. "Let me go first."

Bella started to object before remembering his earlier admonition about putting herself in danger despite his warning. While she didn't agree with the assessment, there was no sense in giving Jax cause to ban her from the investigation. "All right," she murmured before stepping aside.

Jax entered the cottage with his gun drawn. His gaze scanned the small entry hall and stopped on the side table. "There's an envelope." He went to pick it up. "It has your name on it."

Surprise filled Bella as she crossed to take the missive from him. "That's odd," she said before opening it. "It's from Mr. Neece. He says due to the bad weather and not feeling well, he went home, and he left a check to pay for the balance of his stay."

"May I see it?" Jax asked, a frown on his face.

"Of course," Bella replied as she handed the missive to him.

He quickly scanned the contents. "Evidently, he left very early this morning. If he's ill, it seems funny that he didn't simply rest here today. It's an hour's drive to Toledo, and not an easy one with steady rain."

"Maybe he was anxious to get home before he got worse," Bella suggested, although she agreed that Neece's behavior was questionable.

"I need to keep this."

"Of course," Bella agreed. After all, it could be evidence, and arguing over it would be silly. Jax slipped the paper back into the envelope. "I asked Abbott about his acquaintance with Neece, but he was very terse. I don't feel like I got the entire story." Jax searched her face. "Did he say anything to you that might be important?"

Bella hesitated. Abbott had, but she needed to be careful not to reveal her own questioning of the man. "Not much. Neece is the one who indicated there was a problem, and he didn't want to see any of the men in Monticello's group. Mac recognized him and mentioned he used to come with two foursomes, but not for a couple of years. At least not until yesterday. Anyhow, Mr. Neece dismissed Mac's comments and hurried out." Abbott had told her that Neece had caused the problem. Had he also revealed the information to Jax? "What did Mr. Abbott have to say to you?"

"Not all that much. Like I said, I don't think he told me everything he knows. It's unlikely that he's the killer, but not impossible. I have to keep all possibilities in mind."

A long, low breath left Bella. Jax needed to know what Abbott had said, so she couldn't withhold the information any longer. "From what I gathered, Mr. Neece had a serious issue with Mr. Monticello about something. Abbott said Mr. Neece blamed Mr. Monticello for something that wasn't his fault. I don't know what. Just that the group felt Mr. Neece was in the wrong."

Jax studied her face for a moment. "I'm not going to ask how you found out, because I'm guessing I won't be happy to hear the reason."

Bella licked her suddenly dry lips. "It isn't very useful information." The excuse sounded weak even to her own ears.

"I don't know. It certainly puts Neece in the spotlight." He removed his cap and shoved his fingers through his hair. "I wish I'd been able to search his car last night. I'd like to get his home address. Hopefully, I can reach him by telephone today. I want to speak with him as soon as possible. I assume you have some information on him, and that you'll let me have it."

His irritation was obvious in his voice and expression. Bella averted her gaze as she replied, "Of course. His address and telephone number are on my desk. I'll make sure you have them before you leave."

Chapter Eight

They spoke little as they headed back to the inn. Irritation kept Jax silent. Clearly, Bella had questioned Abbott. Exactly when, he didn't know. Not that timing mattered, but he'd invited her to take notes without realizing her deception, which only added to his dismay.

"Do you want to look at the bridge while we're out here?" Bella asked before they got very far.

Since she had stopped, he did, too. Briefly, he fought an inner battle—tell her to go to the inn without him or let her come along. He was still deciding when she spoke again. "I'm sorry I didn't tell you I talked with Mr. Abbott about the case."

The apology sounded sincere, and Bella looked contrite. Jax massaged his taut neck muscles.

"I know you don't think Abbott could be involved, but we don't know for sure."

"He started talking, and I took advantage of his openness. I didn't say anything to you right away because nothing was really important, and I knew you'd be mad."

Mad didn't describe how he felt. Disappointed and worried were closer to the mark. He admitted neither. "I'd appreciate you telling me if you learn anything more from anyone else."

"Of course."

Because there's no good reason not to examine the bridge with her, Jax said, "Let's look at the side entrance since the drizzle has let up." When they got close, he continued.

"More than one vehicle has been down this way recently. The ground isn't as soft as I figured it would be after the rain. Even so, the tire prints aren't clear and there are branches broken off those shrubs like a vehicle hit them," he noted, pointing to a line of elderberry bushes. His attention went to Bella. "You said Mrs. Mars came this way yesterday, but there are a lot more tire tracks than one car coming and going would make." He gestured toward them.

Uneasiness shone in her dark eyes. "I see what you mean. You heard what Mac said about roping it off with Dad. Some guests like taking a shortcut to the highway, but until we have a lot more business, I can't see spending the money on clearing the brush or repairing the bridge. We may need to completely block it off with boards instead of rope. I don't want someone crashing into the creek or using it for some bad purpose."

"Probably a smart idea." Jax continued his trek with Bella at his side. When they got to the bridge, he stopped to grab the rope hanging from one of the side rails. Before speaking, he looked at the other end of the expanse. "Whoever used this route drove right through the ropes." "And knocked some boards loose," Bella observed.

He followed her gaze and saw several gaping holes in the surface. "Those boards weren't missing pieces before now, were they?"

She shook her head. "Not that I know. Looks like some have rotted right through. Using it isn't safe."

"Not for a vehicle, but I'm going to walk to the other side. I want to see if there are better tire tracks." Jax met her gaze. "Stay here. I'm not sure if the remaining wood would support both of us, and the creek is high right now. I'd rather not take a mud bath." He aimed for a note of humor and, when Bella smiled, Jax knew he'd hit the mark.

"Me, either."

Because he'd been serious about not testing the wooden slats too much, Jax proceeded with care. After studying the rope at the other end, he looked at the dirt path and sighed with frustration before rejoining Bella. "Although I can tell vehicles went across, I can't even be sure about the timing. We know Minnie drove along here yesterday, but it's hard to say when the other tracks were made. You said you haven't been out this way lately. Has anyone else?" "The twins might have been. They like to explore when there's free time. Mac warned them not to ignore the ropes and use the bridge, so I'm sure they would have told one of us if they saw evidence of someone else doing it."

"I'll talk to them again. With luck, they may have been out here within the past couple of days."

On the way back to the inn, Jax's mind whirled with all the work yet to do on the case until Bella's voice broke into his thoughts.

"Dick and Dale should work around the golf shop, but Mr. Abbott will probably be in his suite. I wish you'd speak with him so he can get on his way."

When Jax turned to Bella, he saw her troubled expression. "I already said I'd like to consult Richard first."

Her frown deepened. "I know you consider Abbott as a suspect, and I agree it's possible he drove down the lane, killed Monticello, and went back that way before checking in. Possible, but not at all likely. If you turn up solid evidence against him at some point, you can still make an arrest. After all, Toledo isn't very far."

Fresh annoyance filled Jax. Everything she said was true, but he disliked being second-guessed, especially by Bella. Despite his dismay, he tried for a conciliatory tone. "I know you don't want disgruntled visitors, but I have other considerations. Besides, who's to say he'd go back to Toledo? He'd be just as apt, probably more apt, to go elsewhere."

Bella gave a slight nod. "Hurrying home where he'd be easily located wouldn't be wise, which is another reason he's probably not the murderer. The man has a law practice and a family. Why kill his friend and have to abandon both?"

While Bella made good points, Jax resisted agreeing. "I still think he should stay a little longer. What if Abbott killed Monticello, and I let him leave? It will look like I didn't use good sense in protecting the community."

For a moment, she simply stared at him. "Releasing someone who is likely not guilty seems most sensible to me."

Jax's jaw tightened. Could he do nothing right in her eyes? After a brief fight for control, he replied. "I may let him leave after we speak again. Now, if you'll excuse me, I want to do that before finding the twins and getting on my way." With that, he took the porch steps two at a time and disappeared into the inn.

***

As Bella had suggested, Abbott was in his suite. While the man remained hostile, he allowed Jax in but didn't invite him to sit down. Jax didn't ask for that nicety. Instead, he withdrew his notepad and pencil before speaking. "You said you were aware of the side lane. Did you go that way yesterday?"

"No, of course not. I came from Toledo, so there was no reason for me to veer off and enter from that end. Besides, if I recall correctly, it's rough going from the road into the property. I wouldn't want to damage my Cadillac."

"I see," Jax murmured. "And you didn't walk out that way, either?"

Abbott's nostrils flared with a sharp intake of breath. "Constable, only minutes passed between the time I got a key from Miss Stewart and walked into the cottage to find Malcolm dead. I didn't have time for any jaunts around the property."

The man's anger was palpable, and if he was innocent, Jax couldn't blame him. On the other hand, he wasn't ready to eliminate Abbott. "Did you stop in Moreley on your way here?"

"No, I did not. Why would I?"

"But you came that way."

"I already said I did."

"Then, you must have passed by the filling station."

A puzzled look replaced the man's angry expression. "Of course, I did."

"Did you see any vehicles there?" Jax really wanted to know if someone at the place might have seen Abbott take the side route into Ballantyne. If this man proved to be a solid suspect, he'd ask the owners if they'd seen a Cadillac, and when.

"Young man, I don't keep track of other vehicles and such, and I don't appreciate being accused of killing one of my best friends."

Jax noted the change in title—he'd gone from being called *constable* to being referred to as *young man* quite quickly. Not that Abbott's opinion of him mattered. After all, Jax was doing his job, but he couldn't help but consider the possible repercussions to Ballantyne if the man spread his anger far and wide. "Sir, I haven't accused you of anything. I'm simply gathering evidence. I know you want the crime to be solved quickly and so do I." Abbott's demeanor didn't change. "You'll solve it more quickly if you stop harassing me. Now, unless you plan to arrest me—and you have no evidence to do so—when can I leave? I spoke with Smedlay and Forrester. They're releasing Malcolm's body today. I've spoken with his wife, and an Auto Hearse will come for him. I'd like to accompany him."

A long sigh escaped Jax. Disagreeing about evidence was impossible because he didn't have enough to arrest anyone, and Bella was right. Toledo wasn't far. Since Abbott had a law office there, he wasn't likely to disappear. Besides, Jax could easily empathize with the man's desire to escort his dead friend home. The last factor made him relent. "Any time, sir." The man gave a slight nod. "Then, I will bid you good day and be on my way."

"Thank you for your cooperation," Jax replied, straining to maintain a neutral tone.

When he got back downstairs, Jax saw Bella back at the front desk. Her expression was almost as forbidding as Abbott's had been.

"Dick and Dale helped Mac. Now, they're in the kitchen."

"Thank you," Jax said. "I'll speak with them and get going." She remained angry and upset.

"I told Abbott that he can leave." Almost immediately, the tension drained from her face.

"Good."

Jax gave a brief nod. Although he wanted to keep her out of the case, letting her listen to his discussion with the twins couldn't hurt. It might even help since she would be privy to some information—just not enough to put her in danger. "Why don't you talk to the twins with me?"

They'd probably be more comfortable. They were before.

Something akin to surprise flickered in her dark eyes before a half-smile tugged at one corner of her lips. "All right."

Bella preceded Jax through the kitchen door. "Jax wants to ask the two of you a few more questions."

Both boys immediately tensed, so Jax hurried to reassure them. "Nothing to worry about." He held out a chair for Bella and then sat down at the table himself. "We were just looking at the lane running from cottages to the back road. Bella said the two of you occasionally walk out there."

"Yes, sir," Dale replied while his brother nodded in agreement.

"Have you been out that way in the last few days?"

The two exchanged a glance before Dick answered. "We were out there a couple of days ago.

Tuesday, I guess."

Jax nodded. "Did you cross the bridge?"

Dick frowned. "No, sir. Mac said to stay off. There's rope at both ends." "Did you see the rope when you were there?" Jax asked.

"Sure," Dale replied in a confused voice. "But we didn't duck under it or nothing. I think the bridge would be safe to walk on, but Mac said we shouldn't, so we don't."

"We listen to Mac," Dick put in. His attention went to Bella. "And to Miss Bella, too." "Very good." Jax smiled at the boys' responses. "Thank you again." He got to his feet. "Thank you, too," he said, looking at Bella. "Now, I need to get back to my office. First, I need Mr. Neece's address in Toledo. That will help Bertha put a call in. Since she's new as an operator, she takes longer."

Bella went to the front desk, jotted some information on a slip of paper, and handed it to Jax.

"Thanks."

As he left, she said, "I'll walk you out."

Jax grimaced. Of course, Bella would want to discuss her thoughts on the twins' revelations.

Since that wasn't hazardous, either, he merely nodded.

Once they were outside, he turned to her. "We know the rope was there on Tuesday, so it's likely that the killer used the lane to come and go from the cottage." "Then you can eliminate the twins, since they don't have a vehicle."

"I can certainly move them down the list. It's likely the killer's vehicle drove through the ropes, but that doesn't mean it's the only possibility. I still have to explore other ideas."

Bella chewed on her lower lip. "I wish there were good tire prints."

"I do, too," Jax heartily agreed. For a moment, he considered the current suspects. The twins, Abbott, Neece, and even Minnie Mars remained at the top of his list. Abbott was leaving, but where was Neece? Not knowing was a major factor in Jax's anxiety. "I still can't narrow the list of suspects down a lot, so you need to be careful. Even though the twins don't have a vehicle, they could have pulled the ropes down to make it look like someone else came and went that way."

"That's ridiculous, Jax. They're sixteen-year-old boys, not skilled criminals."

Her tart response annoyed him. "But you can't deny it is possible. It's also possible they just lied to me. I'd like to find someone else who was near the bridge in the past couple of days." "I'll ask Curt and Carl when I see them."

Jax immediately regretted his lapse. "Don't go asking questions on your own."

Her chin lifted a fraction. "I thought you eliminated them."

Annoyance gripped Jax. "I'm not going over my investigation with you. I appreciate your cooperation, but stay out of the case."

Twin splotches of red rose in her cheeks. "So, I can help when you deem it necessary, but otherwise, you bark orders and I'm supposed to follow them."

Once again, Jax regretted involving her at all. Bella yearned to help, and he wanted her well out of it. "It's a police matter. There's a killer somewhere, but I don't know who and I don't know where. Poking around on your own could be dangerous."

"You must need to do more interviews. I could help with those."

For several moments, he weighed her words. Refusal would likely lead her to ask questions herself, so Jax relented. "If I talk to more people, I'll let you know." The bright smile curving her rosy lips appealed to him far too much. Jax touched the brim of his cap and went to his car.

***

After saying goodbye to Bella, Jax steered his Chummy out of the parking area and on to the road toward town. As he drove, he couldn't help but think about his exchanges with her. He understood why she wanted the murder solved quickly, but she needed to leave it to him. A killer was on the loose, and they had several suspects. Getting involved could be perilous, but she didn't seem to understand that. Or maybe she didn't want to understand. They were often at odds, which made everything harder.

After Matt's death, a chasm had opened between him and Bella—a chasm created by his cold indifference that day in October 1918. Clearly, she had expected commiseration and comfort from him, but he hadn't been able to offer either. He'd been so shattered himself, felt so guilty, that simply seeing Bella had nearly undone him. All he'd been able to think about was escape. Even worse, during their meeting, Celeste Bouchard had appeared and Jax had been forced to walk away with her for fear that the French nurse would reveal a deep secret, one that he had promised to keep from Bella. A promise her brother had made, too.

Guilt and fear still weighed him down. Guilt about Matt's death and fear that, if he let Bella get involved in the case, he might end up responsible for her death, too. Some way, somehow, he had to protect Bella as he hadn't protected her brother.

That meant he had to find the killer, and he had to do it quickly. Preferably with only minimal involvement from her.

***

When Jax parked in front of the office, he saw Senior Constable Jenkins getting out of his car.

He hurried to the older man's side. "Good afternoon, Richard. Thank you so much for coming." Despite a few additional lines on the man's broad face, he appeared nearly the same as he had last December—tall and muscular, with close-clipped gray hair and a neat gray mustache that still held a trace of black. Although Jenkins no longer wore a uniform, he looked every inch the lawman he had been for all his adult life.

"It's good to see you again, son." Jenkins stuck out one callused hand as a broad smile curved his lips. "I'm happy to help, if I can."

Jax shook the older man's hand and nodded. "Come on in," he said before ushering him into the office.

"Afternoon," Nolen called from behind the narrow counter.

After a further exchange of pleasantries, Jax escorted Richard into his small office. "Sit down and make yourself at home." He gestured to the round table in one corner.

Battered and scarred from years of use, it wasn't much to look at it but, while it might be short on charm, it served the purpose. "How about a cup of coffee?"

"No thanks. I just had my lunch. Why don't we get started?"

Jax scooped up the file sitting on his desk and pulled a notepad out of his pocket before joining the other man at the table. "I'm afraid we have little to go on."

Jenkins skimmed the file contents. "You've covered all the basics." He glanced at the small notepad that Jax handed him. "And you've reviewed a lot of information with the witnesses today. That's a good start." He looked at Jax. "Have you been able to eliminate any potential suspects?"

"Only Bella, Mac, and the Molitor brothers. Nolen talked to yesterday's players this morning.

I haven't had time to look at his report to see if it confirms what the Ironton twins and the Molitor brothers said, but it's right here."

Jenkins scanned the deputy's notes. "It looks like none of those who played in foursomes is a suspect since they vouch for each other."

"That's a step forward," Jax said. "I spoke with all but one of the Ballantyne employees today. You'll remember Curt and Carl from last winter." When Richard nodded, Jax went on. "Curt has been helping his brother on the course and doing odd jobs for Mac, when necessary. Dick and Dale Ironton were hired a couple of weeks ago. The boys help with various tasks around the resort. Curt and Carl can be ruled out since Mac talked to them until they headed to their cabin shortly after three-thirty. They also have each other as alibi witnesses, and absolutely no motive to kill Monticello. It's a slightly different story from the twins. For one, they usually eat dinner with Mac and Bella. Last evening, they went to the café without telling anyone. Both said they'd gotten big tips from guests, so they spent some of that money on dinner." He explained the rest of what the twins had told him. "They took particular note of Monticello appearing to be wealthy."

Jenkins looked back at Jax's notepad and flipped through a few more pages. "I see that one of the boys went to the cottage with Monticello when he arrived, and the other helped Abbott, but he left without going inside. Neither twin was seen at Ballantyne after that because they came to town for dinner."

"That's right," Jax agreed. "They live in the suite off the kitchen, but there's an outside entrance. Golfers gave them a ride to town. You'll see that Nolen talked with Sam Push at the café this morning, and he confirmed that Dick and Dale were there from around six until eight. They left with two friends."

The senior constable removed his spectacles and wiped them on his handkerchief. When he looked back at Jax, his gaze was clouded with dismay. "I see that both Monticello's money and gold watch are missing, and you only found half of the mashie."

"Yes," Jax replied before explaining where he had already searched. "I'd like to look along the road from Ballantyne to town, and farther along the side drive. It may be a waste of time. With the river going by the resort and a creek leading from it to town, I'm guessing the killer would have tossed the shaft in one of them. As high as the water is, finding it will be hard."

Jenkins shrugged. "I don't think that's a top priority. I saw the river and creek. Anything that's tossed into either one won't be found soon."

"All right," Jax agreed. "I planned to speak with Ernest Neece this morning. When we noticed his car was gone, Bella and I went out to the cottage to check on him. A note and money were there. He said he left early due to being sick and the weather." Jax found the excuses weak and wondered if Richard would, as well.

"Do you believe he went home because he's sick?"

Jax shrugged. "If he was really ill, driving back to Toledo in a steady rain would be difficult. Of course, it depends on how sick he is." He stopped to glance at his notes. "I tried to talk with him last night, but he wasn't at Ballantyne. He told Bella he planned to visit his son after playing golf. The whole situation seems odd, so I want to talk with Neece as soon as possible." "That could provide some additional clues," Richard observed.

"I think so, too. Bella gave his address to me, so I thought I'd have our operator place a call this afternoon."

"That seems like a good idea. Do you know if he was acquainted with the victim?" "Yes, he was. In fact, Neece used to be part of a group of eight who came to Ballantyne before the war. I got very little out of Abbott regarding the situation. Bella discovered that there was some sort of falling out. I hope I can talk with Neece soon, but you know how long-distance calls are. Who knows when we can get a line?"

Richard smiled. "Yes, I do. Anything else I should know?"

"While we were checking on Neece, Bella and I walked down the side lane." He briefly described the location, bridge issue, and roping. "It looked like a vehicle had pulled them loose, although I suppose they could have been yanked away. But there are tire tracks—enough that one car didn't make all of them—in the lane and on the bridge. That's in addition to some broken boards."

"You think it would take the weight of a vehicle to break the wood?"

"I believe so," Jax replied. "I wish the tracks were clear, but the road is fairly muddy, so it's impossible to identify a particular set of tires." He paused for a moment. "What do you think?"

"I didn't know about the old lane," Richard replied, "so, I'm guessing a lot of others don't, either. Local people and guests who stay in the cottages, I suppose. Maybe a few who used it as a shortcut. Or was it more heavily traveled in the past?"

"Not heavily traveled, but when the bridge was safe, the lane wasn't so bumpy or overgrown. I looked at Abbott's car last night, and it was dirty. Of course, he drove from Toledo in the rain and the primary drive into Ballantyne and on to the cottages is dirt, too."

"At least we know the killer could have, and very well might have, used the lane with little chance of being seen."

"That's my main theory, but I don't want to eliminate the twins. Even though they don't have a vehicle, they were very interested in the man's money and watch."

Jenkins leafed through the notepad. "It looks like we can eliminate the Molitor brothers as suspects. What about Minnie Mars? You noted she is the housekeeper-cook. Does Arabella have the notes on that interview?"

Jax shook his head. "I haven't been able to talk with Mrs. Mars yet. She lives with her sister- and brother-in-law in town. They own the mercantile. I thought I could catch her at Ballantyne this morning, but she wasn't in yet." Jax glanced at his pocket watch. "She should be there now. I told Bella that we'd be out to interview the woman."

"Good. Talking with her may lead to some key clues, if she saw or heard something."

Richard looked at Jax. "Do you know her very well?"

"No, she moved here from Toledo last summer, not long after I took this job. She and her husband had a grocery store there, but both he and their son died in France. She worked in the mercantile for a while, but she's not too friendly. At Ballantyne, she need not work directly with the guests, so that seems to be better for her."

"I see," Richard murmured. "It's a long shot, but she might have known Monticello in Toledo."

"I definitely plan to ask her about Monticello." Jax shared Bella's story about the housekeeper's odd reaction to the victim.

"I don't know that she's a strong suspect, but it's worth looking into any ties." The senior constable laid the notepad aside and looked back at Jax. "The crime could have started as a robbery. If the killer was surprised by Mr. Monticello, he could have grabbed the mashie in desperation."

"That's what I thought, too."

Jenkins braced his elbows on the table and leaned forward. "We'll know more after you talk to Monticello's boss, Neece, and the two others who were coming for the weekend. One of them may provide a substantial lead. It seems very coincidental that Neece came the same weekend as Monticello." Jenkins looked over the file Jax had hastily compiled the previous night when he'd returned from Ballantyne. He glanced back at Jax. "The interviews should prove helpful."

"Other than talking to them, what do you think my next step should be? I was considering a trip to Toledo. That's where the victim lived. The two friends, the ones who canceled, live there, too. I might learn more about him after speaking with them in person, and I figured I would see his boss as well."

"Those are all good ideas. Face-to-face interviews are preferable to my way of thinking. While you're there, you could also speak with the victim's family. Was he married?"

"Yes. Married with two children." Jax leafed through his notepad. "They're eighteen and nineteen. They're both away at college now. He also has a brother and a sister. The brother lives in Cleveland, and the sister is in Pittsburgh. I was able to get those details from Abbott, although I didn't get much else."

"Abbott is the friend who found the body." The older man scanned the papers again. "You're right. He had little useful information, but that's not unusual. Finding a body, especially the body of a close friend, is a shock. He may think of something more later."

Jax pinched the bridge of his nose to quell a building headache. "I hope so, but he seems to suspect the twins. What with Monticello's money and watch being gone and the boys not having strong alibis..." Unable to complete the thought, he let his voice trail off. "A victim's friends and relatives are always anxious to have the killer found right away, Jax. That doesn't make their judgment sound. We can talk to the boys again together, which should satisfy Abbott for now. After you go to Toledo, you may find other information that leads us to the killer."

"I haven't taken Abbott off my list, either," Jax admitted. "Bella disagrees, and I know he's not a likely killer, but it is possible."

Richard sat quietly for several moments. "The person who finds a body is sometimes the killer, so I think you're right to keep Abbott on the list. If you talk to folks in Toledo, you may learn more."

As he sorted through the rest of Nolen's notes, Jax nodded. "We also had calls from reporters this morning. Evidently, Monticello's two friends in Toledo called some contacts last night and got the story published. Nolen took the calls, so I need to call them back. From what the men said, the stories put Ballantyne in a bad light."

"Reporters can be a help or a hindrance," Jenkins observed. "I can stay at the front desk while you make your calls. Then, Nolen could make the regular rounds." The older man paused before continuing. "That's if you think it's a good idea."

Jax appreciated that Constable Jenkins wasn't sweeping in and taking over, but he also appreciated the suggestion. "That would be great," he agreed.

A slight smile lifted the senior constable's lips. "How is Arabella?"

The question and Richard's expression gave Jax pause. "She's fine." His tone sounded off, but maybe Richard wouldn't notice. "She's eager for the case to be solved," he continued before revealing that some guests had already canceled for the weekend, and a few had withdrawn from the four-ball. He ran a hand over his face. "Not only do we have an unknown killer, Bella and Mac really need the case settled quickly."

"You said Arabella took notes for you again."

Jax hesitated. Should he tell the older man about Bella's insistence she help and his reluctance to let her? Unsure, he offered a benign response. "My handwriting isn't any better now than it was in December," Jax admitted, "and there are a lot of notes to take." His excuses were weak, but he quickly pulled out the papers and spread them across the table. Maybe Richard wouldn't ask about Bella if Jax stuck to the case.

***

Once they had reviewed all the notes, Jax went to the outer office, where Nolen was still sorting papers. Richard stayed at the table and went over the paperwork in more detail.

"Richard and I are going out to Ballantyne, so why you don't you make the rounds now? I have more calls to complete, but I'll be finished when you get back," Jax said.

Nolen hurriedly agreed. When the deputy was gone, Jax placed his calls. All of them connected in record time.

When Jax returned to his office, he relayed what he learned to Richard. "I set times for tomorrow with Mr. Monticello's boss, Howard Harrig, and with the two playing partners who canceled. I actually spoke with Harrig for a few moments, and he said Neece works for an insurance company in the same building as the bank."

"That's a rather convenient coincidence," the senior constable observed.

"I thought so, too. I tried to reach him there, but the receptionist said Neece took the rest of the week off to play golf. I suppose there's no reason for him to call in sick when they weren't expecting him anyhow." Even so, Jax was suspicious.

"No, probably not. When you go to Toledo, you may find him back at home, or at least learn where he might have gone."

"I wish we knew where the son lives. It must be in this area, but that doesn't help much." Jax sighed.

Nolen's return interrupted any further comment, so Jax and Richard headed to the Chummy.

As he steered on to the main road, Jax reconsidered, revealing some of Bella's displeasure with him. He cleared his throat and said, "I should probably tell you that Bella wants to help with the investigation. That's why I let her take notes; not that it wasn't a help, but she wants to be more involved."

He had waged an internal battle about revealing her interest to Richard, but Jax knew Bella would plead her case to the senior constable. Being one step ahead of her seemed wise.

Jenkins took a moment to reply. "I don't know the girl as well as I know my Jenny, of course, but Bella was instrumental in the last case. We discussed her service in France then. That couldn't have been easy. The operators went ahead of most of the expeditionary force, which took a lot of courage. I'm not surprised that Arabella wants to take part in another investigation."

The senior constable's statement was undeniably true. Bella was courageous, perhaps too much so in Jax's opinion. General Pershing had wanted lines of communication in place before his main contingent of soldiers was in battle, so the women operators started leaving early in 1918. They did a great job, and at a much faster rate than their male predecessors had. He brushed away the memories and addressed Richard's comments. "Bella applied when the first call for women who were fluent in French went out without telling anyone. Her parents tried to talk her out of going, but it was too late. Matt and I tried, too, but she wouldn't listen."

A low chuckle rumbled out of Jenkins. "Do you think she would have listened if any of you had warned her sooner?"

The question needed little reflection. "No, I don't think it would have made any difference at all." He didn't add that, unlike her parents and brother, Jax had tried several times to stop her from going. Jenkins laughed again. "That doesn't surprise me. As far as Arabella helping, it's up to you, because it's your case. However, if you think she's going to investigate on her own, I'd consider bringing her in so you can keep an eye on her. For instance, we might have her present when we speak to Mrs. Mars, and she could sit in on our group discussions. That worked well last winter. What do you think?"

"She could get in harm's way if one of the interviews alerts the killer. She did in December."

A look of bewilderment blanketed the older man's face. "I'm not sure what you mean."

"When we confronted the killer, I told Bella to stay in the car, but she didn't. She got out and she could have been shot."

Richard's expression softened. "She didn't get out of the car until after the killer shot himself, Jax." He paused briefly to study the younger man. "It may not have seemed that way to you because you worry about her so much. Concern for the people we care about alters our perceptions."

Heat flooded Jax's face. His immediate impulse was to deny the older man's assertion. Instead, he said, "Her brother was my best friend, and Bella tagged along with us for a lot of our growing-up years. Matt asked me to watch out for his family if he didn't make it back. His parents are gone, but Bella isn't and I don't want her getting hurt." The observations sounded reasonable and objective.

"I understand," Richard said, "but I don't see any danger in having her take notes for you tomorrow. It isn't like anyone you see in Toledo is apt to go to Ballantyne and seek her out for retribution. Nor is it probable that any of them will become violent during an interview. If you don't take her along, she may poke around here on her own. Since we can't be sure if the suspect in this area or not, that isn't a good idea."

Because that possibility seemed far too likely, Jax said, "You could be right."

"I believe I am, son. Arabella shouldn't be in any danger if she's only taking notes for you. If you think she'll strike out on her own, allowing her to participate in that way may be a way to ease her concerns."

Again, Jax considered Richard's words. "I think that may be my only option. If I keep her out, she's likely to investigate on her own, which could be dangerous." If she was with him, Jax had a chance to protect her. If she wasn't...his mind veered away from the consequences. "I agree," Jenkins said. "It might help to know that I worried about Jenny whenever she assisted me, but I was always careful. Very careful. She is precious to me, and I would never put her in danger, but Jenny deserves to live her life, not be hidden away because of my fears." He grinned. "Her words. Arabella might feel the same way."

"I suppose so. What about Jenny? I thought she might come with you."

"She wanted to come, but one of the teachers at our local grade school had to have her appendix removed. Jenny is taking her place. Of course, she'll want to know all about it when I get home evenings, so we'll have her input."

"Good," Jax replied. "Her insight was a big help in the Schwarz case."

"So was Arabella's," Richard said with a smile.

To that, Jax merely nodded.

***

When they entered the inn, Bella was at the front desk. Her pinched, pale face made Jax falter. What else could be wrong now? Slowly, not eager to find out, he followed the senior constable.

"Good afternoon, Richard," Bella said as Jenkins stopped at the desk.

"It's good to see you again, Arabella," the older man said. "I'm just sorry it's under these circumstances."

"I am, too, but I'm grateful that you are helping with the case," she said with obvious sincerity. "Isn't Jenny with you?"

"I'm afraid not," the older man said before repeating what he had told Jax.

"I'll miss her, but I'm glad she'll have some input."

"We're both happy to do what we can. Jax has already gotten a lot of information and is on the right track. Unfortunately, he can't be in more than one place at a time and with only Nolen on his staff, they're really strapped. That's why I offered to help."

Bella's attention moved to Jax. "Is Mayor Cawlings going to let Nolen work full-time?"

"He will while we investigate this case," Jax replied. "The council will decide whether or not to hire him full-time at their next regular meeting tonight. Of course, they've discussed it more than once and never agreed. The town's funds are low, which is the key problem." "In the meantime, you're doing a fine job under difficult circumstances," Richard put in.

The older man's words were more than kind, Jax knew, and he was grateful. When he saw pink rise in Bella's cheeks, he saw she got Jenkins' point, and he could only be glad. Maybe it was left over from adolescence when he had wanted to impress her, but Jax didn't like her effusiveness over the senior constable's help. They all knew Richard was far more experienced than Jax. However, Bella's reaction seemed like a vote of no confidence in him.

"Yes, of course," she murmured, but she kept her attention on Jenkins and away from Jax. "I suppose you want to talk with Minnie Mars."

"Is she back? We don't want to keep her from her work, but if we could speak with her for a few minutes, that would be helpful," the older man said. Bella nodded. "There isn't much for her to do except bake treats for the golfers and fix dinner. Luckily, the weather improved this afternoon and we still have some guests coming for the weekend, although none from Toledo. Evidently, an article about the murder appeared in all three Toledo papers this morning." Her expression grew troubled. "Monticello's two friends not only canceled here, they spread the news far beyond their acquaintances last night and early this morning. Since they evidently both have contacts at all the papers, the stories are not exactly filled with facts."

"I know," Jax said. "Several reporters called our office while I was here earlier. I'll call them back to try and ease the damage."

Bella's expression didn't soften. "Did you look for the rest of the mashie on your way back to town? You said you would."

The question caught him off guard. "I didn't have time," Jax murmured in frustration. "I'll try to get to it yet this afternoon." Weariness tore at him as he considered how to get everything done. He hadn't told Bella, or anyone, that he planned to search for the other half of the golf club immediately, though finding it was highly unlikely.

Jenkins turned from Bella to Jax. "With the river and creek running fast and high, it's very unlikely that we'll find it. With so many other leads to pursue, putting a search for the shaft on the back burner seems wise at this point." After a moment, Bella nodded. "I suppose you're right."

"Did you get calls from reporters?" Jenkins asked Bella. "A couple. I gave them brief statements. Just the bare facts which, as you know, are few. That won't provide much material for more stories. We get many guests from the Toledo area, so more negative stories could hurt us."

"The less we all say, the better," Jenkins put in. "I know it's hard to remain silent, especially if the victim's friends have been talking and, probably, wildly speculating. None of the reporters is likely to drive out here at this point."

"Good," Bella said. "I know you want to speak with Minnie. She's in the kitchen, but I can get her. Would you like to talk in the library? It would be the most private place."

"That would be perfect," Jax agreed. He cleared his throat again before continuing. "If you have time, maybe you'd take notes again. It would be a big help, and Mrs. Mars might be more at ease if you were present, too."

Bella glanced from Jax to Jenkins and back. "It's unlikely that we'll have people dropping by, and we have no reservations for today. Let me get the twins to answer the telephone in case people call." She disappeared momentarily and returned with both boys, who looked at Jax and Richard with wide, scared eyes.

"I'll get Minnie now and meet you in the library," Bella said.

Jax introduced Richard to Dick and Dale before leading the senior constable to the library. He didn't mention his plan to speak with the boys again. While the pair was not likely to disappear, Jax didn't want to give them an opportunity to prepare stories. Undoubtedly, the brothers had already discussed their earlier interviews.

***

It didn't take long for Bella to locate the housekeeper. "Constable Hastings and Constable Jenkins are here, and they'd like to speak with you," Bella told the woman.

"Who is Jenkins?" Minnie asked in her usual tart tone.

"He's a retired senior constable from Karsten. Since Moreley only has one full-time officer, he agreed to help on this case. He assisted with solving the Schwarz murder last winter." Minnie's frown deepened. "I can talk with them, but I don't know a thing that would help." Her usual grim expression was firmly fixed on her lined face. While Minnie could not have been more than forty-five, she appeared weary and care-worn, and she had every reason to be. Once again, Bella's heart softened. Like Minnie, she knew how it felt to lose her entire family.

"Neither did I, but I was still interviewed," was all Bella said in response as she led the way into the cozy library.

Chapter Nine

Jax and Richard had taken the two chairs facing the fireplace, but they rose as the women entered the room. "Minnie," Bella began, "I believe you know Constable Hastings, and this is

Senior Constable Jenkins, who is assisting with the case."

"Thank you for taking time to speak with us," Jax said as the ladies sat on the sofa at a right angle to the hearth. Once they were settled side-by-side, the men sat back down.

"I don't think I'll be of any help," Minnie said, her voice was as flat and emotionless as her expression.

"You never know," Jenkins observed in a friendly tone. "You may have seen something that will help us and not even realize it."

Minnie shrugged, but said nothing more. Bella had picked up a notepad on her way into the room, so she laid it in her lap and took a pencil from her pocket. When she felt Minnie's gaze on her, she smiled. "The gentlemen have asked me to take notes for them."

One of Minnie's typical harrumphs left her. Bella sighed with resignation. Evidently, the woman wouldn't be any more pleasant to the constables than to anyone else.

"Bella told us you saw Mr. Monticello when he arrived," Jax observed. "Since you're both from Toledo, did you recognize him?"

"Toledo is a big city," Minnie replied in a curt tone. "I don't know everyone in it."

"So, you didn't recognize him," Jenkins filled in. His voice and expression remained pleasant.

A moment of silence preceded her reply. "No, I did not," the housekeeper said.

"But you didn't like him on sight," Jax observed.

The housekeeper's pale eyes widened as if in surprise. For several moments, she simply stared at Jax. "I didn't speak with him." Minnie folded her big hands in her lap.

Bella frowned, but said nothing. She had already told Jax and Richard about Minnie's reaction to Monticello, but the woman was acting like she hadn't had a response at all.

"Arabella mentioned you said he looked pretentious," the senior constable put in. "What caused you to think that?"

The woman shrugged again. "His clothes were flashy. Some folks like that. I do not." Minnie's clothes were far from flashy, Bella thought, but the woman's reaction to their guest involved something more than his expensive attire. Even so, she said nothing. Instead, she continued to jot down the conversation. Later, Bella could mention her thoughts to Jax and Richard.

"I see," Jax replied. "So, you were not a customer at his bank?"

Minnie opened her mouth and quickly closed it. She cleared her throat. "I don't know what bank was his. There's more than one in Toledo."

Bella frowned at the woman's sharp retort. Of course, Jax and Richard knew the city had more than one bank.

"He worked at Toledo City Savings and Loan," Jax explained. In response, she shook her head. "We never did no business there." "By *we* do you mean you and your husband?" Jenkins inquired. "Yes."

If either Jax or Jenkins was frustrated by the woman's terse replies, neither showed it. Bella hoped she wasn't showing her aggravation, either. While she didn't believe that Minnie was guilty, Bella thought the woman might be more helpful. At least, she could try. Of course, if she didn't know anything, how could she be of assistance? Once again, Bella had to admit Minnie's brusque manner got on her nerves.

"I understand you and your husband ran a grocery store in Toledo," Jenkins said in his usual casual, pleasant manner. "I suppose that was a difficult task after he and your son left for France."

Bella felt Minnie stiffen beside her. "I managed."

The woman's voice sounded husky, almost hoarse. When Bella glanced at her, she saw Minnie blinking quickly. The housekeeper drew a handkerchief from her pocket and wiped at her eyes. The show of emotion, although slight, surprised Bella. This was the first evidence of genuine sorrow from the older woman, and Bella's heart constricted. Loss and grief were familiar to her, too.

"I know you lost both of them," Jenkins said in a soft, soothing tone, "and I'm very sorry."

"Thank you." Minnie's voice was still thick and her pale blue eyes still brimmed with unshed tears.

"We don't have many more questions, but we would like to finish today. I hope you feel you can continue." Again, Jenkins spoke with kindness.

"Of course," the woman murmured.

A moment of silence passed before Jax asked, "Did your husband or son ever speak of Mr. Monticello?"

"No, of course not. We didn't know him." The sadness was gone, replaced by Minnie's usual annoyed impatience.

"I just wondered if your husband might have gone to him for a loan," Jax explained.

Minnie's eyes looked like chips of ice when she replied. "We didn't need no loan. The store belonged to my husband's folks. When they passed, he got it since his brothers and sister died young."

"I see," Jax said. "What about your family? Were any of them able to help you once your husband and son went to France?"

"My sister is my only kin. She and her mister couldn't leave their own store here to help, but I managed," Minnie replied.

"Running a store is a lot for one person," Jax pointed out. "Especially handling the deliveries and all. A lot of heavy goods to move about, too." "I had no trouble with that. I was already strong from helping for years, and I hired a boy to work during busy times and make the deliveries."

"Even so, your husband must have been worried about leaving you," Richard suggested.

Minnie turned her pale, piercing gaze on him. "He was, but the draft board said he had to go and do his duty. Turned out his duty was to die."

"We're all sorry that happened," Bella put in. "Very sorry."

The older woman glanced at her. "You've lost your people so you know how it feels."

Bella nodded. "Yes, I do," she murmured.

Once again, Jax and Richard exchanged a long look before Jax posed another query. "Did you know an Ernest Neece?"

A moment of silence preceded her reply. "The name is not familiar."

"We're looking into several leads, and his name came up," Jax said in explanation.

Minnie hesitated for a moment. "We had many customers in the store. Some were regulars, but others only came occasionally. If I remember anything, I'll say so."

The woman's sudden show of cooperation surprised Bella, but she continued writing. Maybe Minnie would be of some help, after all.

"When you left yesterday, did you see Carl and Curt? They would have been heading to the cabin about that time," Jenkins put in.

She shook her head. "No, I never saw either of them yesterday afternoon. Do you have other questions?" the housekeeper asked as she again dabbed at her eyes.

Jax and Richard exchanged a look. Then, Jax spoke. "What about the twins? Did you see them? They were still working late in the afternoon."

Minnie stiffened. "Working? Ha. Those two are lazy and don't do no more than someone makes them. They spend far too much time wandering near the river and through the woods. They like to play around the old lane."

"Did you see either of them out that way yesterday?" Richard asked.

"No. I'm only saying they like to dilly dally in the area whenever they can." "Bella said you used the bridge yesterday. What time did you leave here, ma'am?" Jax asked.

Something flickered in Minnie's gaze before she looked toward the fireplace. When she again focused on Jax, her face was expressionless. "Between three-thirty and four o'clock, I s'pose. I put a roast in the oven, cleaned up the kitchen, and went on home." "Did you see anyone when you left?" Richard asked.

"No, I didn't see nothing." She paused a moment before continuing. "Can I go now? I've got work to do."

Jax and Richard exchanged nods before the younger man said, "Thank you, Mrs. Mars. If you remember anything that might help, please let us know."

"I will." Minnie got to her feet and said to Bella, "I'll finish in the kitchen. I baked cookies already, but I need to prepare dinner. After that, I'll go home unless you have something else for me to do."

"No, nothing. In fact, since the rooms are all ready and we have no guests arriving until Saturday, you don't need to come for the next two days. If things change, I'll call you." Minnie nodded and hurried from the room. When she was gone, Bella looked at the two men.

"I'll transcribe my notes, but I guess she wasn't too helpful."

"Not a lot of information, but she confirmed she handled the store easily, which had to involve lifting heavy bags and boxes," Jax said. "She's a big woman, and evidently strong, too."

His comments evoked anxiety in Bella, which made her voice the questions swirling through her. "Do you think Minnie might have killed Mr. Monticello? Her initial reaction to him seems odd. Why would she be so critical of a stranger?" She chewed on her lower lip. "But I can't imagine her planning a robbery. Besides, she sold the store, so she isn't destitute. Her sister said

Minnie only works to keep busy."

"Women commit crimes, even murder, and it isn't only poor people who steal." Jax hesitated briefly before continuing. "I agree about her response to seeing him. The trouble is, we don't know if she's usually quick to judge or not. I'll have Nolen ask other merchants on Main Street about their impressions of her, but I don't know that we'll learn much since she keeps mostly to herself." "That's a good idea," Bella replied.

"Yes, it is," Richard said. "She's an imposing woman. Taller and broader than some men, and likely stronger, too. Moving heavy items takes muscle. As far as theft, Jax is right. People steal for reasons other than need of money."

Bella couldn't deny the observations. "That makes sense." She looked from one man to the other. "So, the number of suspects is the same." "I can't eliminate anyone else yet," Jax said.

"Jax may turn up some good leads tomorrow in Toledo," Richard pointed out. "People there may know if Mrs. Mars and Monticello were acquainted and if she's quick to judge and criticize folks."

The revelation about Jax going to Toledo surprised Bella. Would he have revealed his plans to her if Richard hadn't?

Somehow, she doubted it. Once again, Bella was happy that the senior constable was involved. He was far more likely than Jax to support her assistance. "How many people do you plan to see tomorrow?"

Jax shrugged. "I'm not sure. A few at Monticello's office. I also want to talk with his two friends who canceled and, hopefully, to Mrs. Monticello, and to Ernest Neece. I may stop by Abbott's law firm."

"That's a lot of note-taking," she observed, "and a long drive."

"Yes, it is," Jenkins said before Jax could reply. "Perhaps you could use some help, son. Arabella did a great job on the Schwarz case." He gave her a broad smile before looking at the young constable.

A frown furrowed Jax's brow, and long moments passed before he spoke. "I'd hate to take you away from your work here, Bella."

Jax's tone and expression weren't encouraging, but if she could go, welcome or not, she would. The murder was not only a tragedy for Mr. Monticello's family and friends, the crime—if unsolved—could have a devastating effect on Ballantyne and Moreley. While Bella knew Jax was working hard on the case, she wouldn't rest easy until the killer was caught. "We haven't been busy, and we probably won't be until the murder is solved. Word spreads quickly, unfortunately. The twins can handle the front desk tomorrow, not that I expect much activity."

"If you're sure it won't be a burden," Jax said.

"I'm sure." The words were firm, and her expression was fixed.

"Wonderful. While you two are gone, Nolen and I will be here," the senior constable said

with a smile, "waiting to hear your report."

Chapter Ten

The next morning, Bella pulled into a parking space in front of the constable's office. She glanced at the watch pinned to her shirtwaist and smiled. It was only seven-fifteen, and Jax planned to leave at seven-thirty, so she had time to spare. Her smile faded as she looked up and down the street and saw no sign of Jax or his distinctive roadster. Had he left her behind? She'd thought coming early would keep him from using that as an excuse to leave without her. Maybe she should have arrived at seven o'clock.

A sigh escaped Bella as she grabbed her pocketbook and notepad before climbing out of the vehicle and entering the office. If he was gone, she would have no choice but to go home, an idea that infuriated her. Once inside, she saw Nolen at the front desk. "Good morning. Is Jax here?"

"Good morning," the young man replied. "No, he called a few minutes ago to say he needed to stop at Mrs. Adams' house. She was sure she saw a light in her shed early this morning. He's going to check it, but he said you'd be coming and to tell you he might be a few minutes late." Relief spread through Bella. Jax hadn't left without her. "Fine. Thank you, Nolen." She took one of the old beat-up chairs that sat across from the counter. They'd gotten fresh coats of varnish regularly when she was a girl. Now, bare wood showed through in some places—another sign of the town's overall decline. Last December, Jax had told her the town council didn't like to spend money unnecessarily, especially in the constable's office, but the faded, worn look of the place was dispiriting. Bella wondered how Nolen and Jax coped daily. With the population smaller, money was tight. Once again, she hoped turning Ballantyne around would also help Moreley. With effort, she pushed the negative thoughts from her mind. "How is your mother?"

The young man shrugged. "She's feeling better, so she's looking for work but hasn't found nothing. Since we don't have a car, a job would have to be in the area and there aren't any. I was lucky to get a part-time position here." His boyish face held a grim expression. "The council voted last night on being full-time. The answer is still no."

"I'm sorry," Bella said, and she was. Nolen's concern was obvious. It must be hard for him and his mother to make ends meet. His father had died in a vehicle collision while Nolen was in France. Shortly afterward, his mother had gotten a severe case of Spanish flu that had led to a lengthy recovery. Last winter, she had contracted bronchitis and then, pneumonia. Prior to the pandemic, Mrs. Rogers had worked at the hotel in town. Since the place had closed, she was jobless.

The whole town needed a boost. A big boost. Two days ago, Bella might have been able to offer a part-time position at Ballantyne to Mrs. Rogers, but that wasn't possible now. Since Bella didn't want to extend false anticipation, she simply said. "I hope she finds something soon."

"Thank you. I hope so, too."

The little bell on the front door chimed to signal Jax's entry. "Good morning," he said to her before crossing to stand by the counter, where he turned his attention to Nolen. "There was no sign of an intruder, but I told Mrs.

Adams that you'd be in the office all day, so she only needs to call for help. You know how she is, so try to reassure her. Senior Constable Jenkins will be here around one o'clock. When he arrives, make the usual rounds, and stop by to see her. That should ease her mind." "Sure thing. She is a sweet lady, but anxious at times. I'll do my best to help her," Nolen replied.

"Good man." Jax looked back at Bella. "Let me get my file. Then, we can go."

She nodded and got to her feet. Jax was back in moments. When they were outside, he stopped. "I want to speak with Mrs. Downing before we leave. They don't open the mercantile until later, so we'll have to stop by the house."

Surprise rounded Bella's eyes. "Why do you want to talk with her?"

"Mrs. Mars said she left the resort by four o'clock. If so, she should have been at the Downing place no later than four-fifteen." "The mercantile doesn't close until five," Bella remarked.

"True, but Mrs. Downing leaves by four o'clock. With that in mind, she should have gotten home just before or right after her sister. If Minnie was there, it would make her less of a suspect because she wouldn't have time to kill him, get rid of the club shaft, and get home."

Bella caught her lower lip between her teeth. "That makes sense. I didn't actually see her drive away, but she said the Packard was near the cottages."

A grimace furrowed Jax's forehead. "If she took the side road to the highway, she could have more easily escaped notice. That route would bring her out nearer the Downings' house. Since it's at the end of the street with an empty lot between it and the road, she didn't have to go through town."

Bella considered his comments. "Mr. Neece could have taken the same route."

"Yes, he could, but I only want to check on Mrs. Mars right now."

"All right," she murmured with reluctance. Jax's suggestions were viable, but Bella hated thinking a resort employee might be guilty.

"I'll drive," he said before opening the passenger door for her.

"What about your arm?"

"It'll be fine for now. You can drive back."

Within moments, Jax parked the Chummy in front of the Downings' gray frame two-story home. Neat hedges ran the length of the front porch while a few tulips were peeking out along the walk. He hurried to open the door for Bella before following her up the sidewalk. Shortly after Jax rang the bell, Mr. Downing answered. A look of surprise spread across the older man's round face.

"Good morning," he said. "How can I help you?"

"I wanted to speak with your wife," Jax replied. "I know you must be getting ready to leave for the store, but this won't take long."

"Come in." Mr. Downing stepped back before leading them into a tidy parlor. "My wife is in the kitchen. I'll fetch her."

"Is your sister-in-law here?" Jax asked.

The shopkeeper paused. "Yes, but she's sleeping," Downing said before leaving the room.

Bella and Jax had no chance to talk because the husband and wife appeared within moments. "Good morning, ma'am," Jax said to the woman.

"Good morning," Mrs. Downing replied in a tentative tone. Her eyes were wide—with surprise or dismay, Bella wasn't sure. "My husband said you want to speak with me, but I cannot imagine why."

"It's simply routine," Jax reassured her. "We need to know about anyone who was at Ballantyne yesterday."

"I wasn't there," the woman murmured.

"No, but your sister was. In order to eliminate her as a suspect, I have to confirm what she told me about when she got home."

Mrs. Downing looked at her husband, who laid his arm around her shoulders. "Just answer the constable's questions."

A weak smile formed on her lips. "Of course."

"What time did you get home yesterday afternoon?" Jax asked.

"About four o'clock. I usually leave then since we aren't busy late in the day," she replied.

Jax looked at Mr. Downing. "Is that right, sir?"

The older man nodded in agreement. "Yes, it is."

"I see," Jax responded before looking back at Mrs. Downing. "Your sister was home when you got here?"

Her eyes moved away from Jax to a point somewhere beyond his right shoulder. "Yes, she was home." She cleared her throat. "Since my husband had a meeting, Minnie and I had a light supper later."

"What time did you get home, Mr. Downing?"

"It was close to eight o'clock," the older man replied. "Minnie had already gone to bed, so I didn't see her."

"I see," Jax said before looking back at Mrs. Downing. "You and your sister had a quiet evening together?" "Yes, we did."

Briefly, Jax glanced at Bella, who gave a slight nod. "Thank you, both of you," she said with a smile. "We're sorry to have disturbed you, and I hope we didn't disturb Mrs. Mars, either."

"Minnie is still sleeping," her sister said. "She told us you wouldn't need her today, so she'll help in the shop this afternoon."

"That's right," Bella replied. "The constable and I are taking a brief trip to Toledo today since I'm not busy at Ballantyne myself."

The older woman nodded, but said no more.

Mr. Downing turned to Jax. "Is that all, constable? If so, we have to get ready to leave for the store soon."

"Yes, that's all for now," Jax replied before escorting Bella out of the house and to the Chummy. Once there, he opened the passenger door for Bella, walked around to the driver's side, got behind the wheel, and headed out of town.

"I suppose we can take Minnie off the suspect list," she murmured when he said nothing.

"You thought Mrs. Downing was being honest." It was both statement and question.

"Yes, I did. Why? Didn't you?"

He exhaled sharply. "She seemed tentative and anxious."

"Being questioned by a constable may have upset her, Jax."

"I suppose so, but she's known me since I was a little boy."

"You aren't a boy now. You're a grown man. A lawman."

Her observations reminded him of how much his life had changed. How much he had changed. Not all the townspeople accepted him in the role of constable. If the Downings did, he ought to be grateful, he supposed. "You're most likely right."

After a few moments of silence, Bella spoke again. "I transcribed my notes last night," she began. "As I did that, I revised my list of potential suspects, even remote ones, and put them in order."

Jax glanced at her and quickly back to the road as annoyance rippled through him. How could she make a list when she didn't have all the facts? "I see," he replied. Jax heard Bella sigh and braced himself for her next comments.

"I know you only let me take notes yesterday and come along today because Constable Jenkins told you to. At least he thinks women can be useful. Or maybe you just don't think I can be helpful." Her hurt tone slipped past his defenses. "Bella, it's not that. I know you're perfectly capable, as much—even more so—than many men. It's just that..." His voice trailed off as he struggled with how to reveal his concerns. Revealing the depth of his fear for her was likely to destroy the barriers he had constructed, and he needed those barriers, especially if she wasn't as indifferent as he'd figured.

"Just what, Jax? I don't understand you anymore. Sometimes, I feel like I don't know you at all."

His nostrils flared with a sharp intake of breath. This line of conversation was exactly what he wanted to avoid. "I told you I'm not the same guy who left for France two years ago."

She chewed on her lower lip. "No one who served is exactly the same. How can we be? I wasn't in the trenches, but what I saw..." Her voice grew tremulous. "I can't even imagine what it was like for those of you who were at the front."

What he had seen and done would always haunt him, but it was his role in the death of his best friend, Bella's brother, eating at his soul. Allowing her to know the depth of his remorse was something he wanted to avoid, so Jax relentlessly pushed the thought from his mind. "You operators worked under difficult, dangerous conditions. We all knew that and admired you ladies."

"Working in Paris wasn't bad, but being near the front lines was challenging," she admitted. He hadn't seen her after she started serving close to the trenches, but he wouldn't have called it *challenging*. To his way of thinking, *dangerous* was a better word. "I'm sure," he finally replied.

"I was never sorry that I volunteered for the Signal Corps or worked close to the front."

Her statement hung heavily in the air between them because it acted as a reminder of his insistence that she'd be better off safe and sound at home—not serving in harm's way. They'd reached an understanding in Paris, but his opinion hadn't changed. He just hadn't voiced it again, and Bella hadn't referred to it, either. Not even when she'd complained about him trying to keep her out of the last case. Because Jax preferred to avoid references to the past, he responded with care. "You did an important job under arduous conditions, from what I know." He hadn't heard details from her, only from others.

Bella shrugged. "It was often hard, very hard. Ida and I thought our college dormitory room was cramped, but we shared a smaller space with two other operators for the last few months of the war. The only saving grace was we worked opposite shifts so, mostly, only two of us were there at the same time. But the place was cold and drafty. It seemed like we never got warm that fall. We were dry, though, which is more than those of you at the front could say."

Her words weren't overly expressive, but they revealed more than she had in the past. With that in mind, Jax opened up. "I never knew how much it rained in France. Icy rain and so much mud. Not to mention the rats and the lice." Abruptly, he stopped. Why was he rattling on? "Sorry..."

"I heard much the same from other soldiers who had been in the trenches. We always had some officers billeted near us. Staff officers. None of them spent much time on the line, but they told horror stories about their brief sojourns, so I have some idea of how awful it was. We had to ask them to stop sharing their experiences at meals."

Some indefinable emotion nipped at Jax. "I didn't know you ate with officers." *Male officers* was what he meant. How had he missed that information? Although he hadn't seen much of Bella in France, finding out she and other operators had socialized with staff officers was unsettling news. Almost immediately, he inwardly chastised himself for feeling disquieted. He had no right to be.

"Like I said, some were billeted close to us. We ate meals together and, when there was time, we'd sometimes have sing-a-longs and such."

Jax wondered what she meant by *and such*, but he didn't ask. He'd had no claim on her when they'd been in France. He didn't have one now, and he never would. It wouldn't do to get too close, but always being at odds with Bella wore on him. Besides, he didn't think Matt would want that. Not when he'd asked Jax to look out for his family if he didn't return from France. The thought sent his spirits plummeting. Matt. His friend was never far from his thoughts, and being around Bella only intensified his guilt and shame.

Once again, he reminded himself he'd been her brother's best friend. If he played that role alone, how would he react to her revelations? Casually and nonchalantly, Jax decided. Surely, he could manage that. "I'm sure they appreciated your efforts to maintain morale."

"I hope so. We tried to conceal our own doubts and fatigue in order to keep their spirits up.

They needed and deserved that much from us."

Bella's disclosures revealed more than she probably realized. Suddenly, Jax thought of the two photographs in his desk drawer, especially the one taken in Paris. Bella was quite capable of maintaining a calm and cheerful façade to cloak deeper feelings. Was she doing so now? Bella's reply about the war changing everyone joined with her latest admissions. Now he knew both remarks were personal feelings, not general observations.

Mostly, Jax not only avoided her; he avoided thinking about her—a challenge. Now that he was, some things were becoming clearer. On the surface, Bella seemed much the same. When she had arrived home in December, she had been thin and tired. Now, she looked much more like herself. But that was external. How did she feel inside? Mac had mentioned her tendency to worry too much. That wasn't like the old Bella at all. Before the war and the pandemic, she had been carefree and confident. His first memory of her was as a happy, exuberant, fearless little girl with a loving, indulgent family. Now, with her parents and brother dead, much of that support was gone. As Bella had said more than once, she still had Mac, but he was nearly seventy. She had to realize he wouldn't always be with her. How did she feel about another loss? Was it one of her worries?

Ever since picking her up at the train station in December, Jax had mainly focused on his own feelings and reactions. Now, he resolved to be more aware of Bella's emotional state. Barriers—necessary ones—would always be between them, but he could be a better friend to her. Matt would expect that much of him. The thought guided his next words. "I suppose many of your sister operators changed after being in such a dangerous situation," Jax said in what he hoped was a careful, cautious observation. Avoiding a personal comment seemed best. He cast a sidelong glance at her to gauge her reaction.

Bella didn't reply immediately. "I guess so. We were well-trained and well-prepared. Of course, the reality of war isn't something that anyone can truly understand without firsthand experience. But you know that."

Her last statement neatly turned the conversation back on him, something Jax realized she had been doing all along. Whenever the subject of the war came up, Bella talked about the soldiers and civilians in harm's way, not the operators. While he had disclosed little about his own experiences, Bella had said virtually nothing at all about hers. Jax tried again. "I never got to your posting, but I know you weren't very far from the front at the end." It was on the tip of his tongue to say he'd tried—more than once—to get a day's leave simply to see her. He bit the comment back because it would be too revealing.

She shifted restlessly in the seat beside him. "Close, but not right at the front."

"You don't talk much about it."

A moment elapsed before Bella replied. "You and I don't talk much about anything except your cases, and that's only when you feel you have to let me be involved."

Her words confused him. In December, she'd been clear about Ballantyne being her sole focus, which was as it should be. His life had taken a decidedly different turn when he became constable, which meant their primary common bonds—golf and the resort—were gone. They might have bridged those gaps, but his role in her brother's death was a major barrier. Heaven knew, he worried every time they got into a private conversation. Now they were spending the entire day together. If he retreated, it would not only be unpleasant for both of them, it would go against his decision to be a better friend. "You're right. I'm not comfortable talking about the war for a lot of reasons that I can't fully explain." Jax could present explanations—worthless, selfish ones—but he didn't. Maybe he was protecting himself as much as Bella, but with them traveling different paths, what good would it do? Matt had wanted and expected Jax to look out for her, and that wouldn't happen if Bella knew the truth. When he responded, he concentrated on Bella's experiences, not his own. "I suppose you and Ida have discussed your service."

"To some extent, yes. We talked about it on the way home and when I stayed with her family for a few days last December," she replied in a guarded tone.

Jax wanted to ask more questions, but Bella didn't seem open to answering them. He couldn't blame her. Candor required connection, and theirs was now tenuous. His next observation was benign. "That's good." He went on as if Bella hadn't rebuffed his attempt to draw her out. "How is Ida doing?"

A soft sigh escaped Bella. "In her letters, she says she's fine, but I don't know. Losing Alan was very difficult for her. When we were still in Europe, we were busy, so she didn't have as much time to think. Now, she isn't working or going to school. That gives her a lot of free time, which isn't good."

Jax didn't respond to Bella's reference to Alan Brewster. The man didn't deserve Ida's continuing grief. Not for the first time, Jax wished he hadn't promised to keep Brewster's secret.

"Does she want to go back to college?"

Bella stared out the window at the passing scenery, as if the answer to his question was there. "I don't think so. She asked me if I planned to, but Mac needs me at Ballantyne, and it's where I want to be. Ida could teach without finishing her last year, and she may. She says it would give her something to do with the rest of her life."

Jax frowned. "She could meet someone else and get married." Bella shifted to look at him, and he felt more than saw her dismay.

"She was deeply in love with Alan Brewster. He was such a good and kind man, and he died a hero. You know that. Ida doesn't want to marry someone else. At least not right now, and maybe never."

Guilt pricked at Jax's conscience because he knew a lot more about Ida's dead fiancé than

Bella did. "Alan died saving one of his men, but he was hardly perfect."

A low gasp escaped her. "If you see Ida, please don't say something so callous to her. She's still grieving."

The words were a reprimand, and Jax felt stung by them. He wanted to explain his comments, but doing so would mean breaking a solemn pledge to Brewster. "I wouldn't do or say anything to hurt her, Bella, but no one is without flaws."

Silence followed his remark. Finally, she said, "No, everyone has shortcomings but, right now at least, it helps Ida to revere Alan. It's been less than two years since he died. With time, she may open her heart to someone else. I hope so."

"I do, too," Jax replied. He hoped someone could find joy in the aftermath of loss. He doubted he ever would, but Ida was more deserving than he was. After a moment, he steered the conversation back to the case. That was a safer topic than the war. "So, tell me about your list." After flipping open her notebook, she began, "Mac and I were at the resort, but we have decent alibis so I put us in the unlikely column. Curt and Carl are very unlikely suspects. They don't have a motive at all." She paused to let him speak. "I agree."

"Dick and Dale are equally unlikely, but their alibis aren't as strong. I know you believe a robbery could have led to the attack."

"It's a possibility, not a foregone conclusion. Added to that, the twins were both surprised that a golf club could be a dangerous weapon. One blow, maybe the first, was to the back of his head. Another one likely happened as he fell. If it was the twins, they might have simply grabbed the mashie out of his golf bag because it was in the doorway to the parlor. They may not have planned to kill him, just to knock him out, and get away before he recognized them."

"I suppose Mr. Abbott and Mr. Neece would know how much damage a mashie could do." "Yes, but if one of them is the killer, I don't think robbery is the motive. We don't know what caused the problem between Monticello and Neece, but that could be a reason. As far as Abbott,

I think we'll either eliminate or highlight him after today's meetings."

Bella gazed out the window at the passing scenery. "Mrs. Mars isn't much of a possibility since she was home with her sister."

"A family member isn't the best alibi witness."

Immediately, she shifted to look at him. "Do you think Mrs. Downing lied?"

"I'm not sure. She seemed uncomfortable. You may be right that being questioned by a constable caused her reaction. We've both known her for a long time, and she's always been a forthright person. Even so, I don't think her assertions are a powerful reason to eliminate Minnie. I wouldn't with anyone else."

A long, inaudible sigh escaped Bella. "I guess you're right. I'll keep Minnie in the possible suspect column. So, we don't have any strong suspects."

"No, but Ernest Neece is near the top of my list," Jax pointed out. "Yes, I included him. I hope you can speak with him soon."

"I tried calling him early this morning, but no one answered."

"Maybe he's too sick to come to the phone," she suggested.

"Possibly, but we can stop at his house and see if he's actually there."

"That sounds like a good idea," Bella agreed before stifling a yawn.

Jax took a quick look at her before returning his attention to the road. "If you're tired, take a nap. We have an hour before we get there."

"I'm fine," she said, but another yawn escaped her.

"If you keep yawning, you'll have me doing it and that's not a good idea for the driver," he said with a chuckle.

"I suppose not. Maybe I will rest my eyes."

"I'll wake you when we get there," Jax replied, but Bella said nothing. She was already asleep.

Chapter Eleven

Jax didn't need to wake Bella. She roused as they arrived at the outskirts of the city.

"Feel better?" he asked when she stirred.

"Yes, I do. I'm sorry I wasn't more company." She sat up straight and rolled her head to ease the stiffness.

"Not a problem. I'm used to my own company."

The admission surprised Bella. Jax was usually more careful with his words, but so was she. Both had made revelations during the trip. Did he realize he'd admitted he was now a loner? A sidelong look at him told Bella that he didn't. He still appeared to be completely relaxed. Since she didn't want to make him regret the acknowledgement, Bella was careful with her response.

"I chatter too much."

"Some things don't change."

The words and tone made her look back at him. A slight smile curved his firm lips. Maybe the changes in him weren't permanent. Maybe the old Jax was still there somewhere. She hoped so. As things stood now, she only had Mac who remembered the old days. If nothing else, Jax could be another link to her past—a happy past. Bella needed that more than she was usually willing to admit. Sometimes, late at night when sleep was elusive, she felt adrift and alone. While Bella was lucky to have Mac, he was getting older and—although she hated to think about it—he wouldn't be around forever. But Bella couldn't force Jax to spend time with her or at Ballantyne. She didn't want to force him, of course. With determination, she brushed off her troubled thoughts and tried for a casual note. "Very funny," she said with mock dismay.

He chuckled again and then turned his attention to the street names. "The bank is on Madison. I'll try to park close."

"I don't mind walking," Bella told him. "Just park any place."

Jax pulled over to a spot on the side of the road. Once they were out of the Chummy, he led the way to the building where Neece worked and, when they were inside, headed toward the company's suite. An attractive young receptionist greeted them as soon as they stepped into the main office. Her auburn hair was cut in a stylish bob, and she wore a neat ivory shirtwaist that set off her creamy complexion and green-gold eyes. "Good morning," she said, offering Jax a welcoming smile.

With a sigh, Bella glanced at her own attire. Suddenly, her perfectly serviceable—but unadorned—white shirtwaist looked lackluster as did the navy skirt hitting halfway down her calves. Although she couldn't see the height of the receptionist's hem, Bell felt sure it was close to the knees, not well below them.

Bella couldn't help but notice that the girl, and she was probably only nineteen, didn't spare her a look. Her smiles were for Jax, who grinned at the receptionist in return. "Good morning, Miss..." He glanced at the nameplate on her desk and then, back at her.

"Miss O'Casey. I'm hoping you can help me."

His use of *me* instead of *us* annoyed Bella, but she bit her lip and remained quiet. Interfering wasn't likely to help.

"I hope I can, too," Miss O'Casey replied, batting her long lashes.

Bella had to look away. The girl's coquettish manner annoyed her. Jax, on the other hand, seemed to soak it up. His reaction was surprising. Even before he'd gone to France, Jax had never engaged in flirtations. Both he and Matt had been preoccupied with golf and, while they'd occasionally stepped out with one young lady or another, there had never been one particular girl on a regular basis. Bella had never had a serious beau either, although several young men escorted her to college events, Jax included. But he'd never been flirtatious, and she'd certainly never acted as silly and coy as Miss O'Casey. Nor would she.

"I'm Constable Jackson Hastings from Moreley," Jax said, a smile still on his handsome face.

"And this is Miss Stewart."

Miss O'Casey briefly glanced at Bella before returning her attention to Jax. The quick dismissal clearly indicated that the girl didn't see Bella as any actual competition. Of course, she wasn't. She didn't want to be. Even so, the interplay between Miss O'Casey and Jax annoyed her far more than it should have.

"I'd be happy to help you in any way I can, Constable Hastings."

The receptionist's tone dripped sugar. Bella cringed, but fought to remain expressionless. Getting information was all that mattered. If Jax flirted to do it, she shouldn't care. She didn't care, but she couldn't help but notice. He certainly didn't appear grim now.

"Miss Stewart and I would like to speak with Mr. Neece. Would you ask him if he has time now?"

Miss O'Casey's little bow of a mouth went from a smile to a frown. "I'm so sorry. Mr. Neece isn't in today."

Jax's smile disappeared, too. "He won't be in at all?"

"I'm afraid not. He took the end of the week off to play golf. He called yesterday to say he would be out until Tuesday at least," the girl replied.

His jaw tightened, and Bella knew he must be as frustrated as she was. Other than the staff at Ballantyne, Neece seemed to be a likely suspect. Then, there was Abbott, who Jax hadn't eliminated, either.

"Does Mr. Neece often take time to go play golf by himself?"

O'Casey shrugged her slender shoulders. "I've worked here almost two years, and this is the first time. I know he plays golf most weekends when the weather is good, but as far as I know, this is the only time when he's gone off and rented a place by himself. He said he wanted to get away and have solitude."

"Do you know if he often plays alone or does he play with friends?"

"He plays with friends and colleagues. Some of the other men who work in the building have golfed with him in the past, but not recently. At least I've heard that in the lunchroom."

"Do you know why he stopped going with them?" She shook her head. "No, I'm sorry I don't."

"Thank you, Miss O'Casey. You've been very helpful," Jax told her, his charming grin evident once again.

The girl blushed prettily as she turned her full wattage smile on him. "Is there anything else I can do for you, constable?"

"No, you've been a tremendous help. We appreciate it."

Bella noted he had gone back to *we*. Evidently, he hadn't forgotten her presence entirely.

Within moments, they were out of the office and back by the elevator. Bella took a long look at Jax but said nothing.

"What's wrong?" he asked. He wiped both cheeks with one hand. "Did I miss a place shaving or something?"

"No, you didn't miss anything." Bella heard the tart note in her voice, but she didn't quell it. As reserved as Jax could be with her, he acted warmly—very warmly—toward Miss O'Casey.

"Then, why are you looking at me like I did?" Confusion clouded his green eyes.

Since she didn't want to comment on his flirtation with the receptionist, Bella merely shrugged. "I didn't realize I was looking at you in any odd way. I was just thinking." Curiosity replaced confusion. "About what?"

"Just about the case," she replied. After all, that was the reason for their trip to Toledo. If Jax now made a habit of flirting with strange women, it was none of her concern. The image of the French nurse rose in her mind's eye. Had the woman been another flirtation? That seemed out of character for the Jax of her childhood and adolescence, but Bella already knew he had changed. He had said so more than once. She needed to believe him and not wish for a re-emergence of her childhood friend and girlhood crush.

His voice broke into her thoughts. "We need to get to the bank now. Once we leave there, we can go over your notes from yesterday and whatever we learn in the next interviews on the way to Neece's house. If he's really ill, he'll most likely be home."

All traces of charm had disappeared from him. Only bone-deep fatigue remained, as evidenced by the dark circles beneath his green eyes. Odd how Bella hadn't noticed them at all when he was chatting with Miss O'Casey. She brushed the thought away. "I suppose you're right." Bella paused briefly before continuing. "Are you planning to speak with Mr. Abbott's colleagues?"

Jax absently rubbed his shoulder with his other hand. "No. I thought I would but, as it is, we'll be getting back to Moreley late. I can call his office tomorrow."

With that, the two of them took the elevator to the first floor. There, the security guard, a man in his fifties, nodded when they entered the bank.

"We're looking for Mr. Harrig's office," Jax told him. "We have an appointment."

"Over there," the man replied, gesturing to the far side of the expansive lobby where a double door labeled *Offices* sat. "Thank you, sir," Jax replied before ushering Bella ahead of him.

Once inside the doors, a secretary greeted them. "How can I help you?" Her tone was gruff, as if she didn't really want to help and only did so since it was her job.

Bella immediately observed that this woman was three times the age of Miss O'Casey. Her gray hair was pulled back into a tight bun, and her equally gray eyes held no hint of admiration when she looked at Jax. If anything, she seemed imperious.

"I'm Constable Hastings, and this is Miss Stewart. We're here to see Mr. Harrig. I made an appointment with him yesterday."

The woman looked at the desk calendar. "I will let him know you're here. Please sit down for now."

Jax and Bella took seats across from the desk and waited. Within moments, Harrig, a tall man clad in a gray three-piece suit, emerged. With his silver hair and mustache, he was a study in monotones.

"Good morning," the man said to Jax as he extended a hand.

Jax rose, shook the man's hand, and introduced Bella. "Miss Stewart is here to take notes for me," he explained.

"Fine," the banker said. "If you'll follow me, we can talk in our conference room. Then you can meet with the others there."

Bella and Jax followed Harrig down a narrow hall and into the room. Once all of them were seated at the gleaming mahogany table, Harrig sighed. "As you might expect, everyone is devastated by Malcolm's death. Such a terrible shock."

"Yes, I imagine it was," Jax put in. "I don't want to add to the grief, but we want to solve his murder as quickly as possible, and I'm hoping someone here may have a clue that helps."

"I thought you had suspects already," Harrig said. His heavy gray brows pulled down until they nearly obscured his eyes.

"We've spoken with all the Ballantyne employees and most of the players from that day," Jax replied. "We haven't been able to single out a strong suspect, so we need more information. We want to get the right person, of course."

Bella noticed he avoided mentioning Neece and Abbott. Surely, Jax had a reason. "Of course," Harrig agreed, but he looked uneasy. "However, no one here could have done it. No one else was out of the office at the same time."

"Yes, sir, you mentioned that on the telephone. However, someone who worked with Mr. Monticello may have useful information," Jax said in a calm voice.

For the next few minutes, the men reviewed their conversation from the previous day. Bella continued to take notes, even though Jax had recorded the information then. Perhaps Harrig would add something new.

"You said Mr. Monticello was well-liked at work and in the community, so you don't know of anyone who had a grudge against him?" Jax asked.

The banker fiddled with his bow tie. "No. Not really. He was head of the draft board during the war. There were a few pacifists in the area, and I know the board heard from them until the Sedition Act passed. No one was jailed here, but when some of their ilk were imprisoned in other places, they stopped their protesting," Harrig said in a tone that indicated he agreed with such measures. This information was not new, but it made Bella cringe. While she hadn't agreed with the peace movement, the penalties levied against protestors had been harsh. During the war, freedom of speech had been curtailed—a mistake in her mind. After all, President Wilson had argued that going to war was critical to keeping the world safe for democracy. In Bella's mind, freedom of speech was an important element.

"You don't know of any personal threats against Mr. Monticello?" Jax inquired.

"No, but he seldom discussed the draft board here. I only know about the pacifists because articles were in the newspapers. Some draftees protested their inductions to the review board. That wouldn't have involved Malcolm, though. The local draft boards did what they were told to do: see that eligible men were registered, classify them, and select draftees from the Class One group. Objections went to the review board. Many folks didn't understand those facts, and a few complained to draft board members like Malcolm."

"The classification system caused some controversy," Jax agreed. "I went over with the Thirty-Seventh Division, and no one I knew objected, but most of us had been in the National Guard and others volunteered. I met some men who were drafted and didn't think they should have been."

"You were in the National Guard," Harrig observed.

Jax shifted in his chair. "Yes. Our local unit was merged into the Thirty-Seventh with some other units."

"The Buckeye Division," Harrig observed. "You served with distinction."

"The division did, sir," Jax replied in a clipped tone. "Do you know if the local draft board had anyone who was really angry or upset? A family member of a draftee who was angry, perhaps?"

Briefly, Bella looked up from her notepad. Jax's expression was hard and his gaze was cold. Why did he sidestep taking any credit for his service? He'd always been humble, though. Harrig shook his head. "No, Malcolm seldom discussed the board's work in the bank. I know he found it to be an arduous task. Sending men to war is difficult. But as far as a particular problem, I never heard of any."

"Thank you, sir. I appreciate your time. If I have other questions, I hope I can rely on you to be equally cooperative then," Jax said.

"Of course. I want the murder solved quickly," Harrig said. "I'll send the others in one at a time, if that's good with you." "I appreciate it," Jax replied.

When the banker left, Jax turned to Bella. "What do you think?"

Bella tapped her pencil on the table. "He didn't provide any real leads, but the draft board could be an angle. It's funny that Mr. Abbott didn't mention it, though."

Jax nodded. "I agree, but the man wasn't forthcoming at all. Mostly, he complained about not being able to leave sooner."

"Someone else in the bank may know more," Bella suggested.

***

But no one did. Each of Monticello's colleagues could only confirm what Jax and Bella already knew—he was a wonderful man, and he had rarely spoken about his service on the draft board. By the time the last employee left the conference room, Jax was once again tired and frustrated.

"None of them knows much more, but I'm still hoping to reach Mrs. Monticello," Jax said as he ushered Bella out of the office.

On the way to the reception area, he and Bella stopped to again thank Mr. Harrig. Jax mentioned calling Monticello's widow.

Concern blanketed the banker's face. "She is grief-stricken. She and Malcolm were childhood sweethearts, and they'd been happily married for over twenty years. I'm not sure she is up to talking with you, or anyone, yet."

"She may know something crucial to the case, sir," Jax pointed out. "I understand she is grieving, and I won't take more than a few minutes of her time."

Harrig adjusted his already perfect bow tie. "Perhaps I could call and speak with her first."

The man's hesitation was obvious, and Jax understood his desire to protect Mrs. Monticello. He had known grief and anguish himself, and the sorrow of a widow had to be more profound than that of a platoon leader or a best friend. "Certainly. Please tell her I will make our talk as brief as possible."

Seemingly satisfied, Harrig nodded. "If you will excuse me, I'll try to contact her right now."

While the man made the call, Bella and Jax waited in the outer office. When he came out, Harrig shook his head. "I spoke with her sister, who is at the house helping. Mrs. Monticello, the boys, and Malcolm's mother are at the funeral home. Mr. Abbott is with them. From there, they'll be going to the church to speak with their minister. The sister isn't sure when they'll be home, but I let her know how to reach you. She will tell Mrs. Monticello, although she didn't know if you should expect a call today."

"Thank you," Jax replied. "I appreciate you contacting her for us."

When they got out in the hall, Jax turned to Bella and said, "Lumley and Earl have offices on the fifth floor. I said I'd be here early this afternoon. I know it's almost one o'clock, but will a late lunch do?"

"That's fine," Bella assured him.

They took the elevator again. When it reached the right floor, a sign saying *Lumley and Earl—Public Accountants* was on the door directly across from them.

"Looks like we're at the right place," Jax observed as he held the door open for Bella and followed her into the offices.

Once they were inside, another receptionist, young and pretty like Miss O'Casey, greeted them. Bella noted she smiled at both of them.

"How can I help you?" the woman asked.

Again, Jax made the introductions. The receptionist immediately nodded. "They said you would arrive this afternoon. I'll let them know you're here." She was only gone a moment. When she returned, she said, "Follow me, please."

When they arrived at an open door, she told them that both accountants were inside, so Bella and Jax entered the room. The two men immediately stood up. The tallest one, a man in his fifties, reached out to shake Jax's hand. Jax introduced Bella, and they all took seats at a large, round table in the room's corner. The other man—shorter and rounder, but the same age—simply nodded.

Lumley immediately spoke to Bella. "I'm very sorry we had to cancel, Miss Stewart."

Despite the words, his tone indicated he wasn't sorry at all. When Earl said nothing, she nodded in response and murmured, "We are, too."

Earl focused on Jax. "We don't have much time, constable. A client will be here in thirty minutes, so I hope you can wrap up quickly."

"I believe we can, sir. I just want to ask a few questions in case either of you knows something that would help solve the case," Jax replied.

"If we knew something, we would have contacted you," Earl shot back. His pale eyes narrowed on Jax as if in accusation.

Lumley was slightly less antagonistic. "We probably don't know anything helpful, but we have a little time to talk, constable."

Jax maintained an impassive expression. "I appreciate that. We've learned a few things that have opened another avenue of investigation."

"*We?*" Lumley asked. His attention moved to Bella. "Is Miss Stewart assisting you with the case?" His tone and expression indicated something between dismissal and disapproval.

"As I said, she is here to take notes," Jax replied. "However, a retired senior constable is helping with the case, as I only have a part-time assistant." "I see," the man went on, but he didn't appear to be mollified.

Maybe he did, Bella thought, but he didn't have to sound so curt. She wanted to reveal that she had helped with a previous case, but that was unlikely to move either Lumley or Evans. On the other hand, it was likely to annoy Jax. Bella kept her peace. "What have you discovered that you want to ask us about?" Lumley inquired.

"Mr. Harrig mentioned that Mr. Monticello served on the draft board during the war," Jax responded.

"Yes," Lumley replied. "He was the head of it."

"Do you know if he had any issues with any draftees or their families?" Jax asked.

Lumley glanced at Earl and then back at Jax. "When the draft age range was expanded, Malcolm said they got more complaints and more requests for exemptions. All the requests were referred to the review board. Most were denied, and a few of those men, and their relatives, were quite unhappy. Several contacted the board to complain even after their reviews were turned down. Of course, when the review board turns a man down, that's the end. The draft board couldn't intercede."

"Was there anyone in particular that more than complained?" Jax asked. "Anyone who was especially angry?"

"Malcolm mentioned that someone had been harassing him about a decision made by the review board. He didn't seem overly concerned. More annoyed. Malcolm said it went with the territory, but his wife was upset. Evidently, one person came to their house a couple of times," Lumley replied. "Did he give you any indication of who that person might have been?" Jax asked. Both Earl and Lumley said he hadn't provided any additional details. "He only talked about it once, and that was when someone asked if they got many complaints," Lumley said. "Malcolm mentioned one problem, but he brushed it off."

"I also wondered if either of you is acquainted with Ernest Neece, who works at an insurance company in the building," Jax said.

Lumley nodded. "We both know Ernest. We used to have two foursomes that played together most weekends. A few times each year, we all went to Ballantyne or another resort for a long weekend."

"You said you *used to* play with Neece. Does that mean you don't anymore?" Although he had already heard that information, Jax wanted clear confirmation. If this pair knew anything that would make Neece a stronger suspect, he needed to find out. Conversely, if they could offer support for the man, that could still help lead to a faster conclusion.

Earl scowled. "No, we don't. Ernest was against American involvement in the war. When both of his boys were drafted, he became even more adamant, and he asked Malcolm how he could live with sending young men to die in a foreign war. When his older son was killed, Ernest became much more vocal and volatile. He brought up the war and the draft in every conversation. He even accused Malcolm of taking bribes from others to keep their boys out of uniform, which was absurd. He was far too honest to do such a thing." The man released a dismissive snort.

"I agree Ernest was wrong to make such a spurious accusation, but his grief overtook his good sense," Lumley put in quickly. "He was furious with Malcolm for being involved with the draft board. He made it impossible for us to play golf together, and Ernest took to playing alone most of the time. I was sorry about it, and I still am, but he was wrong to blame Malcolm for his boy's death. Or for the younger one's fragile mental state. Malcolm was doing a civic duty, a very difficult one."

A frown creased Jax's forehead. "What do you mean? Does his younger son have some sort of problem?"

"The kid came back without his senses," Earl said. "Ernest laid that at Malcolm's door as well. But no one is to blame for the boy's own frailties."

Bella and Jax exchanged a long look. She saw his jaw tighten to keep from chastising Earl for his lack of compassion and understanding. Very few Americans realized what trench warfare had been like. While Bella wanted to tell the accountant that he had no idea what soldiers had suffered, she knew berating him for his ignorance was useless. Still, she wanted to say something. Before she could construct a logical response, Lumley spoke.

"I believe Irwin's ailment is called shell shock."

His partner snorted. "No matter what it's called, nothing that happened was Malcolm's fault, and Ernest should have realized that. His ranting was ridiculous."

Several moments passed before Jax spoke again. "It is my understanding that Mr. Neece planned to visit his son while he was at Ballantyne. Does the young man live in the area?"

"He's institutionalized somewhere not far from Ballantyne," Earl replied with obvious disdain. The man's derisive tone wore on Bella's patience. "He must have suffered greatly," she observed, "to need special care." Not that most of the care afforded to shell shock victims was helpful. In fact, some of it was dreadful.

Again, Lumley hurried to reply. "Irwin's brother died in his arms, which I believe started the problem, but the boy continued to serve. I only saw him once after he got home." His expression was grim. "His hands shook badly, and he said nothing. He simply stared into space. I knew both boys before they went to war, but Irwin didn't seem to know me. Ernest said his son had horrible nightmares. Some nights neither of them slept at all due to that. After a while,

Ernest couldn't keep Irwin at home. He needed rest himself, and he was afraid to leave the boy without supervision."

"I've heard of cases like his," Jax said. He cleared his throat. "So, Mr. Neece found a place for Irwin near Ballantyne. Do you know the name of it?"

"I believe it's called Poplar Pines," Lumley replied. "A new place, just opened recently. It's a half-hour or so to the south of the resort. I occasionally run into Ernest here in the building, and he told me he tries to get down there at least once a month. More often if he can." "Have you seen Mr. Neece recently?" Jax asked.

Lumley's brow furrowed, as if he was pondering the question. "Yes, I ran into him a couple of weeks ago."

Bella looked up from her notes to see Jax looking alert and interested. His question to the accountant didn't surprise her. "Did you mention your plans to spend a weekend at Ballantyne?" "I believe I did," the man replied. His gaze went to his partner and back to Jax. "I agree. Ernest should not have blamed Malcolm for what happened to his boys, but I can understand his feelings. I don't have children myself, but if I did and if they had both been so horribly harmed, I'm not sure I wouldn't feel the same way."

Bella noted Earl pursed his lips as if he had just tasted something nasty. People without compassion or empathy were hard for her to accept, and she wanted to rebuke him, but Jax didn't give her the chance.

"Thank you for your help," he said. "Both of you."

"Of course, constable. We want the murder solved, and we're glad to help, if we can," Lumley assured him. "Please let me escort you and Miss Stewart out." Once they were in the outside hallway, the man spoke again. "My partner has children, two boys and a girl. Neither of his sons was old enough to serve, but I would think he'd have more sympathy for Ernest." He paused for a moment. "You don't regard Neece as a suspect, do you?" The question was directed at Jax.

"Sir, I don't know. Right now, I'm gathering evidence. Once we finish today's interviews, we should have a better idea," Jax told the older man.

Lumley nodded. "Of course." Then he bid them farewell, went back into the office, and closed the door behind him.

Chapter Twelve

Jax was silent until he and Bella were riding down in the elevator. "Abbott had to know most of those details, but he didn't share them and I have to wonder why. I know he wasn't impressed by me, but he should have mentioned the draft board. On top of that, he had to be aware of what happened to Neece's sons."

Bella chewed on her lower lip. "I don't know. He was terribly upset, so that may be why he wasn't cooperative. As you said, he seemed more focused on leaving Ballantyne than anything else."

With one hand, Jax rubbed his forehead. "Yes, but I don't like that he withheld so much. Still, the timing of his arrival makes him a less likely suspect. Monticello had clearly been killed at least an hour, maybe more, before Abbott arrived. We already discussed the possibility of him using the back road. Possible, not probable. Even so, it bothers me when someone isn't forthcoming. He was a close friend of the victim. As such, he should want to do everything in his power to help find the killer. So far, he hasn't."

The man hadn't shared that information with her, either, but Bella withheld the observation. "It is odd, but I still think he may have been traumatized by finding his friend murdered. In addition, he seemed to be fixated on Dick and Dale as the killers."

A harsh sigh left Jax. "That's true. I'd like to talk with him again, but if he's with the Monticello family, I'll have to wait." Jax looked at his watch. "It's already after one-thirty.

Let's eat lunch, and I'll try to call Monticello's house afterward. If his wife was upset about someone harassing them, she may have important knowledge." "That's a good idea," Bella murmured as they left the elevator and went out to the street.

***

They found a small restaurant down the block and went inside. The place was still crowded with lunch hour diners, but they located a booth near the back and sat down across from one another. A waitress appeared before they had even gotten settled. She placed two menus on the table, turned a smile on Jax and asked, "Can I get you something to drink?"

He smiled back at her, but not with the enthusiasm he had shown Miss O'Casey. Of course, Bella noted, the waitress was over forty and somewhat stout. Her gray-streaked hair was pulled into a sloppy bun and the only color in her face was from two spots of red rouge and a matching bright lipstick. Even so, she focused on Jax with a girlish grin. Despite the fatigue lining his face and shadowing his eyes, he was still handsome, and most ladies reacted accordingly. They always had, and he'd always seemed oblivious. Until today.

Bella focused on her menu and tried to marshal her thoughts.

"Bella," he said, "what do you want to drink?"

"Coffee, please," she said with a glance at the woman, who continued to keep her attention on Jax.

"I'll have the same," he said to the waitress.

"Be right back," she assured him before stepping away.

"What sounds good to you?" he asked.

Bella glanced up from her menu. His clear green gaze met hers. For several moments, she lost the thread of their conversation. It would be easy—so very easy—to be swept into the past. Almost immediately, her resolution to focus on the future emerged. With that in mind, she looked back at the menu. "The meatloaf and mashed potatoes sound good."

"Yes, they do," he agreed.

When the waitress returned with their coffee, Bella and Jax placed their orders. The woman asked Jax to let her know if he needed anything, while Bella was virtually ignored. Once again, the image of him walking away with the French nurse flashed in her mind. With effort, she forced it away. Solving the case was her goal, and while she wished the two of them could return to their old camaraderie, Bella needed to control her feelings and her words.

"We didn't learn as much as I hoped at the bank," he said with a sigh. "The draft board seems like a good lead, and both Evans and Lumley had interesting details about Neece's relationship with Monticello."

"That's true," Bella agreed. She gripped her coffee cup in both hands and let the warmth invade her palms. "I met a few soldiers who were drafted and mad about it, too. I can't blame them. The entire process seemed subjective."

"It was. I know some boards avoided drafting any man who had a family. Others didn't find that to be a reason for an exemption. They had quotas to fill, which complicated the entire process. Most folks didn't understand that, especially the ones who were against the war." She nodded.

"I met an officer who had four children. The family owned a drugstore, and the board told him that his wife and the oldest two could run the business. His wife kept it going, but he knew it was hard on them."

A frown knit his brows. "Do you know what happened to him?"

"He was wounded and lost his sight in one eye."

"He got sent home then."

"Yes, he did. In that way, his family was fortunate. I hate to think of four children without their father, but many are. Too many here and far more in Europe." When she looked back at Jax, Bella saw anguish in his eyes. She knew he'd lost men, some of them boys, really. The Meuse-Argonne offensive in September 1918 had gotten off to a terrible start for the men from Moreley. A half-dozen had died, and more had been wounded. Matt had been among the former. She swallowed over the lump of grief that still, far too often, threatened to choke her.

Anxious to discuss less troublesome issues, Bella moved the conversation back to Neece. "Evidently, Mr. Neece made a habit of playing alone. However, it seems very coincidental that he was at Ballantyne when Mr. Monticello was. I need to check and see exactly when Neece made his reservation, but if Lumley told him that Monticello would be at the resort before then, I wonder if that played into his decision to come for a long weekend himself."

"I wonder about that, too. Whether or not Neece made his reservation before or after talking with Lumley, he knew Monticello would be at Ballantyne."

Before replying, Bella took another sip of coffee. "Mr. Neece losing one son and having another who suffers from shell shock is very disturbing."

"Yes, it is. He has had a lot to handle," Jax said. "Putting the boy in a sanatorium had to be a hard decision."

"The symptoms that Lumley described were very serious. His brother dying in his arms had to be devastating. I'm surprised Irwin didn't collapse right then."

Jax stared down at the table. "The kid probably let himself be shamed into staying on the line. Even if his lieutenant wanted to relieve him of duty for a short time, the next officer up the chain might not have permitted it."

Bella studied his bent head. "Did you ask for any of your men to be relieved temporarily or permanently?" When his face, an ashen mask of anguish, came up, she knew the answer.

"We had good commanders when we arrived in France, men who knew us because they trained us before we shipped out. But everything got turned around once we got to the front. Officers and men were shifted to other units, and it got even more mixed up as casualties mounted. Some officers didn't want to hear about any man not being mentally or physically fit for duty. In those circumstances, about all a platoon sergeant or lieutenant could do was to keep a close watch over the soldier and hope for the best." His voice was hoarse with suppressed emotion. "It was much worse in the British army. Years of trench warfare took a heavy toll in casualties and shell shock. I met officers who were completely shattered by losing not only many of their men, but most of their friends."

"I heard some tragic stories," she agreed. "The Belgian, French, and British armies suffered great casualties." Bella took another sip of coffee before continuing. "So many deaths, but also horrible wounds. People have more sympathy for physical injuries. Mental problems aren't very well understood, and the treatments can be brutal. Have you heard of the place that Lumley mentioned?"

Jax shook his head. "I have, but I know little about it. I agree many treatments are barbaric." He leaned back in the booth. "Poplar Pines is a private facility. It must cost Neece a lot of money."

Bella ran one forefinger around the edge of her cup. "Another reason for him to have a grudge against Mr. Monticello."

At that moment, the waitress, who had identified herself as Molly, brought their food, ending their line of conversation. For several moments, neither spoke.

"It's delicious," Bella said with a smile.

"Yes, it is."

During the rest of the meal, they talked only about the food, the weather, and their next steps. "Neece seems like a strong suspect, but would he really have followed Mr. Monticello from Toledo to Ballantyne?"

"If a person has a big enough grudge, and Neece definitely had one, it seems quite possible." Jax let his fork rest on the side of his plate. "Although I'd like to talk to him today, I'm not counting on him being in town." "If he isn't, that's another bad sign," Bella pointed out.

"You're right," Jax agreed. "Like I said with Abbott, a guilty man is likely to hide out."

Since she had thought the same thing, Bella nodded. "Are you still planning to drive by the Mars' store?"

"I'd like to do that. Nolen got the address for me, and I tucked it into my pocket. It's on Erie Street, so not far from Abbott's apartment. I'd like to see if we can find him first. Then, we can head to the store. We have a lot of puzzle pieces, but some big ones are still missing."

A long sigh escaped her. "A lot more information is needed. Hopefully, we'll get closer to a solution today."

***

He didn't reach Mrs. Monticello because she remained away from home. Unfortunately, no one answered at Neece's home, either.

When Jax returned to the Chummy, he revealed the outcome of the calls to Bella. "Let's head to Neece's house. Even if he isn't there, we might get some information from a neighbor."

The drive took less than ten minutes. "It's a lovely neighborhood and close to downtown," Bella observed when Jax pulled over to the curb. Large frame homes lined the wide street. Towering trees were just showing shoots of green, while daffodils, tulips, and narcissus already bloomed in many yards. Under other circumstances, the scene would have charmed Bella.

"Yes, it is. From the address, Mr. Neece must live in a duplex or apartment building. The street address is 5928, and his number is One A."

Bella twisted to look out her window. "This is the right house," she said, "and it certainly looks large enough to accommodate several apartments."

Jax followed her gaze. "It does, and there's a lady sitting on the front porch. Let's see what she has to say."

Before Bella could get out, Jax was opening the door for her. She smiled and preceded him up the sidewalk. When they got close to the porch, the older lady sitting there stood up and met them at the steps.

With one hand, she patted her white hair, which was pulled back into a loose bun. A smile curved her lips and her blue eyes twinkled as she looked from Jax to Bella and back. "Did you see my advertisement in the *News Bee*?" she asked. "The apartment is perfect for a young couple."

Heat invaded Bella's cheeks and, when she glanced at Jax, she saw color infuse his face, too. At that moment, she let him respond.

Jax shifted from one foot to the other and cleared his throat. "No, ma'am, we aren't here to look at the apartment."

"It's a lovely place." The lady looked back at Bella with a twinkle in her eyes. "I have one of the nicest buildings on the street. Several other units are for let, but I really think you and your husband would be happiest here. My rents are higher than some, but I would consider lowering it for a couple just starting out."

Husband. When Bella glanced at Jax, the emotion darkening his green gaze confused her. She had little chance to consider what it might mean because he was rushing ahead to explain their reason for coming.

"Actually, we came to speak with one of your tenants. Mr. Ernest Neece."

The landlady's smile fled, and a disappointed frown replaced it. "I'm sorry, but I thought...well, the two of you look like..." She halted. "None of my business." She indicated the four wicker chairs grouped on her porch. "Let's sit down. Don't have as much energy as I used to." She returned to the seat she had vacated and waited for Jax and Bella to join her.

Jax introduced himself and Bella. "Miss Stewart is taking notes for me, ma'am."

The woman again looked from one to the other. "I see," she replied. "Ernest isn't home. I haven't seen him since Wednesday morning," the elderly lady, who introduced herself as Dolly Daniels, said.

"Is it unusual for him to be away?" Jax asked.

She pursed her thin lips. "He seldom travels anymore except for going to see his son. This weekend, he planned to go golfing and visit Irwin. That's his son." A sad expression crossed her face. "Poor boy."

"Did you know Irwin and the other son?" Bella asked.

"Oh, yes. Two wonderful young men." She shook her head. "Aaron died only a week after landing in France. Ernest was beside himself, of course, but grateful Irwin made it. We all were.

Then, the war ended and Irwin came home." One hand went to her throat. "But he isn't the same at all. Such a shocking change."

Mrs. Daniels' sorrow was obvious, and Bella's heart turned over. The war continued to cast a long shadow over many lives. "We've heard he's in a sanatorium."

"Yes," the older woman agreed, "and it costs Ernest a pretty penny. He couldn't keep the boy at home, though. Irwin stayed in his room all day. I never saw him, although I took lunch over. Sometimes, he would eat, but often the food sat outside their door until Ernest got home. Then, there were the nightmares." Her expression became grim. "My apartment shares a wall with theirs, and I could hear Irwin's screams. I never complained, but Ernest apologized over and over. I said not to fret. Heaven knew, he had enough on his shoulders already." "Is that why Mr. Neece took his son to a sanatorium?" Jax asked.

Mrs. Daniels shrugged. "Part of the reason. Ernest got little rest himself, so going to work became a chore. He also worried about Irwin being alone all day. I think he feared the boy might take his own life." She took a handkerchief out and dabbed at her eyes. "Now, Ernest can only visit once during the week and on the weekend. It's hard for him to get there in the evening after working all day. Since he missed a lot of work when Irwin was here, he often goes to the office on Saturday and even Sunday. That means he only gets to see the boy every few weeks. Such a terrible state of affairs."

"Yes, ma'am," Jax agreed in a soft voice.

Her gaze narrowed on him. "Did you serve, constable?"

"Yes, I did." Jax glanced at Bella. "So did Miss Stewart."

Surprise widened Mrs. Daniels' pale blue eyes. "Were you a nurse?"

"No, ma'am. I was with the Army Signal Corps as a telephone operator," she replied.

"I've heard of them. Very brave young women. Made me wish I was younger, but I imagine your family and..." She looked at Jax. "Friends worried about you."

"Yes, they did," Bella admitted. Before the older woman asked any more personal questions, she hurried on. "How did Mr. Neece feel about his sons going off to war?" They knew the answer, but hearing the landlady's perspective could be helpful. When she glanced at Jax, she saw him give a nod of agreement, signaling he approved of her question.

"He didn't think we should fight any European wars, and he was very upset when they were drafted," the landlady said. "When Aaron died, Ernest was beside himself." She took the handkerchief and dabbed at her damp eyes again. "Who could blame him and then, when Irwin came home in such awful straits...it's enough to bring anyone to his knees."

"Yes, it certainly is," Jax agreed. "Was Mr. Neece upset with a particular person?"

"The government and draft board, but I never heard him speak about someone in particular," Mrs. Daniels said. "It's all been a sore trial for him. His wife left him shortly before he moved here five years ago, and he has no other family. Growing old alone isn't easy."

"No, ma'am. I understand that," he replied before pursuing the new piece of information. "Do you know where Mrs. Neece moved?"

"Ernest said near the sanatorium. That's one reason he chose Poplar Pines. Even though his wife left him, she stayed in touch with her boys. From what he said, she was crushed when Aaron died and distraught when she saw Irwin. Of course, it was a terrible shock to her." "Did she come here to visit?" Bella asked.

"Oh, yes," Mrs. Daniels replied. "After Irwin came home, she visited every week or two. For a while, I thought she might move back. Heaven knows, Ernest could have used more help."

"Did you have the chance to speak with her when Mr. Neece was at work?" Bella inquired. "Only a few times. She kept to herself, and I didn't intrude. She first left to care for her ailing mother. After the woman died, Mrs. Neece came back for a bit. She evidently prefers living in her family homestead." Mrs. Daniels sighed. "I had the impression she wanted Ernest to join her. Don't know why he stayed here. I know she was upset when he continued to play golf with someone on the draft board. More than once, I heard them arguing about it, but he told her he'd stopped associating with the man long ago. When they noticed me on the porch, they lowered their voices, so I don't know more."

Jax absently tapped his fingers on the wicker chair arms. "The boys must have still been in school when she left the family."

The woman nodded. "Aaron had graduated from high school about when they moved here, and Irwin was a senior. Both attended the university before going to war. Maybe the boys didn't want to leave Toledo. I don't know. They were polite young men but busy with their activities, so I seldom spoke with them at length," Mrs. Daniels explained.

"I see," Jax said. "Do you know the name of the town where Mrs. Neece lives?" "Riddling. I believe it's quite small. Never heard of it," she replied.

"Yes, it is. I've been there once or twice myself, but years ago," Jax told her. "I wonder if you might know of a grocery store here on Erie Street. The long-time owners were named Mars, and I'd like to stop there while we're in town."

"I patronize our neighborhood grocery and rarely go to Erie Street for shopping. It's only a ten-minute drive, but I don't have a car. I can't walk to stores any longer, but they all deliver."

The landlady smiled. "Good for us old folks."

"Delivery is nice for everyone," Bella agreed.

Jax got to his feet. "Thank you for your time, Mrs. Daniels. We appreciate your help. If you hear from Mr. Neece, will you have him call me?" Jax handed her a slip of paper with his name and how to reach the Moreley constable's office. "I assume you have a telephone."

"Yes, I do. I'll certainly let you know if I hear from Ernest," the landlady assured him. Her bright blue gaze moved back to Bella. "It was lovely to visit with both of you."

"It was also a pleasure for us," Bella told her

Once they were back in the car, Jax released a pent-up breath. "Even though Neece wasn't home, we learned quite a bit."

"Yes, Mrs. Daniels was very informative and sweet, too." Bella hesitated for a moment. What had the woman noticed when she looked at the pair of them? Some lingering connection from the past? That was all there was, all there ever would be now. With determination, she brushed the question away. "It's very unusual that Mrs. Neece left her family and didn't come back. I can understand her taking care of her mother, but she had two sons. Even though they weren't small children, I can't imagine a mother leaving."

"It is unusual. It was interesting that they argued about Neece's association with Monticello. That had to be who they meant."

"I'm sure it was, and I agree. Mrs. Neece was evidently even angrier than he was." Bella chewed on her lower lip. "If she lives in Riddling, she isn't far from Ballantyne. A bit to the north. I wonder if she knew Mr. Neece planned to spend the weekend with us."

"Neece could have gone to see her or even picked her up. Riddling is off the primary route from Toledo, so he'd be going a bit out of his way, but it is possible. Could he have taken her to the cottage with none of you noticing?"

Bella's brow furrowed in concentration. "Dick went with him. Although he didn't stay long, he would have seen someone else in the car."

Jax turned to look at Bella. "Then, she wasn't with him, but I still want to find out more about

Mrs. Neece. She could have influenced her husband to confront Monticello."

"That seems likely," she observed. "What we've learned today—about the draft board and the Neeces—gives us plenty to consider."

His hands gripped the steering wheel until the knuckles showed white. "You're right. I just want to solve this murder without anyone getting hurt."

"You will," Bella assured him.

When he glanced back at her, Jax's expression softened. "It's still a team effort, so we will." With that, he pulled away from the curb.

Bella didn't comment further, but his reply was encouraging. "Some shopkeepers in Minnie's old neighborhood should know how she reacted to people. If she was judgmental of some."

"I agree. After that, I'll try to contact Mrs. Monticello and Neece again. I'd especially love to talk with him."

Sadness filled Bella. "He is a strong suspect, but I feel sorry for him."

Jax released a harsh breath. "He and Minnie Mars are at the top of my list. It's still possible that Monticello surprised a thief. I don't want to lose sight of that."

Bella knew he was still thinking the twins might have robbed and killed Monticello. Although she didn't like Jax continuing to keep the boys on the suspect list, Bella couldn't prove they were innocent. Since she didn't want him to accuse her of being biased, she phrased her response carefully. "Then, you're mostly thinking about Neece, Minnie, and the twins. Or are you still considering Abbott?"

"He could have used the side road, killed Monticello, and driven around to the inn. But we haven't found any motive. Killing a close friend and then, going with the grieving widow to make funeral arrangements would be very cold and calculating. Abbott isn't a warm person, at least he wasn't to me, but it's hard to see him being so devious."

"Does that mean you're ruling him out?" Bella didn't even try to keep a note of triumph from her voice. "Pretty much."

"Then, I was right to insist you let him leave."

With one forefinger, he tapped the steering the wheel. "Pretty much."

Despite his grudging admission, Bella laughed as she glanced back at Jax. When his lips quirked, almost in a smile, she felt vindicated and returned to the case. "Talking to Mr. Neece and Mrs. Monticello could be key factors in the investigation." Although the comment was repetitious, it was safe.

"I think so. I don't know that we'll learn a lot from the current owner of the old Mars grocery or other shopkeepers on the block, but we're so close that it's worth a try," Jax said. "I looked at a city map this morning, so I can get us there without too much trouble." He was as good as his word and, within ten minutes, they were parked in front of a small grocery store.

Jax held the door for her and followed Bella inside. Rows of bins filled the center of the shop, while shelves lined three of the walls. A tall, broad man in his early thirties greeted them. "I'll be right with you folks. I'm just finishing a delivery order in the back room." "Thank you," Jax replied.

Within moments, the shopkeeper returned. "I'm Will Orling, the owner. How can I help you?" he asked with a smile.

Jax introduced himself and Bella before explaining the reason for their visit. "We're in town doing interviews to help solve a murder in Moreley."

Shock widened the man's eyes. "What would I know about that?"

"Nothing about the murder, I'm sure," Jax hurried to tell him, "but the crime took place at Ballantyne, a resort just outside town. Minnie Mars works there, and we understand she and her family used to own this store."

"Yes, they did," he said, confusion still clear in his expression.

"Did you buy the store directly from Mrs. Mars?" Jax asked.

The grocer hesitated briefly, as if uncertain why they were asking. "I did. I'd knowed her and her husband for years since my folks shopped here. I was in France myself when Al and Mikey were killed, although I didn't never learn about their deaths 'til I got home. Minnie was still grieving and angry. Her sister suggested moving to Moreley. I saved up some money before the army, so I bought the place." The man's expression grew troubled. "I can't believe Mrs. Minnie would be involved in a murder. Before losing her menfolk, she was a sweet soul. She'd always sneak me and my brothers some sweets when we come to shop with our ma."

"I don't know that she was involved," Jax replied, "but you said she was angry. Toward someone in particular? Or, mostly in general?"

Orling's forehead wrinkled. "I dunno. She talked on about the draft board a lot. Said Al should never have been sent over to France."

"Did Mrs. Mars manage the store completely alone after her husband and son left?"

Orling shook his head. "She hired a boy for deliveries and odd jobs. Mostly, she handled it alone." A smile pulled up one corner of his mouth. "Mrs. Minnie is stronger than a lot of men. I seen her lift fifty pounds of flour with no trouble."

The seemingly offhand comment disturbed Bella. Both Jax and Richard had mentioned Minnie's size and strength, and Orling's words confirmed their view. Could the cook-housekeeper have killed Monticello?

"It's good she didn't have to hire a lot of extra help," Jax observed. "Are many of the shops on the block owned by the same people who were here when the Mars family owned the grocery?"

"A couple of stores changed hands since Mrs. Minnie moved away, but Burt Hollis has been the barber for years. He probably knowed Al's parents. Samson Little is corner druggist. Been there from when I was born."

"Do you recall how Mrs. Mars reacted to people? Was she quick to criticize strangers?" Jax asked.

Orling's brow furrowed. "I dunno. Not sure I ever saw her with strangers. Most customers live in the neighborhood."

"Thank you for the information and for your time, Mr. Orling," Jax said. "Just one more question. Did you ever meet a Malcolm Monticello? He's a banker, and he was on the draft board."

Again, Orling's gaze narrowed as he seemed to consider the question. "Sorry, the name isn't familiar, but I volunteered, so I don't know much about the draft board."

"I see," Jax replied. "Thank you again."

"Surely."

Bella tucked her notepad in her pocketbook and preceded Jax out the door. When they got to the sidewalk, she turned to him. "Not much new, but it sounds like Minnie aired her grudge toward the draft board widely."

"Yes, it does," Jax replied, "but we might get more specific information from some of the other business owners." He glanced down the street. "The barbershop is only two doors down, so let's stop there first."

Bella and Jax entered the shop to find an older man sitting in one chair reading the newspaper. The man laid it aside when the door chime tinkled. "Good afternoon," he said, getting to his feet. "Can I help you?"

Once again, Jax made the introductions and explained their purpose. "Are you Mr. Hollis?" "Yes, sir, I am."

"I understand that you've owned your business for a number of years." A smile creased Hollis' lined face. "Yes, I've been here for over thirty years."

"Then, you knew the Mars family," Jax said.

The barber's smile faded. "Yes. I knew them well. They were such a happy family." His pale blue eyes went from Jax to Bella and back. "I'm sure you know both Al and Mikey died in France."

"Yes, we do," Bella put in. "Minnie is still devastated by their deaths."

Hollis shook his gray head. "She was terribly upset when Al was drafted and even worse when Mikey volunteered. She got word both were killed on the same day." His eyes filled with moisture, and he hastily brushed it away. "She nearly had a breakdown, but we all understood. Our hearts were broken, too. Although I hated to see her go, I thought a change might do her good." His gaze narrowed on Bella. "You said she works for you. How is she doing?"

Bella bit her lower lip as she pondered how to respond. Finally, she decided offering a partial truth would be best. "Overall, she's doing well. She's an excellent cook and housekeeper."

His lips softened into a slight smile. "Good. She deserves to have peace."

"You said she was upset when her husband was drafted," Jax began. "Did she direct her anger at anyone in particular?"

The barber lifted one shoulder in a half-shrug. "At the government, mostly, but I could understand her feelings. We didn't need to be involving ourselves in a foreign war. A lot of darn foolishness."

Jax cleared his throat. "Do you know a Malcolm Monticello?"

"Not a familiar name, and I have mostly regular customers from the neighborhood. If he doesn't live here, I probably never met him."

"You said Mrs. Mars was upset with the draft board, but was she a critical person?" Jax asked. "Not sure what you mean," Hollis said.

"Did she find fault with how people dressed or what they did, especially if they were wealthy?" Jax asked.

"Folks around here aren't rich, but I never heard her get after people for their way of dressing." After thanking the man, Bella and Jax walked to the corner. "This may be a futile stop, too," he said.

"At least you're covering all the bases," Bella observed. "That's all you can do."

"I suppose." Jax opened the drugstore door for Bella. The druggist, clad in a white jacket, was in the back behind the counter. For the third time, Jax introduced himself and Bella before explaining the murder and their visit. "Mr. Orling at the grocery said you probably knew the Mars family."

The man's brow furrowed, creating more lines in his already well-wrinkled forehead. "Yes, my father opened this place about the time the Mars family started the grocery business. I don't see what any of that would have to do with your case, constable."

"You probably knew Mrs. Mars moved to Moreley to live with her sister- and brother-in-law. That's quite close to Ballantyne, where the murder occurred." Jax explained patiently.

"What in the world would Minnie have to do with that?" The pharmacist was as skeptical as both the grocer and barber had been.

"She works part-time at Ballantyne, and she was there when the victim arrived," Jax replied.

"He was also from Toledo. Mr. Malcolm Monticello. Did you know him?"

Again, Little looked contemplative before shaking his head. "Sorry, the name isn't familiar." The man's dark gaze narrowed on Jax. "I don't know exactly why you're here, constable, but your questions make me think you suspect Minnie. She grew up in the neighborhood, so I knew her folks, and I remember when both Minnie and Nellie were born. Sweet girls, although to look at them, you'd never know they were sisters. Nellie being petite and Minnie being sturdy. Different in abilities, too. Nellie was better in school. Minnie didn't take to learning much. Al didn't mind about that or her towering over him." His good humor fled.

"Minnie was nearly broken by losing Al and Mikey. She would never kill anyone. It would be completely out of character."

Jax didn't deny their underlying reason for coming. He simply nodded and said, "I'll keep that in mind, sir." He cleared his throat. "You said Minnie was good-natured, but we've heard she was very upset with the draft board."

"She was, and I can't say I blame her. If Mikey hadn't volunteered, she may not have been so angry. But he did, and Al signed for him," the druggist said.

Surprise hit Jax. When he glanced at Bella, her shock was also obvious. "How did Mrs. Mars feel about that?"

"I don't imagine she could have been pleased, but she didn't speak about that as far as I ever heard."

"So, she didn't criticize her husband. Did she find fault with others? Criticize those who had more—better clothes or cars and such," Jax said.

"Not that I know of. We don't see a lot of rich folks in the neighborhood, and owning a car is pretty rare," Little observed.

Jax thanked the man for his time and went outside. Once he and Bella were on the sidewalk, he released a pent-up breath. "Evidently, Minnie is a different person now."

"Many people change after great losses."

A moment passed before he replied. "I can't argue with that."

As they walked toward the car, Bella wondered if Jax was thinking about how the war had changed him. And he had changed, as had she. "Would she change enough to kill someone? After what we've heard, it seems unlikely. To me, Mr. Neece is a stronger suspect."

"Maybe." Jax glanced down the street. "When we walked by the hardware store, I saw a pay phone just inside. I'll run in and try to call Mrs. Monticello one more time. If I can't reach her, we'll head home."

"I'll wait for you at the car."

Within moments, Jax was coming out of the store. When Bella saw him absently massage his wounded shoulder and wince, she climbed out of the passenger seat and met him as he approached the Chummy. "Why don't I drive home like we planned?" "Sounds like a good idea."

Bella got behind the wheel while he slumped back in the passenger seat and released a pent-up breath. "Did you learn anything new with your call?"

"No. The sister was a little annoyed at hearing from me again, but said she'll pass the messages along."

As she started the car and pulled away from the curb, Bella voiced one of her questions. "Do you want to go to Riddling today? The turnoff is about ten miles north of Moreley. Going there wouldn't add a lot of time."

Jax focused on the passing scenery as he considered the idea, which made sense. The trouble was, he hadn't met Neece. What if he was the killer? What if he was armed? Even though a mashie was the murder weapon, the man could have a gun. The thought of Bella getting in the line of fire disturbed him. "I can go tomorrow with either Nolen or Richard."

"It seems silly to wait and make an extra trip when we can do it right now."

Obviously, Bella wasn't worried about the danger inherent in the situation. No surprise. "From what we know, he sounds like an angry, hostile man. I'm not sure how he'd feel about us confronting him."

A moment passed before she replied. "He won't change in twenty-four hours. He'll be just as hostile tomorrow."

She was right, but the observation didn't alleviate his uneasiness. "I know." He shifted to look at her. Briefly, her gaze met his before returning to the road.

"I won't get in your way or ask questions."

He pulled off his cap and ran his fingers through his hair. "I don't like putting you in a possibly perilous situation," he admitted. When Bella didn't immediately respond, he turned back to her. Was she weighing her words, holding her temper, or speechless with resentment? As seconds ticked away, Jax slumped back in his seat. How could he make her see his viewpoint? Being straightforward might be best. "You've always been fearless. Volunteering for the Signal Corps was one major example. I'm sure you'll say you got home safe and sound. Obviously, I can't argue with that. But you don't need to put yourself in danger here."

"If Mr. Neece is armed and volatile, you'll be in danger. Today or tomorrow or whenever you question him."

Jax silently counted to ten before he asserted what was, to him, patently obvious. "It's my job to investigate crimes and question suspects."

Her response came quickly. "And maybe get shot like you did twice in France?"

Neither her tone nor her profile gave away any underlying emotion, but the words surprised him. Jax wished he could see her entire expression. What was she thinking? "My dad was never shot in fifteen years as town constable and five as a deputy, so it's not likely I will be, either."

Her attention flitted to him for a moment before going back to the road. "He never had a murder case."

"No, he didn't," Jax agreed, "but we're getting away from my point. I appreciate your help. However, in all good conscience, I can't put you into a possibly risky situation."

"Because you're the town constable and responsible for the welfare of us residents."

Again, Jax couldn't gauge her sentiments. Although the urge to agree and move on was strong, a partial explanation might be more convincing. "It isn't the entire issue, Bella. Of course, I want to keep the townspeople safe, but you must know you aren't just another citizen to me. We've known one another for over twenty years. I was your brother's best friend and your friend. The three of us spent a lot of time together for all our growing-up years. You and I are going in different directions now, but I still worry about you." He held his breath, wondering how she would react.

"You don't need to," Bella murmured.

Because her words and tone revealed very little, Jax again considered what might persuade her. She had dismissed his advice about staying out of harm's way during the war to the extent that his repeated warnings had put a wedge between them. Clearly, admonition wouldn't work. Finally, he decided that divulging his discussion with her brother was necessary. Jax only hoped she wouldn't want a broader talk, since he wasn't ready for that, and probably never would be.

Before he spoke, Jax took several deep breaths. "Matt and I knew going to war would be bad, but it was worse than what we imagined. By the time we came to Paris to see you, we discussed that one, or both, of us might not be coming back."

Bella took a quick glance at him. "You talked about that?"

"We did." Jax still wondered how much to reveal. Not everything. Not his role in Matt's death. In December, he had admitted his worry for her, but not his promise to her brother. Maybe doing so would finally make her understand. "Matt asked me to look out for you and your parents if he didn't make it home, and I said he didn't need to ask because I'd do it anyhow." When she didn't reply, he turned to look out the side of the car. "I know I let you down, Bella, and I'm really sorry. Sorrier than you can know."

"Let me down? How?"

The confusion in her voice made Jax look back at her. "At the end of that weekend in Paris, you said to take care of myself. I told you I would, but I also promised to take care of Matt, and I didn't." Regret and remorse roughened his voice until it was nearly inaudible.

"Jax, how could you take care of him when you both had platoons to lead? I didn't take your words as a promise to make sure he didn't die. I knew that was impossible. Surely, you knew, too."

For long moments, Jax considered her words. She was right about saying he couldn't have protected her brother every moment, but Bella didn't know what had really happened. What if he told her the truth? Just thinking about doing so made his heart race and his breathing shallow. He couldn't tell her. Not now. Not ever. "I suppose I did, but not being able to keep that promise to you doesn't mean I can't keep the one I made to him."

An audible sigh left her. "No matter what my brother wanted, you aren't responsible for me."

He looked back at Bella. "I know you don't want or need anyone telling you what to do, and I won't."

"But you have more than once."

Again, Jax wished she was looking directly at him so he could read her expression. "I suppose my promise to Matt has been in my mind all along," he said, although that was only part of the reason. Despite no longer sharing a lot, Jax would always want her to be safe and happy.

"Neither you nor Matt was so high-handed when we were growing up. In fact, you used to believe I could do almost anything. We discussed this in Paris. Then, you said you still did. I haven't brought it up again because we have such a hard time talking about anything other than your cases and such. Were you simply saying what I wanted to hear then?"

For several moments, he considered her words. "No, not at all. I still believe you can do anything. That doesn't mean I think you should. Especially when it involves danger." Talking about the Paris weekend made him uneasy, which was why he hadn't brought it up, either. Doing so now was probably a mistake, but the words were out.

"I spoke with Mr. Neece, Jax. He wasn't happy to hear Monticello was coming, but he showed no signs of being volatile, and we don't know that he has a gun. Even if he does, how likely is it that Mr. Neece would shoot me for taking notes while you talk to him?"

Several moments passed before he answered. "You're probably right."

"Does that mean we can go to Riddling now?"

The eagerness in her tone evoked a chuckle. Despite his continuing concern, Jax had to admit the situation wasn't likely to be hazardous to either of them. "Yes, take the turnoff."

The smile that she shot him could only be called triumphant. He didn't mind at all. Seeing her smile was still a tonic and probably always would be.

***

As they continued toward Riddling, Jax directed the conversation back to what they'd learned in Toledo. Bella thought she must be making credible contributions to the conversation, but her mind was on his revelations. Although she didn't want to be coddled, Bella better understood Jax's overprotectiveness. He'd made a promise to Matt. That didn't mean she had to do what Jax suggested, but she wouldn't resent his bossiness so much.

Once they were close to the town, Bella posed a question. "Do you want to stop some place and ask where Mrs. Neece lives?"

"Yes, let's stop at the post office over there."

Bella parked the Chummy in front of the small brick building. When she got out, Jax spoke again.

"I'll run in and find out."

He was back within a few minutes. "She lives five blocks down this street. The postmaster said it's a two-story white frame house with a porch on two sides. He said the forsythia bushes are blooming, so we shouldn't have trouble finding it."

Within a few minutes, the house came into view, and Bella once again parked the Chummy. "It's a lovely home," she observed when she joined Jax on the front walkway. "I can understand why Mrs. Neece would want to stay here instead of going back to an apartment in the city."

"It's certainly different," Jax replied as he fell into step beside her. When they reached the front door, he spoke again. "You're probably right about Neece not being unpredictable, but I'd like to talk with him and his wife out here. The weather is pleasant, and the lot is big, so no one else will hear us."

Bella scanned the wide porch. A swing and two chairs were on the end that wrapped around the corner of the home, which gave them plenty of space. She glanced back at Jax and saw the tension in his expression. He was worried about her safety. Although Bella still thought he was being overprotective, she resisted the urge to argue. "That sounds fine."

His response was to knock on the door. A minute passed before it swung open to reveal a petite woman in her forties. "Good afternoon. Are you Mrs. Neece?" Jax asked.

The woman might have been pretty, but the scowl on her face made her features appear like a brittle mask. She glanced from Jax to Bella and back.

"What do you want?" her voice was as cold as her blue gaze.

Jax maintained a pleasant expression as he introduced himself and Bella before explaining their presence. "Is your husband here, ma'am?"

As she spoke, Neece appeared behind her. He glanced at Bella. "What brings you here, Miss Stewart? I left a note and money in the cottage for you." The man, a head taller than his wife, peered over her shoulder.

Before Bella could reply, Jax spoke. "That's not why we came, sir."

Neece focused his cold gray gaze on Jax. "Who are you?"

"Jax Hastings, the constable in Moreley. I wanted to talk with you about Malcolm Monticello."

"We don't want to talk about that awful man," Mrs. Neece said.

Her husband patted her arm. "What do you want to know about Monticello?"

"He's dead, sir."

"Dead? What would I know about that?" Neece asked in a flat, hard tone.

"Perhaps nothing," Jax said, "but I would still appreciate a few minutes of your time." Several moments ticked by before Neece nodded. "All right." "Why don't we sit over here?" Jax said, pointing to the corner of the porch.

Neece nodded again and led his wife to one of the chairs while he took the other, leaving Bella and Jax to share the swing. Once she was seated, Bella pulled out the notepad and pencil while keeping her attention on Neece. His lack of reaction to the news about Monticello's death was unnerving.

"The note you left for Miss Stewart said you were going home to Toledo because you're ill," Jax began.

"Ernest came here because it's much closer to Ballantyne, and he wasn't up to a long drive," Mrs. Neece said before her husband responded.

The woman's tone and expression hadn't softened and, while her observation made sense, Bella wasn't at all sure of its validity since Mr. Neece looked and sounded fine. She took a sidelong glance at Jax. If he was suspicious, he hid it well.

"I hope you're feeling better, sir."

"I am, constable. Now, what are your questions?"

"Did you see Mr. Monticello at Ballantyne?"

"No, I didn't. I played the course, cleaned up, and went to see our son," Neece replied. "I don't know what that has to do with Monticello dying. I assume he had a heart attack. Despite his penchant for walking, he loved rich foods and good cigars."

His disdain was obvious in his tone and expression, which only increased Bella's certainty that he was the killer. Jax was probably right to question the man outside, in full of view of passersby and neighbors.

"It wasn't a heart attack, sir," Jax said. "He was murdered."

A low, humorless laugh left Mrs. Neece. "I'm not surprised."

Her husband shushed her. "Why would you think I know about it?"

"He was killed in the cottage next to yours. Perhaps you saw something," Jax suggested.

"I saw nothing. As I said, I went to see our son."

The man's lack of concern troubled Bella. It was as if Jax had said Monticello had a bout of indigestion. Mrs. Neece's reaction was even worse.

"Where is he living?" Jax asked.

Although Mrs. Daniels had told them about Poplar Pines, Bella felt sure Jax was testing the Neeces to see if they would be honest.

"You don't need to be bothering our boy," Mrs. Neece said. "He doesn't know Monticello, and he wasn't at Ballantyne. Ernest, you need to keep this man away from Irwin."

Anger sparkled in her pale blue eyes as she spoke. Bella glanced at Neece, who had laid a hand on his wife's arms. "I will. I will. Try not to get upset."

The exchange between the pair puzzled Bella. Why were they so anxious to keep Jax away from their son? Was he involved in the murder? Had he escaped from the sanitorium? If so, where was he?

"I won't bother your son, ma'am. I simply want to know where your husband went to visit him." Neece turned a dark scowl on Jax before speaking again. "He's at Poplar Pines." His fingers grasped his wife's hand. "He suffers from shell shock and needs special treatment." "I see," Jax murmured.

"Do you, constable?" Mrs. Neece asked. "Do you know what it was like in the trenches?"

"Constable Hastings knows quite well," Bella said before Jax had a chance to reply. "He served in France himself."

Surprise rounded the woman's eyes as she focused on Jax, but it was her husband who spoke. "Then, you know about shell shock."

"I do. I've known more than a few soldiers afflicted with it."

Neece nodded. "Not everyone understands. Monticello was one who didn't. His boys weren't quite old enough for the draft, and they didn't volunteer. That was true of most on the board.

They sent other folks' sons to war, but not their own."

"And that's what led to the end of your friendship?" Jax asked.

"Do you have children, constable?" Mrs. Neece asked.

"No, ma'am."

"Then, you can't possibly understand how it is to have your babies sent off to fight a foreign war by a man who could have done something, but wouldn't," the woman shot back.

Bella paused in taking notes and looked at Mrs. Neece. Her flushed face and fiery gaze went along with her furious tone. When the woman's hands balled into fists, Bella felt relief that Jax was out of reach because, otherwise, he would have gotten hit in the face, she was sure.

Evidently, Mr. Neece had much the same thoughts because he laid one of his big hands over both of his wife's smaller ones.

"Being on the draft board didn't give Mr. Monticello the power to keep able-bodied men out of the service," Jax pointed out.

A low snort left Neece. "You're rather naïve, constable. Or you're pretending you don't know what went on. Not all eligible men went. Some who were in the mix were pulled out because their families had influence. Unfortunately, we didn't."

The implication that Monticello might have helped those with money stay out of the draft deeply disturbed Bella. Draft boards decided on exemptions, of course, but she had never heard of any bribery being involved.

"Mr. Neece, I understand you lost one son in France, so I'm sure it's difficult. Draft boards voted on exemptions, but not due to influence or money, if that's what you're suggesting," Jax said in an even tone. Neece's nostrils flared with a sharp intake of breath. "Malcolm could have kept our boys out, but he refused."

"He would have kept his own sons out, if they'd been eligible," his wife said, her voice shrill. "I know he would have. I even tried talking with his wife, but she was as hard-hearted as he was."

The admissions from the pair continued to disturb Bella. Evidently, they had thought Neece's friendship with Monticello would pave the way to keeping their sons out of uniform.

"So, had you seen Mr. Monticello since you last played golf with the group?" Jax asked in the calm tone that Bella identified as his constable's voice.

"Unfortunately, yes, since we worked in the same building. Far too often, in fact. Even when our oldest was killed, he showed no sympathy," Neece replied.

"He said death is part of war," his wife said. "Can you imagine saying that to grieving parents?"

Shock filled Bella because she couldn't fathom anyone being so cruel. To dismiss the loss of a child as a by-product of conflict was heartless. A shiver rippled through her. Abbott's high opinion of Monticello had lost almost all credibility.

"I'm sorry, ma'am. That was uncalled for."

"Yes, it was, constable," Neece agreed. "Malcolm put up a good front as a fine family man and good citizen, but he had little concern for those outside his circle. I'm not at all sorry someone killed him, because I thought about doing it myself." "Did you?" Jax asked.

For long moments, the question hung in the air. Finally, Neese snorted. "No, I didn't."

"What time did you leave Ballantyne, sir?"

"Around four-thirty."

Jax studied the man before continuing. "You didn't come back until late, but left very early in the morning, due to your illness."

Neece leaned back and folded his arms across his chest. "Are you insinuating that I wasn't sick, constable?"

"Not at all, but you left very early. Isn't that the case?"

"Yes, I did."

"Then, you came here instead of going to your apartment in Toledo. Why was that, sir?"

Jax's cool restraint was admirable. Bella would have liked to shout at the man to explain himself. As time passed with no reply, Bella wondered if the other man was going to answer the question. Why was he so reluctant to explain himself? Was he the guilty party? Had he and his wife confronted Monticello? After hearing their anger and resentment, that wouldn't be surprising.

"Mr. Neece, please answer me," Jax said in the same reasonable tone he'd been using.

Some emotion flared in the man's gaze before he spoke. "I picked my wife up when I went to visit our son. Irwin was pleased to see us together, and he hoped we'd both be back soon." He looked at his wife. "I spent the rest of the weekend with my family, but that was no one else's business. I paid for the entire time."

"What time did you finish your round?"

Bella looked up to see Neece blink at the sudden change in topic. When he didn't immediately answer, she wondered if he was thinking about who might have seen him leave the course.

"I didn't finish due to the rain."

The admission only added to Bella's suspicion since the man hadn't indicated that earlier. If he had started his round shortly after leaving the inn, he could have finished all eighteen holes well before four-thirty. Now, he said he'd left the course early due to the rain, which had started close to four o'clock. He could have easily killed Monticello, and left when he'd stated.

"When did you go back to the cottage?"

A negligible shrug lifted one of Neece's shoulders. "I'm not sure."

"Did anyone see you, sir?"

"No, I used the back door to the cottage since it faces the course. No one saw me, and I didn't see anyone." Neece maintained his stony expression.

"Did you see signs of anyone in the cottage next door?"

"I didn't bother to look, constable. I knew Monticello was there, if that's what you're getting at. But I didn't care to see him. And I certainly didn't kill him." "I never accused you of that, Mr. Neece," Jax said.

A humorless laugh left the older man. "No, but that's what you're getting at. I had a powerful motive, and I could have done it. I wish I had in some ways because he deserved to die."

"Yes, he did," his wife agreed. "Now, his wife will know some of the grief that I've carried all this time. She deserves that."

Jax cleared his throat. "Thank you for your time, Mr. and Mrs. Neece. If I have more questions, can I reach both of you here?" He got to his feet and extended a hand to Bella.

She allowed him to help her off the swing, but kept her attention on the couple. Both looked hostile enough that Bella felt uneasy. Nor did she balk when Jax grasped her elbow and led her to the porch steps, where he stopped to glance back at the Neeces.

"We'll be here or visiting Irwin," the older woman said. "But you'll be wasting your time if you contact us again, just like you wasted it today."

Jax's response was to put his cap on his head and escort Bella to the Chummy. Once they were headed toward the main road, he leaned back in the passenger seat with a sigh. "What did you think of that pair?" he asked.

"Some of my sympathy for them disappeared. Losing one son and having the other in a sanitorium must be terrible, but they have so much anger toward Monticello. Hatred really. It was more than disconcerting."

"I agree. They made it sound like the man took bribes to exempt men from the draft, and that is extremely unlikely. It doesn't even make sense. One board member couldn't keep someone out of uniform."

"That bothered me, too. Do you think they actually believe he was corrupt?"

"I'm guessing their grief and pain have overcome their good sense."

"You're right. What did you think about Mr. Neece as a potential killer?"

Jax shifted to look at her. "He has a lot of anger, and it's easy to believe he might have confronted Monticello despite his protestations."

"He admitted he had motive and opportunity. I suppose that could have been a way to throw us off," Bella said in a thoughtful tone.

"It could. What did you think of his responses?" Jax asked. "I think he could easily be the killer. He didn't seem at all surprised to hear about Mr. Monticello's death. In addition, he and his wife hate Monticello and, as you say, Mr. Neece might have gone to the cottage to berate him. Neece could have lost his temper and grabbed the mashie. I really think that's the most likely scenario. What about you?"

Jax ran one hand over his face in a gesture of weary frustration. "I agree with you. Mrs. Neece admitting that she called Mrs. Monticello was revealing since we know some woman harangued her and her husband. The trouble is, I don't have enough evidence to arrest Neece."

"Maybe Mrs. Monticello will call yet today. She might have called already."

"I hope so. Learning more from her is most likely the key to the case."

"That's probably true." After that comment, Bella lapsed into silence. When he didn't speak for a while, she took a quick glance his way and found him sound asleep. Since Jax clearly needed the rest, she focused on the road for the rest of their trip.

Chapter Thirteen

Bella was pulling on to Main Street in Moreley when Jax woke up. He rubbed his eyes with the heels of his hands. "I wasn't much company," he murmured in a voice thick with sleep.

"I slept all the way to Toledo, so turnabout is fair play," she replied with a smile. "Besides, you slept a much shorter time."

Jax chuckled, sat up in the seat, and glanced at his watch. "It's after five o'clock." As Bella pulled the Chummy into a parking space next to the Model T and killed the engine, he looked at her again. "Thanks for driving home."

A genuine smile touched her lips. "Thank you for letting me drive. I enjoyed it. The Chummy is sportier than our Model T, but she's reliable and roomy. And the side curtains are great in cold weather."

He couldn't help but smile back. Although he had dozed off, her pleasure in driving had been obvious, and a bonus was that he'd been able to rest his arm, which still hurt, but no longer throbbed insistently as it had earlier. "It was nice to be a passenger for a change."

When they got out of the car and entered the office, she handed him the keys. Both greeted Nolen, who was behind the counter. "How did the day go?" Jax asked the younger man.

"Fine," Nolen replied with a smile. "I spoke with Mr. Penn when I was on patrol, and he wants to talk with you."

"Did he say about what?" Jax asked as he crossed the room to stand at the counter across from the younger man. Bella followed him.

"He did when I told him you'd gone to Toledo." He glanced down at a tablet of paper in front of him. "You know, he lives out past the side road to Ballantyne. He said he went by there Wednesday night about five-thirty and saw the Ironton twins."

Jax frowned. The brothers had gotten a ride into town shortly after that, but he didn't actually know where they'd been picked up. He and Bella had both been sure Neece was the leading suspect, but they could be mistaken. "I can drive out there later." He wished Penn had given the entire story to Nolen, but the man was a councilman, so he probably thought Jax should talk to him.

"He said he'd stop when he saw your car, since he had more errands in town today," his assistant replied.

Jax and Bella exchanged a long look. "Maybe I should transcribe my notes now."

"That's not necessary," Jax told her. "You've spent most of your day—a long day—working with me, so go on home. I can come out and get them later."

Before Bella could respond, Richard Jennings entered the office. He nodded to Bella and Nolen.

"We gathered interesting information today," she told the senior constable before glancing at Jax.

Jax revealed the pertinent details about Minnie and Neece. "According to what we were told, Mrs. Mars was a sweet person and never criticized people. As far as the Neeces, they've suffered by losing one boy and having another with shell shock. Neither seems at all sorry to hear about Monticello. Neither seemed to be surprised, either. At this point, Neece may be our strongest suspect."

"What about Mr. Penn seeing the twins near the old lane around four-thirty?" Nolen asked.

Richard frowned. "When did you hear that?"

Nolen revealed his conversation with Penn.

Nolen revealed what Penn had told him. The senior constable nodded. "We need to talk with him, but I agree about Neece. His situation bears a lot more scrutiny."

Jax nodded. "I don't think we can rule Minnie Mars out, either. Will Orling, who bought the grocery store from her, confirmed that she did a lot of heavy lifting herself."

"It's as we thought. She's completely capable of wielding a mashie as a deadly weapon," Richard said.

"Why would she seek out Mr. Monticello and kill him?" Bella asked. "I know she was upset about losing her husband and son, but the Neeces are furious. Besides, the other shopkeepers said she was a sweet soul. None of them could imagine her harming anyone, let alone committing a murder."

"But they also said she changed dramatically after her husband and son died in France. We know she isn't a sweet, kindly lady now. You've said yourself that she's prickly and dour," Jax said.

Bella's mouth flattened in a line of displeasure. "That doesn't make her a killer. Earlier today, you said we should keep her on the suspect list, and I agreed. I just don't think she's the top suspect. Besides, her sister said they were home together. Mrs. Downing is a gossip, not a liar."

Jax's jaw tightened. "I told you this morning that I don't consider a relative as a solid witness."

Before Bella responded, the senior constable spoke.

"At this point, it appears that the Neeces should be at the top of the list, but I agree about Mrs. Mars. We can't eliminate her, either. Her sister may be confused about the time," Richard said in a subdued tone.

"Mrs. Monticello hasn't called yet, but I'm hoping she will. I left several messages about a need to speak with her. Of course, it may take a little time." Jax's lips twitched. "Bella long ago schooled me on all the steps for a long-distance connection. Patience is key."

A low laugh rumbled out of the senior constable. "Always wise to listen to the experts," he said.

Bella pursed her lips. "I haven't been an operator in the States, but I had all the training before I went to France." His stubborn refusal to take Minnie off his list, despite her sister providing an alibi, still galled Bella.

"Which makes you an expert," Jax said, his smile more obvious.

His gentle teasing was reminiscent of the old Jax, so Bella didn't object. Instead, she found her pique with him disintegrating. After another moment, she grinned and shook her head.

"Let me find Penn and talk to him," Richard said. "That way, you'll be here if Mrs. Monticello gets back to you."

"All right." Jax glanced at his pocket watch. "She should be home soon, so it's a matter of the call going through." He turned back to Bella. "Why don't you head back to Ballantyne? I'll be out later to get your notes."

Although she wanted to stay and find out more, Bella knew she had no real excuse to do so. Besides, nothing more would happen immediately. If Jax spoke with Mrs. Monticello, Bella could get details later. "All right. I need to pick up a few items at the mercantile, but I'll get to the notes as soon as I get home."

"I'll be out in a couple of hours, if that's convenient," Jax said.

"Of course," Bella agreed. She said goodbye to the men and went to do her shopping before heading home.

***

As she walked down Main Street, Bella once again noted the many boarded-up storefronts. She had been dismayed at the sorry look of downtown when she'd returned from Europe, and not much had changed in the past four months. If she and Mac could restore Ballantyne, Moreley might follow suit. That had been her hope, and it still was. Solving Monticello's murder was crucial.

Bella was surprised to find Minnie behind the counter at the mercantile. Although the woman wasn't currently needed at Ballantyne, she seldom worked in the store. "Good afternoon," Bella said.

Minnie was as glum as usual. "Afternoon. I'm about to close. Do you need something?"

For a moment, Bella tried to see some sign of the woman described by the merchants in Toledo. No trace of sweetness or generosity was apparent now. Minnie was as prickly as ever. "I wanted to pick up some soap for the cottages and candy for the boys before I head home." The boys and Mac.

"I saw you driving that constable's car," the woman said."

Her tone was odd and, while Bella knew she didn't owe anyone an explanation, she replied, "Yes, I was." Minnie didn't need to know details. The woman wasn't very sociable, but her sister was well-known as a town gossip. While the likelihood of any information spreading from Moreley to the Neeces was small, Bella didn't want to take any chances.

The woman's pale eyes narrowed. "Where did you two go?"

Was Minnie asking out of idle curiosity, or was something more behind the query? Perhaps, she liked chin wagging as much as her sister. With that in mind, Bella kept her response brief. "Just visiting people. Now, If I can get my items, I'll be on the way." She ticked her list off and waited. Something that Bella couldn't identify flickered in the older woman's gaze, but it came and went quickly.

"I'll get them for you."

"Thank you," Bella replied. She certainly wasn't giving Minnie, or anyone else, details. Not when Jax was waiting for possibly crucial information. She paid for her goods and took the parcel. "I'll let you know when we need you at the resort."

Minnie's response was a quick nod.

***

After leaving Moreley behind, Bella thought little about her exchange with Minnie. The drive to Ballantyne took only minutes and, when she arrived at the inn, the twins were eager to leave the front desk so to go into town with Carl, Curt, and Mac.

"We're heading to see a picture show, but first we get to eat at the café. Mac said he's only eating dinner because he's supposed to visit a friend, but he'll drive us all there and back. Mrs. Downing called earlier today, and she has our pay ready from the last days we worked at the store. We're going to have ice cream after the picture, too," Dick said.

The boy's words tumbled out in a torrent of excitement, which made Bella smile. "That sounds like fun. Did anyone call for a reservation while I was gone?"

Dale shook his head. "No one called for that, but no one called to drop out of the four-ball, either."

"That's good," she replied, but that didn't help their situation much. After yesterday's cancelations, only eight competitors remained in the tournament field. They needed at least twenty more players to break even, and another twenty would be better. Uneasiness clawed at her. Hopefully, Jax would learn something important from Mrs. Monticello and soon.

Within moments, the other men assembled in the foyer. "Why don't ye join us, lass?" Mac asked.

"I've had a long day," Bella replied. "Besides, Jax will be out yet this evening to pick up my notes, so I need to get them typed. After that, I plan to take it easy."

"Ye need to do more of that," the old pro told her before shepherding the group outside.

Chapter Fourteen

Once the group left, Bella settled at the front desk. She opened her notepad and started the transcription. Within moments, she was absorbed in the task. As she went over the notes, Bella became even more convinced that Ernest Neece was the killer. His wife couldn't have been with him, but her hatred for Monticello and her pleasure in his wife's suffering indicated she was probably an instigator. Thinking about the woman's cold indifference sent a shiver through Bella. Losing one son to death and the other to mental illness had to be devastating. But murder wasn't the answer.

When she heard footsteps in the kitchen, Bella glanced down at the watch pinned to her shirtwaist and was surprised to see that it was nearly seven. From what the twins had said, none of them would be back until much later. Maybe Mac had changed his mind about visiting his friend. If so, she needed to put her notes aside and see if he had eaten at the café. Or possibly, it was Jax to pick up the notes. Hurriedly, Bella finished the last line, added the paper to her pile, and went to the kitchen.

Surprise rippled through her when she ran into Minnie Mars. Bella had seen the woman less than two hours ago, and the housekeeper hadn't mentioned coming to Ballantyne at all. Had she forgotten something? "Minnie, what are you doing here?" she asked in a puzzled tone. "I told you we're not busy now, so I don't know when we'll need you again. Although we have a few guests coming tomorrow, I can handle the meals."

"That's not why I'm here." Her tone was as troubled as her expression.

"Then, why come out this evening?"

"I'm sorry," the older woman said. "Very sorry."

Confusion filled Bella. The emotion underlying the words was unlike Minnie. She thought back to what other merchants in her old neighborhood had said about her. But their observations didn't explain the sudden change in the woman. Besides, she wasn't being sweet. She was simply regretful. But why? "Sorry about what?" Her bewilderment escalated when she saw Minnie withdraw a pistol from her pocket. Bella struggled to come to grips with the scene before her. Shock froze her thoughts. What was happening? "Where did you get that?"

"It belonged to my Al. He gave it to me when he left for France. I was all alone then because our boy went with him. Mikey had to go with his father, you know. He couldn't bear not to be part of the adventure." She shook her head. "But it wasn't an adventure. It was a death sentence for them."

As a fog of confusion engulfed her, Bella struggled to absorb the woman's words and actions. "Why do you have a gun here?"

"You don't know?" Minnie released one of her harrumphs. "You went to Toledo. You must have talked to people who knew that awful man."

"Awful man?" Bella knew she wasn't thinking clearly, but staring into the barrel of a gun clouded her mind. She needed to be cautious and controlled. Perhaps she could convince Minnie to put the gun away.

"Monticello. He was head of the draft board in Toledo. Didn't anyone tell you that?"

Bella's heart raced as the import of Minnie's words hit her. "Yes, we heard he was," she intoned. How did Minnie know about the trip to Toledo? Although that was unclear, a major piece of the puzzle clicked into place. As it did, the picture became horrifyingly clear. Minnie—not Neece—had murdered Monticello. Stalling for time, she said, "But you told us you didn't know Monticello."

"I didn't," Minnie confirmed. "Not really. When my Al got drafted, he tried for an exemption. Because we had the store, and I worked it, the board decided we had plenty of income, even with him gone. And we only had the one child, Mikey. He was seventeen. Too old to really need his daddy, according to them. I called Monticello and said I couldn't handle the store alone. He said we owned it outright, and there was no reason that business would decrease when my man was gone. Besides, he said, I had my son. When I told him that my boy insisted on going with his father, Mr. Monticello laughed and said a little adventure wouldn't do no harm. Awful, awful man. After that, I went to his office, but I couldn't get no appointment. I seen him in passing. Never forgot what he looked like. I saw that heartless face every night in my nightmares." Her brow furrowed as if in pain.

The words tumbled out of her so quickly that Bella could barely follow them. Her heart pounded wildly as her attention riveted on the pistol in Minnie's hand. The woman's pain was understandable, but not her current actions. "I'm terribly sorry for everything you lost."

"Your brother died in that useless war, and your momma and daddy died from the flu. You've already suffered." Minnie quickly wiped her eyes with her free hand. "That's why I'm sorry. So sorry I have to..."

The look of utter devastation on the other woman's face pierced Bella's heart. Minnie wasn't detached or distant now. Not at all. Her grief had turned to anger and that had led to revenge. "You don't have to do anything."

Minnie's expression hardened. "You've been snooping everywhere. And the constable has, too. This morning when you stopped to see my sister- and brother-in-law, I was just getting up. I heard your voices and went to the top of the stairs. That's how I know you went to Toledo, and I knew one of you would figure it out. I had to bide my time today and hope the constable didn't arrest me right when he got back."

The woman's revelation about eavesdropping put her appearance in a new light. But Minnie was wrong on one score. Bella hadn't figured it out, and Jax hadn't, either. They had gone to Toledo and spoken with people. They had learned about Monticello being the head of the draft board and even discovered that someone had harassed him. They had spoken with the Neeces. In retrospect, Bella was sorry she'd convinced Jax to make the side trip since that had focused their attention on Neece. If only they could have spoken with Mrs. Monticello. But they hadn't, and not for lack of effort. Jax had tried again and again and again. They had both thought the widow could be instrumental in solving the case, and she could have been—if only Jax had reached her. At least he hadn't wanted to eliminate Minnie.

That gave Bella a bit of hope. Would he get a call in time to identify the killer? Would he come for her typed notes soon?

Anxiety coiled inside her. What could she do or say now to pacify the housekeeper? "Did you go right to the cottage when you left the inn?" she asked, hoping that a further discussion would delay whatever Minnie had in mind.

"I didn't plan to go there or to kill him, but he was headed that way when I was leaving. I saw his expensive car, and I already seen his fancy clothes." Her expression became hard and forbidding. "I had to sell our store because it was losing money. Had to sell our home, too. If it weren't for my sister, I wouldn't have no decent place to live. That wouldn't have happened if Al and Mikey had been home, and that banker was responsible. He has plenty of money. I followed along, intending to tell him about all that I lost, and I started to do that. Even then, he didn't care. Said I wasn't the only one who had lost loved ones and that my menfolk had served their country, as they should have. But he didn't serve. His boys didn't, neither. He risked nothing. Nothing at all!"

"That's why you killed him?" Bella asked, still trying to keep the woman talking. Mrs. Downing had said Minnie didn't need to work. Had she lied to protect her sister's pride? She'd evidently provided a false alibi for her, so a smaller lie was just as likely.

"He was heartless. Completely heartless. He said I needed to get on with my life. Get on," she repeated. "How can I? I asked him that, and he said I might need to go to an asylum." Her voice grew increasingly shrill as she spoke.

"Was this inside the cottage?"

"Yep. I followed him. He hadn't locked the door, so I walked in. He didn't recognize me, but I told him who I was and he said those awful, callous things." Her lower lip quivered as she spoke. "His golf bag was near the door. When he said I was crazy, that was it. He stole my menfolk, and he didn't give no never mind, so I grabbed the club. At first, he laughed like it was a joke. But it weren't funny to me, and I told him so. When I took the club in both hands and lifted it over my head, he got worried." A mirthless cackle escaped her. "He weren't taller than me or probably stronger, either. Sitting at a desk all day makes a man weak. He talked fast, saying he was sorry, but it were too late. Way too late. And the fool turned away like he was gonna escort to the front door." The woman's breath was coming fast and hard like she was exerting herself to speak. When she gasped for air, Bella spoke.

"What happened then?"

"I hit him. He went down, but he weren't dead, so I hit him again. More than one more time, I s'pose. When he were down for good, I broke the club. It took a lot of effort, but I knowed I needed to take the grip because of fingerprints. Back a while, someone told me about them being clues in some other case. I didn't want to take the clubhead, though. I was afraid blood would get on me, so I stepped on the wood shaft and hurried off with the top part. When I got to work that day, I'd parked out toward the cottages, so I got the car quick and used the side lane to leave."

"What did you do with the wooden shaft?" Bella asked. Nolen and Jax had searched, and so had she, but to no avail.

"Tossed it in the river on my way back to town. It's running high and fast since the heavy rains. That club is probably gone for good."

That seemed quite likely. Minnie appeared neither upset nor brusque now. She looked and sounded pitiless. A shiver ripped through Bella, but she concentrated on continuing the conversation. Jax was coming for her notes, but when? "Why did you take his money and watch?"

For a moment, the other woman simply stared at Bella. Finally, she replied. "I can use extra money. The watch is valuable. It can be pawned."

"There's no pawn shop in Moreley."

A sneer curved Minnie's thin lips. "I'm not staying in Moreley, and neither are you." The grieving wife and mother was gone. In her place was a killer.

Panic threatened to overcome Bella, but she kept her tone even when she asked, "What do you mean?"

"I'm going to Pennsylvania, and you're coming with me. The cops won't try to take me if you're along. Especially not Constable Hastings."

Perhaps Minnie would be safe in another state, but Bella knew she wouldn't be. "You don't have to do this. We can talk to Jax. I'll talk to him. He'll understand."

The other woman shook her head. "It won't do no good. I killed a man. And I'm not sorry. He deserved to die."

Minnie's tone remained icy.

"But you don't want to kill me," Bella began. "I did nothing to you or your family."

The cook-housekeeper started at Bella for a moment before responding. "I know, but I need you with me."

"You don't need to run." Bella stopped. What reason would Minnie accept? Murderers, male or female, were arrested, and most were executed. Another murder wouldn't add to the penalty. She could only be electrocuted once. "And even if you do," she hurried on, "you'll be caught. Your sister must know where you are, and Mac probably saw you arrive."

"Clara thinks I went to Boxwood. Mac didn't see me because he's in town. I saw him, Carl, Curt, and those boys go into the café before I left the store and got the car."

Bella was out of options. Everyone was gone, and Minnie knew it. Her mind raced to think of something else to say. With sunset coming quickly, there was no chance of any golfers happening by. She was alone here. Alone with a murderer. "Mac will be back."

"Not in time. We're leaving now." Minnie's pale gaze swept over Bella. "I got the gun, so you don't have much choice except to do as I say."

The housekeeper's declaration was certainly valid. Bella's mind whirled. If she could find a way to further weaken the other woman's plan, she might have a chance. "Even if you kidnap and kill me, Jax will figure out that you're the murderer and he'll come after you. You can't get away with this, Minnie." That was a certainty, but would Bella still be alive when Jax or others caught this woman?

A period of silence ensued before the older woman spoke again. "I don't plan to kill you right off. I'll have a head start. If he catches up, I'll use you as a hostage. I told you that no cop will hurt me if you're along."

Had Minnie considered all the angles? "Why do you want to go to Pennsylvania? Isn't Mrs. Downing your only family?"

Minnie shook her head. "My Al has cousins living in the mountains of Pennsylvania. Few folks around there. If I get to them, they'll help me."

So, Minnie had a plan. Could Bella convince her it wouldn't work? "You'll have to drive through half of Ohio and part of Pennsylvania to get there. Once Jax knows you abducted me, he'll get word to authorities throughout the area. Even if they don't try to capture you while I'm along, they will eventually."

"But that will take a lot of telephone calls, most of them through long distance. You were an operator in the Great War, so you know how slow it is. I can be at the cousins' cabin long before your friend gets word out. Al's kin will hide me and the car."

Minnie sounded more and more confident, which sent dread cascading through Bella. The plan had some slight chance of succeeding, so she tried another tactic. "Your anger with Monticello is understandable," she began. "People will realize that. Jax will realize."

Minnie shook her head again. "No one understands, and no one will. I killed him, and I'll be electrocuted if I'm caught. I don't want to burn," she said in a trembling voice.

When Bella saw terror in Minnie's pale gaze, uneasiness assailed her. Terror was a double-edged sword. It could make the woman surrender, or it could make her lash out. Bella had to proceed carefully. Very carefully. "There are extenuating circumstances," she said, although she didn't know if the courts would consider Minnie's extreme grief in the mix. Even so, Bella hurried on. "You killed Mr. Monticello out of anguish, but if you kill me...there'd be no excuse for that because I haven't harmed you or your loved ones."

Uncertainty creased Minnie's wide brow. "I can't burn," she repeated.

Obviously, the woman was fixated on the idea of being electrocuted. Ohio had used the electric chair for more than twenty years as an alternative to the gallows. Most people thought it was more humane, but the word *burn* telegraphed Minnie's terror. To get the woman's mind on something else, Bella said, "You can explain why you did what you did. I'll go with you right now. We can talk to Jax. He's a veteran. He lost some of his men and his friends. He'll understand how you feel."

Once again, Minnie brought the gun up and pointed it at Bella. "He can't understand how it is to lose my only child and my husband."

Bella licked her suddenly dry lips. "It isn't the same, of course, but Jax is very compassionate." He'd have sympathy for this woman. Who wouldn't? Her pain and sorrow didn't justify her actions, but anyone with a heart could comprehend her reasoning, as wrong as it was.

"The law don't work for people like me and mine," she insisted. "My husband should never have been drafted. He was almost forty, and I needed his help in our store. And my boy shouldn't have been accepted. Monticello don't care and neither do anyone else. Both of my menfolk died the same day, and I got brief letters saying how brave they were. Like

I cared about that. I only cared about them coming home!" Minnie's voice shook with rage, or grief, or both.

Bella pressed her hands together to still their trembling. Nothing was working. Minnie seemed completely unreachable. Had misery and revenge turned her mind? Unfortunately, that seemed all too likely. "That's terrible," she said, mostly to appease the woman. "I can understand your pain, and others will, too." She tried again to reach the woman.

Minnie shook her head and waved the gun from Bella to the door and back. "Get going."

"Where?" Bella asked, trying to stall for time.

"To the car," Minnie replied in a harsh tone that sounded nothing like her usual dull monotone. She seemed like a completely different person now. When Bella hesitated, she went on. "Now."

Although her legs were shaking as badly as her hands, Bella did as she was told. Somehow, she had to get the advantage, but she didn't know how. Until an idea came to her, all Bella could do was follow instructions, for she feared that, if she balked, Minnie might shoot her where she stood.

During the long drive to Pennsylvania, she might find an opportunity to escape, since they would need to stop for fuel. Despite the fear clawing at her, she walked to the Packard. Minnie seemed impervious to the steady rain just starting. As the pair crossed the short distance to the car, Bella struggled for a strategy to escape. Far too soon, they were standing at the back of the vehicle.

"Open the trunk," Minnie commanded. Once again, Bella did as she was told. "Get in," was the next order.

Bella did that, as well. At least, Minnie wouldn't shoot her here and now.

"Turn over on your stomach and put both hands behind your back." When Bella did not immediately comply, Minnie barked, "Do it now!"

Her captor quickly tied her wrists with a piece of rope. At least she had a little more time to think and to plan. Even though that thought gave her hope, Bella felt a stab of stark terror when the lid slammed shut. Despite the trunk's expansive size, it was dark, dank, and confining.

With her hands bound, getting out seemed impossible. The hard floor provided no comfort and, when she tried to stretch out her legs, they hit the side of the car. Bella wriggled to gain some relief, but moving only made the rope cut into her wrists. Frustrated and dispirited, she slumped back and put her thoughts on how to escape.

Chapter Fifteen

More than an hour after Bella left for Ballantyne, the call from Mrs. Monticello came in.

"Thank you for calling, ma'am," Jax said when the woman's voice came on the line. "I know this is a terribly difficult time for you, and I don't want to cause any more pain."

When she spoke again, her voice trembled, but her words were clear. "I want my husband's murder to be solved, Constable Hastings, so I'll cooperate in any way that will help you find and arrest his killer."

"I appreciate that. I won't take too much of your time, but I have a few questions. I know your husband headed up the draft board," he began. "Two of his friends, Mr. Lumley and Mr. Earl, told me that there were some issues regarding conscription. They said Mr. Monticello had mentioned one person who had harassed him on several occasions and that one of his golf partners had also confronted him."

"Ernest Neece is the golf buddy, and he took Malcolm to task," the woman replied. "He was against the war and was terribly upset when both of his sons were drafted. He accused my husband of taking bribes to exempt others. Malcolm never did such a thing. Some men were deferred, but for good reason. Mrs. Neece was as bad. She called me saying all kinds of awful things. They wanted to know why our boys weren't in uniform. I said they were too young, but she insisted they could go."

Mrs. Monticello spoke in a hoarse, hushed tone that Jax had to strain to hear. Her words confirmed what the Neeces had said.

"Do you think he's the one who sent anonymous notes to your husband?"

"No, not at all," she replied quickly. "The sender was a woman. She tried to get Malcolm to rescind a draft notice. I don't know who was drafted—a father, a husband, a son. He didn't have that power. Only the appeals board did. Later, when her relative died, the woman became hysterical. She blamed my husband, but it wasn't his fault. He only did his job as the draft board chairman. She phoned him at work, and when he stopped taking her calls, she mailed letters. I read them, and they were crazy. She never signed them or identified herself when she called Malcolm and, although he had to know who she was, he never told me." The widow paused for a moment. "I felt sorry for her, but she seemed irrational, which scared me. Malcolm didn't take it seriously. He said she was grieving. I understand grief, but I wanted him to tell the police. Then, he found out that she had left town and said we should forget about her. Mostly, I did."

"Did she move away?" Jax barely got the words out over the lump in his throat. His mind reeled as he tried to put the facts together.

"I think she left Toledo permanently. My husband always wanted to protect me, so he tried to keep the details to himself. He didn't even tell me about her phone calls or letters until she tacked a note on our door. At that point, he revealed almost everything."

Jax's pulse pounded in his ears. He needed more information. "But you don't know her name?"

"No, Malcolm wouldn't tell me," was the reply, "and she didn't sign the notes."

"I thought she came to your house."

"She did, but no one was home, so she left her crazy notes on our front door."

"Do you know anything else about her?" Jax asked.

"I'm sorry. I don't. Once she was gone, we never spoke about it again. The danger seemed to be over." When she spoke again, her voice was barely audible. "But it wasn't, I guess."

"No, it wasn't," he said. Evidently, it had continued and culminated in murder. "Thank you again for calling, Mrs. Monticello. I hope I'll have news tomorrow. Right now, I need to follow up on this information. You've helped me narrow the suspects down to two, and one lives here." And that one could be found immediately, which was exactly what Jax planned to do.

"Of course," she agreed.

Jax put the earpiece back on the receiver and turned to Nolen.

"What's wrong?" Nolen asked. "You look upset."

"It was a woman who harassed and blamed Monticello. From the description that Mrs. Monticello provided, it could be either Mrs. Neece or Mrs. Mars." He summarized what the woman had told him before saying, "Both moved from Toledo. Mrs. Neece went to take care of her mother in Riddling, but that was probably before the war." Jax replayed Mrs. Daniels' revelations in his mind.

"Which means she wouldn't have been in Toledo to put notes on Monticello's door."

Nolen's observation confirmed what Jax was thinking. "Mrs. Neece occasionally went to visit after their son returned." Again, he mulled over the timeframe. "I suppose she could have written notes and harassed, but Minnie Mars seems more apt to be the killer. Not only that, she's here. Find Richard. Try the café first, in case Penn planned to eat in town. I need to call Bella right now."

"I'm on my way," Nolen replied as he ran out of the office.

With a shaking hand, Jax picked up the telephone again, but no one answered at the inn. His heart racing even faster, he asked the operator to call the golf shop. Again, no one answered. Where was everyone? He hesitated for a moment before asking Bertha to keep calling both lines and to let whoever answered know they needed to take care because the killer was still in the area. Then, he hung up before the operator could ask for details. As far as Jax could figure, no one in town was in danger...but those at Ballantyne might be.

The mercantile would be closed by now, but he could seek out Minnie Mars at her sister's house. He immediately called there, but Mrs. Downing revealed Minnie had borrowed their car to go to Boxwood to shop. His alarm grew and a sick, sinking sensation filled Jax. Most shops in the nearby town would have closed more than an hour ago. He gripped the telephone earpiece tighter.

"Mrs. Downing, you told me that your sister came home around four-thirty the day that Monticello was killed. Are you sure about the time?" Silence echoed along the phone line. "Mrs. Downing, I need to know right now."

Another pause filled the line before the woman spoke again. "Minnie hasn't been herself since she lost her husband and son. She couldn't run their store or even take care of herself. She tried very hard, but things got worse and worse. I don't think others knew how she struggled. That's why she came here. She seemed to be doing better, but..." Mrs. Downing's voice trailed off.

"But what?" Jax urged. "I can't afford to waste time. Do you have any information that can help me?"

"Minnie came home late the day that Monticello died." Her voice was barely a whisper. "She said that if anyone asked, I should say she was here with me, so I did. She said she'd stopped on the way home, just to be alone. She was having one of her crying spells and didn't want to burden me with it. Not having an alibi scared her." Her voice broke. "Heaven help me, I agreed, because she's been so distraught. I feared any extensive questioning might break her. I never thought, never believed...I didn't think she could ever harm another person, let alone kill someone." Genuine regret filled her tremulous tone. "I thought she went to Boxwood today for the same reason. Just to get away by herself."

Jax cursed under his breath. "If you see her, try to keep her with you. Right now, I need to get to Ballantyne." He quickly ended the conversation. Mars had a head start on him. She might not have gone to the resort, but he couldn't take a chance. Jax raced out the door to his car and was about to get in the Chummy when he saw Mac leaving the café. Fresh anxiety hit him hard. Immediately, Jax crossed the street. "Did Bella come to town with you?"

Mac shook his gray head. "Nay, the twins, Carl, Curt, and I ate at the café to give her a break. They're at the theater now. Why? Is something wrong?" Confusion crinkled his brow.

"Get in," he called to the older man. "I'll tell you on the way to Ballantyne." As soon as Mac was inside, Jax took off.

"Where are ye going in such a rush?" The older man clutched the door handle.

Jax simply said, "I think Minnie Mars killed Monticello."

The color drained from Mac's ruddy complexion. "Bella is alone at the place. We thought we would save her some work since she was gone all day, so all five of us came to town for dinner."

Cold sweat beaded on Jax's forehead as he briefly outlined what Mrs. Downing had said. "Let's hope Minnie actually went to Boxwood, as her sister said. Or someplace else." Real terror, unlike anything he'd known since he left France, twisted through Jax. If anything happened to Bella, he'd never forgive himself.

A hard rain fell as soon as Jax pulled on to the road to Ballantyne. Despite the torrent, Jax pushed the car to its limits. If anything, his fear had grown. Bella could very well be alone with a murderess. The thought chilled his blood.

"How did you figure out the killer?" Mac asked in a tone filled with his own trepidation.

Jax briefly explained what they'd learned in Toledo and from the Neeces before revealing what Mrs. Monticello had told him. "I still thought it was likely to be Neece since he had motive, means, and opportunity. But Mrs. Monticello put an end to that idea." Silently, he cursed himself. Why had he let Bella go back to Ballantyne alone? The fact that he had no way of knowing the others would be in town didn't halt his self-recrimination. She had wanted to stay and transcribe her notes in his office, but he'd fobbed her off.

"I wish we had nay decided to come to town for dinner. I thought we were being good to the lass. Now, she may be in terrible danger."

"You didn't know, Mac. None of us did." Jax certainly hadn't, and he was the lawman. He should have taken more precautions. "And if anyone is to blame for putting her in danger, it's me. My gut said not to involve her, but she was so angry. I was afraid she'd get in trouble investigating on her own, so I gave in." He sighed. "She tagged after Matt and me all the time we were growing up. That was fine. Neither of us really minded, although we pretended we did. Then, she had to go to France. That was unwise, but other young women went. But this..." His worried words poured out without thought. Finally, fear kept him from saying more, and regret clogged his throat.

"I'm partly to blame, lad," Mac began, "because I dinna try to stop her, either. I dinna see any harm in her helping ye. Solving the crime is important to Ballantyne, but not as important as her life." He cleared his throat before continuing. "We don't know that she's in trouble. She might be soaking in the bathtub and dinna hear the telephone."

"Maybe," Jax replied, but he wasn't convinced. A quick glance at the older man's troubled expression revealed Mac wasn't, either. He mulled over the events of the last hour.

"We don't know why Minnie acted now. Bella went to the mercantile before she headed to Ballantyne. Maybe the woman was there. Maybe Bella let something slip."

"Or Minnie was feeling frantic."

"That's true. Guilty people often ruminate over their crimes and worry about getting caught. Seeing Bella might have sparked additional fear." He halted as he saw a pair of headlights emerge from the gloom. Jax swerved, but the car sideswiped them before speeding off and turning down a side road about fifty feet away. A curse left him.

"That's the Downings' car," Mac called out.

Without a second's hesitation, Jax jerked the steering wheel until the car spun around. On the rain-slick road, the Chummy fish-tailed before he regained control and raced down the narrow lane after the Packard. Once again, he pushed the roadster to its maximum speed. He could only hope he was doing the right thing by pursuing Minnie and not going to the resort. The possibility that Bella could be there, possibly injured or worse, hounded him, but he could only go one way, and catching Minnie before she caused more harm and havoc seemed like the better choice. He only hoped he was right.

Chapter Sixteen

Jax caught up with Minnie within moments. Once he did, he saw only the older woman in the car and his heart clenched. Where was Bella? Again, he wondered if he should have continued to Ballantyne, but it was too late to second-guess himself. If Jax had made a mistake, he'd have to live with it, just as he lived with his mistake in France. He shoved that wrenching thought away. He'd be no good to Bella or anyone else if got lost in the past.

"Are ye going to force her off the road?" Mac asked as Jax pulled the car into the opposite lane.

"I'm not sure there are any other options," he replied. "Hang on, Mac. If she won't pull over, I may have to ram her."

"I'm ready, lad, but be careful. Even though we can nay see Bella, she may be in the backseat or in the trunk."

Jax nodded. "If I have to hit her, I'll clip the front end." His hands tightened on the steering wheel until his knuckles were white. At the same time, his insides hardened into a lump of haunting apprehension. With the same determination he had used when leading his men out of the trenches and into German gunfire, Jax banished all uncertainty. He focused his entire being on bringing his car alongside the Downings' Packard and then, when Minnie sped up, in hitting his own accelerator and steering toward the other car's front bumper.

The impact was negligible, but it made both vehicles jerk. Minnie sped up again, but Jax hadn't pulled away yet and the front bumper of the Packard was scraped by his

Chummy. Keeping in mind that Bella might be in the car's rear, Jax quickly maneuvered so that a small space opened between the two vehicles. He swore when Minnie kept going. While he couldn't see her face, he figured Mars was panicked, which meant she might do anything. If Bella was in the car, she was in grave danger.

***

In the trunk, Bella felt the impact and knew another vehicle had hit them. When the sound of metal-on-metal continued, her heart pounded in her ears. What was the other driver doing? If he wasn't more careful, she wouldn't need to worry about Minnie killing her; an accident would.

Suddenly, an idea hit Bella. Was Jax the other driver? She hoped so, but would he realize Minnie was armed and dangerous? Anxiety gripped Bella.

When the grating ended, Bella breathed a quick sigh of relief. The other driver must have backed off. Still, if someone was in pursuit, she stood a chance of rescue.

Abruptly, Minnie sped up. The Packard seemed to skid, and Bella was thrown from side to side. Unable to keep herself from banging against the lid of the trunk and side panels, Bella hit her head hard. After that, everything went black.

When Jax saw the curve only a few hundred feet away, he had to move out of the left lane in case a car came from the opposite way. Although hesitant to let Minnie get ahead of him again, he eased off the accelerator. Suddenly, the Packard skidded sideways. Within seconds, it was off the road and in the ditch. He quickly pulled up behind it, killed the engine, and reached into his jacket for his gun. Before throwing open the car door, he said, "Stay here, Mac." Jax ran to where he had a view into the vehicle. Minnie was slumped over the steering wheel. Even so, he approached with caution. When he reached the driver's door, he leaned down. She appeared to be unconscious, but he carefully opened the door and reached in. She'd been thrown against the steering wheel, and her head lolled to the side like she was a broken doll. He put his fingers to her neck. No pulse at all. For a moment, he bowed his head. Minnie was dead. A stab of remorse filled him, but when he investigated the back seat and saw it empty, dread disappeared, only to be replaced by terror. Where was Bella?

On shaking legs, he stepped back and gestured for Mac to join him. They met at the trunk. "Minnie is dead, but Bella isn't in the car." His hand went to the trunk latch. For a moment, he hesitated. Jax didn't want to discover the trunk was empty because that would mean she was still at Ballantyne, and he didn't think the older woman would have left Bella there unharmed. Finally, with a trembling hand, he opened the lid. A gasp left him. Bella was there, but she was motionless. Jax's pulse pounded wildly. Was she unconscious or...his mind wouldn't let him finish the thought. His fingers went to her throat. Her pulse was rapid but strong. For long moments, he stood stock-still and stared down at her.

"Lad, we need to get her out of there and get out of this rain ourselves."

Jax glanced at Mac. Abruptly, he realized he was soaked to the skin. "Yes, of course," he said hurriedly. "I'll carry

Bella. We should take her to Doc's house right now. Nolen and Richard can come for Minnie. She isn't going any place."

The words were barely out of his mouth when a car came from the direction of town. Jax immediately recognized it as Constable Jenkins' vehicle. The older man pulled to a stop on the opposite shoulder and quickly crossed the road. Nolen followed close behind him. "When Nolen told me what Mrs. Monticello said, and that you were headed to Ballantyne, we came right away."

"I'm glad you're here," Jax said with relief. "We can use your help." He briefly explained the situation. Then, he swept Bella into his arms and carried her to his car. Mac followed along while Nolen and Richard saw about Minnie's body. Pain radiated through his upper arm and shoulder, but Jax ignored it. His focus was on Bella.

***

All the way to Moreley, Jax fought fear and dread. He couldn't face having anything to happen to Bella. If it did...he didn't allow himself to finish the thought.

Once they arrived at Doc Smedlay's house, he carefully lifted her into his arms and followed Mac to the porch. Fiery fingers of agony clawed at Jax's shoulder, but he didn't falter. Getting help for Bella was his only priority.

Relief filled him when Mrs. Smedlay answered immediately and said Doc was home. Within moments, the physician met them in his office next to the home's foyer. "What happened?" he asked as he glanced from Bella's inert form to Jax, who was still holding her.

"It's a long story, Doc, but she was hurt in an accident. When I reached the car, she was unconscious, but she might have been unconscious before then. I don't know." Briefly, he summed up the incident and finished with, "Richard and Nolen are taking Minnie to the mortuary. One of them will call the Downings, as well."

Doc shook his head. "I'll take care of Bella. The two of you can wait in the parlor."

"We're wet," Mac pointed out. "We dinna want to ruin your furniture."

"The kitchen then. There's a fire going, and my wife has coffee on the stove. I'll be out as soon as I see to Bella."

Jax reluctantly laid her on the examination table. He didn't want to leave. He wanted to know that Bella would be fine. Having no good excuse to stay, he followed the older man down the hall and into the kitchen, where Mrs. Smedlay had already put a tray of muffins, plates, cups, and saucers on the big table. "Sit down, sit down. I've got coffee ready. Both of you look like you could use something hot."

Now that the crisis had passed, Jax was aware of the chill encompassing him. He fought to keep from shivering, but took the chair nearest the fire. While he gratefully accepted coffee, he didn't touch the muffins or chat with Mrs. Smedlay and Mac.

Memories seeped into his mind. His promise to Bella's brother rang in his ears. *Of course, I'll look out for your parents and Bella.* Guilt hurtled through him. He'd done a poor job of shielding her from harm despite his best intentions. Why hadn't he taken Minnie Mars more seriously? Maybe he wasn't fit for the job. Some townspeople held that view.

Lost in his troubled thoughts, Jax was only slightly aware of the conversation swirling around him.

However, when Doc entered the room a bit later, Jax immediately focused on him. "How is she?"

Doc smiled. "She woke up with a nasty headache, but she'll be fine. Evidently, she banged her head on the trunk lid. She's got a few other bumps and bruises from being jostled around, but they'll all heal with no ill effects."

Relief filled Jax, and he slumped back in his chair. Bella would be all right.

"'Tis good news," Mac said as a relieved smile lighted his lined face.

When both older men looked at him, Jax found his voice. "Yes, it is." He cleared his throat. "I need to talk with Nolen and Richard. Mac, I know you'll want to see Bella."

Both men nodded, and Mac said, "I would like to see her before I find the lads and let them know what happened. The picture show won't be over for a while, so I'll wait here. Will she be able to go home with us?" He looked at Doc.

"I'd rather she remains here tonight. You're welcome to stay, too. We have guest rooms that double as our hospital units. It would be no trouble."

When Mrs. Smedlay agreed, Mac said, "Thank you. I'd be grateful to be close to the lass." He glanced at Jax. "Could you let the lads know?"

Bella was in excellent hands, so Jax agreed, bid them all goodbye and left. His guilt was assuaged, but his anxiety was not. More murders in the area were unlikely, but he had to make sure Bella didn't feel free to meddle in other cases. Warnings could wait until later. For now, he only cared about her getting back to normal as soon as possible.

Chapter Seventeen

Jax barely slept. His nagging concern for Bella had him tossing and turning. So did his guilt over her being hurt. Why hadn't he let her transcribe her notes in his office or gone back to Ballantyne with her? Despite Doc's reassurances that she would be fine, Jax was filled with apprehension. When dawn crept over the horizon, he wearily got out of bed. As darts of pain shot through his shoulder and upper arm, Jax glanced at the sheets, where narrow smears of blood appeared. He didn't have to look at his flesh to know more small pieces of shrapnel had worked their way out. That happened less and less often now, so last night's exertions were the likely cause. Of course, the worst damage had been from a bullet tearing through his bicep.

With a resigned sigh, he retrieved a clean cloth and awkwardly wrapped it around the broken skin. Then, he dressed and headed to the office.

At that early hour, the streets were silent and empty. As Jax passed the mercantile, he wondered if the Downings would open it any time soon. Jenkins had gone to their home and informed them of Minnie's death. At some point today, Doc would examine the woman's body, although the cause of death was clear enough. Jenkins hadn't questioned either Mr. or Mrs. Downing, so that was on Jax's list for this morning. He had just started a pot of coffee when the door chime sounded.

"Good morning," Nolen said as he entered the small office. "I didn't think you'd be here so early, or maybe at all, so I figured I should come in."

"Why wouldn't I be here?" Jax's brow furrowed in confusion.

The younger man frowned. "Because you look even more exhausted than you did last night."

Since Jax couldn't refute that statement, he shrugged. "I feel good." That wasn't the truth, but he didn't want the kid treating him like an invalid. Jax didn't want anyone doing that. Unconsciously, he lightly rubbed his shoulder.

Nolen hesitated for a moment before saying, "If you say so." He took off his jacket, hung it on a peg near the door, and moved behind the counter. "I'm still doing paperwork, so I'll keep on it."

"Fine," Jax replied. "I need to complete the report on the murder and about last night. I'll head over to the mercantile. I doubt it will be open, but I need to talk with the Downings in order to fill in some details."

"From what Constable Jenkins said, Mrs. Downing was terrible upset last night, and it sounded like Mr. Downing was having a hard time getting her calmed down."

"Not surprising, considering the circumstances. I doubt if they'll open today or even this week. The whole situation had to be a terrible shock for them."

"You don't think they knew Mrs. Mars murdered Monticello?"

Jax sighed. "I'm not sure. Mrs. Downing is naturally upset over her sister's death. That doesn't mean she knew

Minnie killed Monticello. But I hope she didn't. I hope neither of them knew."

"Me, too," Nolen agreed. "The Downings are such nice people. After my dad died and we had trouble paying the bills, they extended credit to Mother."

Jax nodded. "They've done that for many people." He stopped as the door chime sounded again. This time, Constable Jenkins came in.

"Good morning," the older man called out. "I didn't think I'd find both of you here so early."

"I wanted to get started on the final report, and I need to write up something about last night, too," Jax replied.

"I can help you with last night," Jenkins offered, "but I don't think writing the final report is a necessity right now. You didn't get Arabella's transcription of yesterday's notes yet."

"No, I haven't," Jax admitted. After the crash, he hadn't given a thought to her notes. "Maybe we can go over last night and get that part done so you can head home. I'll get the notes from Bella when she feels better."

Jenkins agreed, so the three lawmen sat down at the table in Jax's office. An hour later, the bell on the front door chimed again, and Mac stood in the door to Jax's office.

Jax's heart raced as he studied the Scot's ruddy face. His expression revealed nothing, which increased Jax's anxiety. After a chorus of greetings," Mac joined the three men.

"Have a seat, Mac," Jax said, indicating the empty chair. He licked his dry lips. He wanted to casually ask about Bella, but the words froze in his throat. Luckily, Jenkins saved him the trouble.

"How is Arabella doing this morning?" Jenkins inquired.

"She seems fine, although she still has a headache," Mac replied. "Doc will most likely let her go home later today. She'll have to take it easy for a few more days. I wanted to stop in here before I head to the course. One twin will pick me up shortly since I let them take the Ford last night." His gray gaze moved to Jax. "We have players this morning and guests checking in this afternoon. With Mrs. Mars gone and Bella ailing, we be shorthanded, so I need to get back. I'm nay sure what we'll do about meals for the guests."

"Mr. MacLendon, if you only need a cook, my mother might be able to help. She's mighty good in the kitchen," Nolen put in.

Mac's attention went to the boy. "Cooking is all I'm worried about right now, lad. If ye mum would help us for lunch and supper over this weekend, twould be a real blessing."

"I'll call and ask her," Nolen said before going to the outer office.

Mac looked back at Jax. "I wondered if I could ask a favor of ye, lad."

Without a second's hesitation, Jax said, "Of course. What can I do for you?"

"Bring Bella home this afternoon, if Doc will let her go."

A knot of dread formed in Jax's throat. He'd have to interview Bella about the events of last evening, but he hadn't thought it would be so soon. His emotions were in turmoil, but he'd already said yes to virtually anything, so he could hardly back out. "Sure, I can do that."

"Thank ye, lad. I'd like to come for her myself, but we'll be busy." He looked over at Nolen, who was just hanging up the phone. "Did ye reach ye mum?"

"Yes, and she'd be happy to help. But we don't own a car, and she can't walk any distance." Nolen looked pensive.

"If she could be ready in a half-hour, she could go with me, and Jax could bring her back after he takes Bella home later."

Nolen grinned. "I'll call her back. I'm sure all of that will be fine with her."

***

The next hour passed in relative quiet. Mac and one of the twins left to pick up Nolen's mother at the appointed time, and no one else came in, leaving only the three lawmen on hand.

Jenkins stretched and rose. "I don't know that I can add anything more to your reports, son. If I can help again, though, you know how to reach me."

Jax stood, as well. "Thank you, sir. You've been a great help. I honestly don't know what we would have done without you last night."

A harsh breath left Jenkins. "It was an ugly situation. I'm sorry Mrs. Mars died, but it may be for the best. Any trial is hard." He shook his head. "A murder trial with a woman defendant. That's one of the worst."

"I can only imagine," Jax said. Despite his anger at Minnie for kidnapping Bella, he felt sympathy for the woman.

"And the good news is that Arabella is recovering," Jenkins continued.

"Yes, that is good news," Jax agreed, but hearing her name brought back all his anxiety.

"Son, I know it had to be a scary situation last night. I can't even imagine how you felt when you realized Bella was in danger," the older man said.

Regret rolled over Jax yet again. "I shouldn't have let her go back to Ballantyne to type up her notes. She could have done it in the office. In fact, she suggested doing that."

The older man shook his head. "You couldn't have known Arabella would be alone there, or that Minnie was the killer. None of us knew." Richard paused for a moment. "I'm the one who said you should probably let her help, Jax, so if you blame yourself, blame me, too."

"It isn't your fault," Jax immediately replied. "I'm the one who sent her home."

"Jax, she'll be fine. You heard Mac say so. Try not to be so hard on yourself." The senior constable focused his gaze on Jax for several moments. "You mistakenly thought she was in danger last December. We've already discussed it. Arabella didn't get out of the car until after the killer's gun went off. He was no threat after that, so she wasn't in harm's way. I don't want to overstep any boundaries, but you clearly feel responsible for her."

Jax shoved his hands into his pants' pockets. "I promised her brother that if he didn't make it home, I'd look out for his parents and Bella."

"It's not only a promise to your best friend making you worry about the girl." Doubt underscored the statement.

The other man's observation and scrutiny made Jax glance away. "It's all it can be," he finally said in a low, raspy whisper.

"Because you had to give up your golf career?"

The question resonated with concern, so Jax was honest. "That's not all of it," he began in a low tone. "Ballantyne is Bella's world. She made it clear back in December that all her interest and energy are on saving the resort, which is as it should be. I can't help her. In fact, I'd be more of a hindrance than anything else." He'd given away a big part of his reasoning. The other element, the worst element, was his role in Matthew Stewart's death. Jax wasn't ready to reveal his selfishness, his mistake. Maybe he never would be.

"You're a highly responsible young man. From what I know, you always have been. But don't take extra burdens on your shoulders, son. You aren't to blame for what happened yesterday. Try to accept that."

After a deep breath, Jax nodded in agreement. "I will," he said, but the affirmation was mostly to assuage Richard. The image of Bella lying motionless in the Packard's trunk wouldn't leave him for a long, long time.

Jenkins smiled and clapped Jax on his good shoulder. "I'll talk with you later."

***

After Jenkins left, Jax shook off his troubled thoughts and turned to Nolen. "I'm going over to the mercantile to see if the Downings are there. If not, I'll go to their house. I want to get statements from them today."

"Will you go to Doc's after that?"

"I need to stop there and see if he'll let Bella go home today, but I'll be back here after that."

"Unless he lets Bella leave right then."

"I doubt that. She probably won't be able to leave until later." With that in mind, Jax figured he might get Nolen to drive Bella home. The key problem was looking like a coward if he did. That could be faced later. "I'll see you shortly," he said before grabbing his cap and heading out.

The *closed* sign was still in the window of the mercantile, so Jax kept walking. The Downings' home was only another two blocks away. Despite the pleasant weather, he passed no one, although he saw folks inside the café. He moved as briskly as possible since he had no desire to answer questions about the previous night.

When he reached the lovely white two-story house, Jax paused at the gate. Not much had changed since he'd last been here, except for the drapes being pulled. Surely, the Downings hadn't left town. Concern nipped at him as he went to the front door. He rapped twice, and when he heard nothing, he rapped twice more. Finally, the sound of footsteps reached him. In a few moments, the door inched open.

Jax thought he saw a man's hand, so he said, "Mr. Downing?"

The door opened wide. "Come in," the man said as he stepped back.

The interior was so dim that Jax had to stop on the doorstep to let his eyes adjust. While he did, he went on. "I wanted to get statements from both you and Mrs. Downing.

I'm sorry. I know you must be terribly upset, and she must be devastated."

"She hasn't gotten out of bed, but she hasn't slept, either. Let me go up and let her know you're here." He gestured toward the couch and two chairs grouped around the fireplace. "Have a seat. I'll be right back."

As the older man ascended the stairs, Jax settled in one of the chairs. He pulled out his notepad and pencil. The room, filled with deep shadows, held an aura of sadness and gloom. Funny how grieving people often gravitated to darkness.

When Downing returned, he flicked on one lamp, which provided weak light. "I'm sorry," he said. "My wife asked me to keep the drapes closed and the lamps off. A couple of people stopped earlier and, as I told you, she hasn't even gotten out of bed. Neither of us has been up to visitors, in any case." A rough sigh left him. "She'll be down in a few minutes. Can I get you anything?"

"No, sir. I won't stay long. I don't want to trouble either one of you, but I need some details."

"I understand."

Within a short time, Mrs. Downing descended the stairs. Jax stood as she entered the room. His heart went out to her. Dark circles, emphasized by her pallor, shadowed her red-rimmed eyes. She wore a shapeless dress that had seen far better days, stockings that sagged below her knees, and battered carpet slippers. Her gray hair, usually neatly tucked into a twist, was completely disheveled. Never had Jax seen the shopkeeper look anything but immaculate. He could easily believe she hadn't slept.

Her husband took her hand and drew her to the sofa, where they both sat down. After patting her arm, he looked back at Jax. "Can you speak with both of us at the same time?"

"Certainly," Jax agreed. He cleared his throat and looked back at Mrs. Downing. "I'm very sorry about your sister, ma'am."

The woman put a trembling hand to her lips. "I knew she was grieving, but I never thought...I couldn't believe." Her gaze went to Mr. Downing, who patted her forearm.

"You did nothing wrong, my dear. Just tell the constable."

Something about Mrs. Downing's words and her husband's reaction put Jax on edge. He wanted to ask what they meant, but he forced himself to remain calm. The woman appeared to be on the edge of a breakdown. Upsetting her would only make matters worse. "Yes, please tell me whatever you think is important."

She nodded. "I don't think I did anything wrong," she began in a tremulous whisper. "I didn't know, didn't imagine." She paused, took a deep breath and went on. "I told you yesterday about the day that Mr. Monticello died. My husband was at a meeting, as you already know. I was home but didn't feel well, so I went upstairs to lie down and fell asleep. Minnie came in some time after that and before Mr. Downing got home. When I saw her at breakfast the next morning, she said I was sleeping when she returned. She said she didn't want to disturb me, so she went to her room." Mrs. Downing swallowed convulsively. "Later, when we found out about the murder, Minnie was so upset about poor Mr. Monticello. She was terrified that you'd put her in jail because she didn't have an alibi. She was here at home, and I was home, but I didn't see her. At least I thought she was home. Now, I know she didn't get here as early as she said, but I didn't know when you first asked me. It was only yesterday that I realized she'd lied to me. Even so, I didn't think for one minute that my sister could kill anyone." Tears streamed down her face as her voice broke. Mr. Downing gathered her into his arms and looked at Jax over his wife's shoulder.

"My wife didn't know anything was wrong, and I didn't suspect, either. I couldn't imagine why Minnie would kill a total stranger. I know his money and watch were missing, but she isn't destitute. The store didn't do well after her menfolk died. She couldn't handle it along with her grief, and she sold when prices were down. Living on her own would be difficult. That's why she came to us."

Jax had been writing steadily, but he paused. Obviously, the Downings didn't know the connection between Minnie and Monticello. He wasn't surprised Richard and Nolen hadn't discussed it with them since the couple must have been in even worse shock last night. "I believe you. But Monticello wasn't a stranger to her."

The Downings stared at him in obvious bewilderment. "What do you mean?" the man asked.

"I didn't know there was a connection until late yesterday myself. Monticello was the head of the draft board in Toledo."

"Oh, my," Mrs. Downing murmured as her hand went to her mouth and her eyes rounded in shock. "I never knew the name of the man, but I know Minnie went to him and said she needed Al in the store. The man told her that, since she worked in it herself, she wouldn't lose any money." A shuddering sigh escaped him. "Then, when Mikey joined up to go with Al, she went back. She begged the man to intercede. He said it would do the boy good. A foolish comment," she said with dismay. "Minnie was grief-stricken when she lost them, and on the same day. Mikey was hit when they were advancing, and Al went to help him. He was shot, too." She wiped at her eyes with the back of one hand.

"I understand it had to be terrible for her," Jax said, and he did. All too well.

"She blamed the draft board and the man who had brushed her off, but she never spoke of it after she moved in with us." Fresh tears cascaded down her pale face. "If she had talked to me, maybe I could have said or done something to help her."

"I doubt that, Mrs. Downing," Jax said. "Did you know your sister had a handgun?"

What little color remained in the woman's face drained away. "Minnie had a gun?"

"Yes, ma'am," Jax replied. "I didn't think you knew, but I had to ask." When neither of the Downings asked for more information, he went on. "I believe I have enough for now, so I'll leave you in peace."

"How is Arabella?" Mrs. Downing asked as he turned toward the door.

Jax looked back at her. "I haven't seen her since last night, but Mac came to my office this morning and said she'll likely be able to go home today."

"I'm so glad. At least Minnie didn't do her permanent harm. When you see her, please say...please tell her I'm so sorry for what my sister did."

"I'm going to Doc's place from here, so I will do that." Jax glanced back at Mrs. Downing. "Again, my sympathies about your sister."

The older woman nodded before burying her face in her husband's shoulder. Mr. Downing patted her back as he also nodded at Jax. "Thank you, constable."

Jax, his heart heavy, quietly took his leave.

Chapter Eighteen

The Smedlays lived only a block from the Downings' home, so Jax continued down the street. He would check on Bella and see if she could go back to Ballantyne later in the day. Jax still figured on getting his deputy to do it. He could use the excuse that Mrs. Rogers would need a ride home. A bonus was that Nolen loved driving the sporty Chummy.

When Jax got to the doctor's house, he found Mrs. Smedlay on the porch swing. "Good morning," she called out as he approached. "Mac said you'd be coming by. I believe Doc will let Arabella go home right after dinner. We'll be eating soon, so I hope you can join us."

"That's very kind, ma'am," Jax replied, although the offer interfered with his plan to have Nolen take over seeing Bella home.

"Nonsense. You look like you could use a few good meals," she said with a smile. "I don't suppose you do much cooking for yourself."

Jax shifted from one foot to the other. "My job keeps me busy, but I often eat evening supper at the café."

"Sam Push serves good food, but there's nothing like home cooking. Dinner should be ready, so let's go in."

When she turned to go into the house, Jax opened the door for her. The motion sent shards of pain through his arm and shoulder, and he couldn't help but wince.

Mrs. Smedlay frowned. "Carrying Arabella last night didn't do your arm any good." It was a statement, not a question. "I think Doc should take a look at it for you."

Jax wanted to argue, but he doubted if it would help. Both the Smedlays could be persistent and persuasive, something he knew through dealing with childhood illnesses. Jax remembered how anxious he'd been whenever he got sick and had to miss days at Ballantyne. Invariably, either Doc or his wife caught him heading out of town and informed his parents. At this point, saving his breath seemed like the best idea. So reluctantly, Jax followed her. After being wounded twice in France, he hated seeing a doctor, any doctor, more than ever. He hated having his weaknesses exposed.

Mrs. Smedlay ushered him into the doctor's office. Doc looked up when he heard them. "Ah, Jax, here to get Arabella?"

"He is, dear, but I think you should look at him. He strained that arm and shoulder last night carrying her," his wife replied before Jax could speak.

Doc's gaze narrowed on Jax. "I thought that might be a problem." He paused before continuing. "You haven't been to see me since you first got back," he observed, "and I rarely run into you."

"I'll give you two some privacy," Mrs. Smedlay said.

When she had closed the door behind her, the doctor continued. "I hoped you haven't been in because your arm is getting better."

Jax didn't admit that he tried to avoid Doc, but the older man looked suspicious, so he'd probably figured that out already. "It gives me trouble when I strain it," Jax admitted.

A frown knit the doctor's brow. "Carrying Arabella and getting soaked last night certainly didn't help you," the older man pointed out.

"No, sir, but I'm sure I'll be fine. Just need to give it some time." Jax's excuse sounded weak even to his own ears. He hadn't thought about his wounds at all. His only goal had been to get Bella to the doctor as soon as possible.

"We talked about the issues with your arm and shoulder when you first got back, Jax. I understand that surgeons in a field hospital did the best they could under very difficult conditions. Not only that, you probably went back to the trenches too soon after the first wound."

Conflicting emotions tore at Jax. "I could have gone back sooner."

Doc released a harrumph. "You haven't told me many details, but a bullet tore through your bicep is what I'm guessing from the scar. Is that right?"

Unable to avoid a direct question, Jax nodded.

"I figured as much. Getting hit with shrapnel probably complicated that injury. So does the remaining shrapnel. I think you should see a surgeon in Toledo. Removing the shrapnel, or at least more of it, is the only thing that might provide real help." Doc paused for a moment. "I know you'd like to be as healthy as you were when you left for France, but you aren't, and it's possible you may never be. The surgeon could give you a better prognosis. I can schedule an appointment for you."

This was not the first time Smedlay had made such an offer, so Jax replied. "I'll think more about it."

"All right," the physician said with a sigh. "I can give you something to help ease the current pain, at least. Take off your jacket and let me give it a look." When Jax hesitated, Doc spoke again. "When we last spoke, you still had bits of shrapnel come to the surface."

"It doesn't happen as often as it did."

"Some came out last night." It was a statement.

"A bit. I didn't notice until this morning, and I put a bandage on it."

Doc clucked his dismay. "Take off the jacket and the shirt."

With reluctance, Jax followed doctor's orders.

"Son, you can't just slap a piece of cloth on these wounds. Surely, before you left France, you were told to seek medical help when this occurred. The bits may be small, but when they pierce the skin, they can cause infection. If they rise to the surface without coming out, I need to remove them for you. Then, I can give you some antiseptic."

Heat rose in Jax's face, and he once again felt like an errant schoolboy. "Yes, sir." He sat quietly while Doc cleaned and re-bandaged his arm.

"There's swelling, but I'm not surprised. You really shouldn't be lifting anything...or anyone. However, I know it was an emergency." The older man gave him a rueful smile. "Rest the arm as much as you can for a few days at least. Come back tomorrow and my wife or I will change the bandage. I'd recommend a sling, but you probably wouldn't wear it."

Jax shrugged, sending another shaft of pain through his upper arm and shoulder. He couldn't help but grimace.

Doc's white brows drew together. "Are you sure it only hurts when you strain it?" Doubt was in his voice.

"It gives me trouble at times," Jax admitted. More times than not was closer to the truth.

"Not surprising." Doc's gaze narrowed on Jax. "If I was in your shoes, I would try anything that might give me relief and let me do more."

"I appreciate your concern, Doc. I really do, and I promise I'll think about it," he said again. Before he became too sidetracked, Jax turned the conversation to Bella. "Is Bella really well enough to go home? She was unconscious for a while."

"Before we move away from you, I'm advising you to take it easy for a few days. Catch up on your rest and eat decent meals. Did you sleep at all last night?"

Jax sighed. "Not a lot." The pain in his shoulder and arm hadn't been the primary reason, though.

"I'll give you some medicine. Take it at night. That should help you rest. But make sure you get to bed at a decent hour. Sleep can be restorative. If you don't take it easy for a few days, you'll be back here and probably feeling a lot worse." Without waiting for a response, Doc went on. "As for Arabella, she is doing very well. I wouldn't let her leave if she wasn't. She still has a bit of a headache, and some bumps and bruises, but she'll be fine in a few days."

"She can go home later?"

Doc nodded. "Yes, she can. Now, I know dinner must be ready, so let's join the ladies."

With reluctance, Jax went to the dining room with Doc. When he saw Bella already seated at the table, he hesitated in the doorway. She looked pale, but how did she feel? Would she really be fine? Despite Doc's reassurances, anxiety continued to plague Jax. Despite Richard's observations, guilt continued to assail him.

"Please sit down, Jax," Mrs. Smedlay said, gesturing to the empty chair across from Bella.

"Thank you." Jax took a seat before looking over at Bella. "How are you feeling?" he asked in what he hoped was a casual tone.

"Much better," she said with a smile, "thanks to Doc and Mrs. Smedlay. They've been wonderful to me."

"Good." Jax couldn't think of anything else to say, so he sat in silence and let the others carry the conversation. When the meal was over, he finally spoke again. "Thank you, Mrs. Smedlay. It was a wonderful dinner."

"I'm glad you enjoyed it," she replied as she turned her attention to Bella. "I suppose you'll be wanting to get home, my dear."

"Yes, I am anxious to get back." Bella smiled as she spoke, "but I appreciate your kindness and care so much."

Doc's gaze narrowed on the young woman. "Remember what I said. You're to take it easy for several days. Mac has lined up young Nolen's mother to cook lunch and dinner, so you stay out of the kitchen and avoid any arduous tasks. He said Dick and Dale will chip in and do whatever needs to be done. Curt and Carl, too, so you have no excuse for overdoing."

"I'm so glad Mrs. Rogers can help us," she agreed, "and I will be careful." Bella looked at Jax again. "Are you still able to take me to Ballantyne? Mac said you could."

He nodded, although tension sang through him. "I can take you whenever you want to go." He stopped for a moment. Why had he said that? She was injured and needed to go home. "My car is by the office, though, and I walked here. I'll get it and be back. While I'm there, I'd like to check in with Nolen, but that won't take long." Now, getting his deputy to drive Bella home seemed impossible. What excuse could he make that wouldn't seem fake and weak? None came to mind.

"That will be fine," she replied.

***

Jax would have liked to linger at his office, but Nolen had no urgent matters for him, so he was back at the Smedlay place in short order. Bella and Mrs. Smedlay were sitting on the porch. Both rose as he stopped the Chummy in front of the house. After Bella again thanked the older woman, they said their goodbyes. Mrs. Smedlay handed Jax a bag with liniment and headache powder. As she did, she smiled at Bella and said, "The medicine should help, but don't hesitate to call if you feel worse in any way. Doc will come out to see you tomorrow. He can come sooner, if necessary."

"I'll be fine, but I will call if I start to feel worse," Bella assured her.

Jax bid farewell to the doctor's wife as he helped Bella down the porch steps and into the car. Once she was settled, he handed her the bag and went to the driver's side. Within moments, they were headed out of town.

***

Silence filled the car, but Jax wasn't sure how to break it. He and Bella had gotten along quite well on their trip to Toledo, but he'd failed her badly yesterday evening. Because of him, she had come close to dying. She didn't act like she blamed him, but this was the first time they had been alone. Knowing Bella, she would never shun or criticize him in front of others. How did she feel? Was she angry, upset, disgusted? He wouldn't blame her if she was all three. Despite Richard's counsel, Jax certainly felt all those emotions and more toward himself. He took a sidelong glance at her and saw that her eyes were closed. Letting her rest seemed like a good idea.

When the car drew to a stop in front of the inn, Bella stirred. "Sorry, I guess I dozed off."

"You need rest," he replied.

For a moment, she studied his face. "You look like you need some, too. Did you have to stay late at the office?"

"Not too late. I waited for Nolen and Richard to come back, and we went over the case."

"You'll need my notes from yesterday," she said. "I had just finished typing them when Minnie arrived."

Fresh remorse hit Jax. He should have let her type the notes in his office. "Don't worry about the notes. They aren't important."

A quizzical expression blanketed her pretty face. "You have to have them to write your final report."

"That can wait."

"Will Mayor Cawlings feel the same way?" she asked with a trace of asperity.

"It doesn't matter how he feels," Jax said. "Doc said you should rest. Now, let's get you inside and comfortable." He hurried to the passenger side and opened the door for her.

As Bella slid out, she swayed slightly. Jax immediately took her elbow. "Do you feel dizzy or anything?"

Her dark gaze met his. "I'm really fine, Jax. Just a little headache and some soreness other places, but Doc says that is to be expected."

He nodded, but as she mounted the steps to the inn's expansive porch, Jax followed close behind. When they got to the front door, she turned to him. Amusement lit her eyes. "I'm reminded of when I learned to ride a bike. You and Matt ran so close to it that there was no chance I could ever fall off. One of you would have caught me."

A warm flush rose in his cheeks, but Jax made no reply. Instead, he gave Bella a bit more space as they entered the front hall. She didn't seem angry, at least. That was good.

"Bella," Carl called to her from behind the front desk. "Welcome home. Good to see you!"

"Thank you, Carl. It's good to be home."

"Mrs. Rogers made sure your room is ready. She's in the kitchen. Would you like me to bring tea or coffee or anything?"

"No, but thank you," Bella replied. "I appreciate the offer."

Jax wasn't sure what Nolen's mother had done to get Bella's room ready. After all, she'd only been gone overnight. Just the same, it was a relief to know she would be in good hands while she recuperated.

Bella went on. "Jax and I will be in the family sitting room, Carl. After that, I'll go to my room for a rest. I feel fine, but those are doctor's orders."

The thin man nodded. "Yes, Bella. You do as Doc says. We're getting along okay. We can all chip in and do whatever is needed while you get better."

"I'm sure you've been a big help to Mac, and I appreciate that." Bella smiled at him.

Carl flushed with obvious embarrassment but also with clear pleasure. "Thanks."

When Bella turned toward the family quarters, Jax followed. Once inside the parlor, he glanced around the once-familiar room. He hadn't been here for almost three years, but he had pictured it hundreds of times when he'd been in France. After his mother's death, Jax had come here when he needed tenderness and warmth. This room had become a haven when his father, dealing with his own deep grief and demanding job, had been too preoccupied to cope with a heartbroken ten-year-old boy.

His gaze went to the fireplace mantel, where several framed photographs sat. Two were copies of the ones in his desk. A shuddering sigh left him. What he wouldn't give to have Matt standing beside him right now.

He looked at the Stewart family picture and wondered again how Bella had managed her own sorrow. They had been such a close-knit and loving family, and he had been lucky enough to be included—along with Mac—in their circle. As Bella had told him, she was grateful for the old pro's continued presence in her life, but she deserved more. So much more. She deserved to have her brother beside her to cope with the sorrow of losing their parents. Matt should not be in a French grave; Jax should, and he knew it even if Bella did not.

The image of her lying bound and unconscious in the trunk of the Packard again rose in his mind. Bella had come far too close to joining the rest of her family the previous night. No matter what anyone else thought, he was to blame for that, too. As anxiety gripped him, Jax remained still and silent.

"Sit down, Jax." His expression bothered Bella. The color had drained from his face, which made the dark circles beneath his eyes appear more pronounced, and he looked like he was a thousand miles away. Four thousand was more like it, since he was probably thinking about France. "Jax," she repeated. She had already taken a seat by the fireplace, but he was still standing in the middle of the room with his attention on the fireplace mantel. She couldn't tell his exact focus, but Bella thought it might be the picture of him and her brother. What did Jax think when he saw an image of Matt? His reaction to her brother's death still bothered Bella. So did his admission about promising Matt to look out for her. She appreciated his loyalty and concern, but Bella didn't want Jax feeling obligated.

Jax seemed to shake off his distraction before taking one of the chairs across from her. "This won't take long, Bella. I just want to make sure I have all the information I need for my report." With that, he pulled his notepad and pencil out of his front jacket pocket.

"There's no hurry," she said with a smile. "I should have asked if you wanted something. Coffee or tea?"

"No, thank you." He licked his lips and stared at the pad. "I already have the basic information. There are a few points I want to go over."

"Of course."

Jax focused on the pad in his hands. "You spoke with Minnie at the mercantile."

Bella nodded in agreement. "Yes. She asked about me driving your Chummy, and I said we'd visited people and nothing more."

"Did Minnie ask any questions?"

"Not really. I got my supplies and came home. I had finished transcribing and typing the notes from yesterday when she came in, but I still wasn't alarmed."

"What did she say when she got here?" Jax asked.

Bella briefly outlined their conversation and revealed that Minnie had pulled the gun out of her pocket almost immediately. "I never thought about her overhearing our conversation with the Downings yesterday morning."

"Neither did I," Jax muttered. "I should have, though. We knew she was in the house."

His self-recrimination wasn't surprising. "Jax, we couldn't have guessed that she eavesdropped." When he said nothing, she knew no words would sway him, so she went on. "Anyhow, as far as last evening, I thought letting her kidnap me was my only option. At least, that gave me extra time."

"You were right to buy time. It made all the difference."

Bella smiled. "You'll never know how relieved I was when you followed us and bumped the car. I know I said so already, but I honestly thought I had no chance until that happened. My options were very limited."

"It was all I could think to do. She was speeding up, and I was afraid she'd lose control of the Packard. Of course, she did anyhow."

"You're right about her speeding up. I'm sure she would have continued to go faster. If she had and then, we crashed, and I probably wouldn't have gotten off so easily."

He swallowed hard before speaking. "I could have put more emphasis on her as a strong suspect, but I didn't until I talked to Mrs. Monticello. I can't believe I was so focused on Neece. It was a major mistake, one that nearly took your life."

For a long moment, Bella studied him. He still looked almost ashen. "You're not to blame for what happened to me, Jax. You didn't know Mac, and the others weren't here, and what the Neeces told us made him the best suspect."

His nostrils flared with a sharp intake of breath. "If Mac had been here, he might have been in danger, too. I shouldn't have let you come back to Ballantyne by yourself."

A frown knit her brow. "You were the one who wanted to keep her on the list," Bella pointed out. "I honestly couldn't imagine a woman committing such a brutal act. I couldn't imagine her doing it, especially after we heard about her being such a sweet, kind lady."

"But we also heard that she changed when her husband and son were killed. I should have paid more heed to that." He drove his fingers through his hair. "I know how war can change people, and I should have taken that into account."

"We both know that, Jax," Bella pointed out. "But we heard a lot more about how Neece had been affected, and his wife, as well. People thought Minnie's grief and withdrawal were understandable because she lost her whole family. Despite that, you were the one who argued to keep her at the top of the suspect list. I thought we should eliminate her." When he said nothing, Bella continued. "You said you spoke with the Downings. Did they know she had a gun?"

He shook his head. "They said they didn't, and I have no reason not to believe them."

"If they didn't know, how would you?"

Her question hung in the air for several moments. "It isn't just the gun, Bella. It's my whole approach to the case. I didn't do a very good job."

Bella sighed. "You expect too much of yourself, Jax. You always have. Without Mrs. Monticello's revelations, I don't see how you could have figured it out. Even then, her description applied to Mrs. Neece and Minnie. They both lost loved ones and moved away."

"Mrs. Neece moved before we got into the war, which made it unlikely that she was the one calling Monticello and going to his home, since she wasn't always in Toledo."

"That's what made you turn to Minnie as the likely killer?"

He nodded. "I was telling Nolen about what Mrs. Monticello said. The two of us made the connection about the same moment."

"We figured she was the key to the case, and she was." When he didn't reply, Bella continued. "I know you think

I'm foolish to reflect on my Grandfather Moore's cases, but not all murders are solved. This one has been."

That comment elicited a rueful smile from Jax. "I don't think you're foolish, Bella, and I was worried that this case might never be solved. My dad didn't have to deal with a murder, but he didn't solve all his cases, either, and Richard hasn't. Sometimes, there aren't enough clues and other times, the criminal acts completely out of character. Or something changes them."

"Minnie certainly became an entirely different person yesterday. After her usual lack of emotion, it was stunning. She was so angry, and she kept saying she didn't want to go to the electric chair; she didn't want to burn. She got really upset. I told her that there were extenuating circumstances. I tried to make it sound like she might not be sentenced to death, but I don't know if that would have been the case." Bella paused before going on. "It was particularly tricky because it was pure happenstance that Minnie came into contact with Mr. Monticello." She reviewed what the woman had said about why and how she had confronted the man.

"Then, she didn't go to the cottage planning to kill him."

"Evidently not. She could have come back the next day with her pistol and had an easier method." A shiver rippled through her. "Killing him with his own mashie. Just awful."

"Telling her she needed to be institutionalized had to be the final blow." He paused a moment before going on. "I'm glad you thought to ask her some questions."

"I was stalling for time because I figured you'd be coming soon."

Some emotion flickered briefly in his gaze, but his reply was purely factual. "We'll never find the shaft now, but at least we know why she took it and what she did with it."

Bella nodded. "The whole thing is nearly unbelievable. It was a complete coincidence that she saw him here, and it was his reaction in the cottage that set her on him. "

"Coincidences sometimes lead to crimes," he observed.

"Do you think the charges would have been lowered because of the circumstances?"

"I doubt it. It was a brutal crime, although not a premeditated one." He cleared his throat and looked back at his notepad. "She forced you into the trunk at gunpoint."

"Yes. I was surprised that she had such an elaborate plan. I doubt if she could contact the cousins before she came back here. That would have alerted Bertha."

Finally, his expression lost some of its severity. "She insists that she never eavesdrops on calls."

Bella rolled her eyes. "Perhaps she does, perhaps she doesn't. However, getting a call through to Pennsylvania would have stood out to her. Once my absence was noted, Bertha would have contacted you. But who knows how far we would have gotten by then? Minnie was counting on you needing to make multiple long-distance calls to try and find us. Getting in touch with her cousins might have been impossible. If their area is remote, telephone service is unlikely."

"Richard is working on getting local law enforcement to question them, but you're right. Minnie probably planned to just show up."

"Her husband's cousins might not have gone along with her plans."

"I doubt if we'll ever know for sure. They aren't likely to admit to it even if they would have. Jenkins had the car towed into town, but nothing in it gave us any clues to her destination. I'll ask Mrs. Downing if Minnie was in regular contact with her husband's cousins, but it's a minor point. I can find out if she tried to reach them. When I spoke with the Downings, they said they had no idea about her threatening Monticello back in Toledo. They also said to tell you how very sorry they are about what happened. Neither of them knew Minnie could or would be violent."

"The whole situation must have come as a terrible shock to them," she murmured.

"It seems that way." Jax revealed what Mrs. Downing had told him about her sister's fear of being under suspicion after Monticello's murder, and her agreement not to reveal that she had not been up when Minnie got home that day. "I'll talk to Jenkins, but I honestly don't see how we can charge the Downings with anything, or that we should do so."

"Oh, no, I don't think so, either," Bella hurried to say. "Mrs. Downing wanted to protect her sister from more pain and trouble. I'm sure she told the truth about never suspecting Minnie." Her brow furrowed. "What about Mr. Penn seeing Dick and Dale? Were they really out at the time he said?"

"Richard talked to Penn, and the man had his days mixed up."

"Everyone does that sometimes," she replied.

"I agree," Jax said, as he snapped his notepad shut. "I don't have any other questions, Bella. I appreciate you talking with me, and I hope you're feeling much better soon. Take care of yourself." He absently rubbed his shoulder.

"I think you need to do the same." Bella studied his face. Despite the camaraderie on the trip to Toledo, she felt Jax slipping away again. Before he did, she wanted to make sure he was okay. "Mac said you carried me from the trunk to your car and then, from your car into the Smedlays' house. Did it do much damage to your shoulder and arm?"

He immediately shook his head. "No damage. Just a bit of soreness."

Her brows rose. "Really? Just a bit?"

His lips twitched into a semblance of a smile. "A fair of amount of soreness, but nothing serious. I'll be fine, and I hope you will be, too."

The dismay darkening his green gaze revealed lingering guilt. "Jax, I already told you that what happened last night isn't your fault. It isn't anyone's fault. Neece seemed like the best suspect. Minnie denied knowing Monticello, and I believed her. Everyone who knew her said she would never harm anyone, and I believed that."

"In part, so did I." Regret and remorse underscored each word. "But a lawman shouldn't be so gullible."

A soft sigh escaped her. "You aren't gullible. Remember, you're the one who refused to eliminate her."

"That wasn't enough."

"You did the right thing, Jax, the best thing," she assured him. "It all turned out fine, except for Minnie, of course, but she may be better off. She was terrified of being convicted and electrocuted. That would have been hard on the Downings, as well."

"Jenkins said the same thing," he admitted. "I'm sorry she died, but living through a trial, imprisonment, and execution might have been worse for her and everyone else." Jax paused for a moment. "She's like Gus Schwarz's killer in a lot of ways."

"I was thinking the same thing myself. Both suffered terrible losses, and both were traumatized by grief."

"Unfortunately, they let grief turn into vengeance."

Bella nodded. "Yes, they did. I'm sorry for the Monticello family and for the Downings, but I'm relieved that you solved the case. It should help us get back on track here at Ballantyne soon. At least, I hope it will."

For long moments, his green gaze focused on her. "I didn't solve it alone, Bella. You, Nolen, and Jenkins helped to resolve everything. In fact, you helped most of all. I appreciate all of your assistance."

She smiled. "I was happy to help and happy that you let me."

"You were the one who said Monticello being on the draft board was probably the key to the solution, and you were right, Bella."

Her smile turned into a wide grin. "I love hearing you say *you were right, Bella.*"

He shook his head, but smiled in return. "I'm sure you do."

"Then, you'll be open to my help next time?" Amusement was in her tone.

A frown creased his brow. "This was only the area's second murder. It isn't likely there'll be another one any time soon—or any time at all."

Bella chuckled. "That's what you said in December after the first murder, but I hope not, too." she said with sincerity. "I think the resort can weather this storm. I'm not sure how people would react if there's another murder around here."

"There won't be," he assured her. "Things should get back to normal now, which will be good for Ballantyne and Moreley."

A sigh escaped her. "We have a lot of work ahead of us."

His green gaze filled with some emotion before Jax glanced away. "You and Mac will get Ballantyne on track again."

"He should take it easy at his age," she said, revealing some of the worry always in the back of her mind.

"I know he should," Jax murmured.

His tone more than his words motivated Bella to voice another thought in the back of her mind. "I know your wounds keep you from playing golf, but a club professional doesn't need to compete in tournaments. Mac hasn't done that for years."

Jax put his elbows on his knees and clasped his hands between his legs. "Mac's age has kept him from competing." He swallowed convulsively. "It isn't the same thing. Besides, he's a co-founder of Ballantyne, and he's been here as a professional or co-professional for thirty years. Before that, he worked as an assistant in Scotland and then, in Cleveland. He has a sterling record in many tournaments."

While all Jax said was true, Bella persisted. "You and Matt planned to be co-professionals. My dad was all for the idea. So was Mac. So was I."

Before he bowed his head, a look of stark agony crossed Jax's face. "Everything is different now, Bella. The war changed it all."

"It changed a lot, but it doesn't have to keep you from working here, Jax. I know you've said it's hard to come and be reminded of your broken dreams. You could still have part of your dream." Seconds of silence ticked away, and Bella wondered if she'd gone too far. She should say she wasn't asking him for closer personal ties. Or would that be too much?

When he looked up, regret shadowed his expression. "Settling for part of my dream might be worst of all," he murmured.

An ache rose inside Bella. She swallowed hard in order to speak with some semblance of grace. "I can understand that. I just thought..."

"I appreciate the thought. I really do, but you'll find the right guy. One who can be a full partner and shoulder his share of the work along with representing Ballantyne at all the big tournaments. Mac and Stew did all that for years. I didn't see them play in their prime, but I saw your dad. He definitely followed in their footsteps."

Despite her disappointment, Bella smiled. "He was an outstanding player."

"He was, and you need a professional with the same skill."

Jax got to his feet. "Doc said you need rest, so I'll be on my way." He put notepad and pencil in his pocket, slipped his cap on his head, and turned toward the door.

Bella watched as he crossed the room and disappeared into the hallway. Her overture had been dismissed on all counts. While she couldn't say she was surprised, Bella was disappointed. Very disappointed.

***

Jax made it to the Chummy before emotion overtook him. A shuddering sigh escaped as he leaned against the vehicle. Sweet heaven. He'd wanted to accept her offer more than he wanted his next breath. Thinking about another man taking the golf pro job at Ballantyne and being Bella's future partner made Jax feel queasy.

Weary in heart and soul, he climbed into the driver's seat. As he put the car into gear and drove off, Jax thought about the surgeon in Toledo. The man might remove the shrapnel, which could eliminate one barrier to his dreams. Unfortunately, that wasn't the only hurdle between himself and Bella. His selfish stupidity had led to her brother's death. If she knew, Bella wouldn't be offering him the pro job—or anything else. Would she?

Full use of his arm would be a marvel. Bella forgiving him for his role in Matt's death would be a miracle. Jax tried to dismiss both ideas, but they stayed with him for a long, long time.

Don't miss out!

Visit the website below and you can sign up to receive emails whenever D.S. Lang publishes a new book. There's no charge and no obligation.

https://books2read.com/r/B-A-JJPN-ZKDPB

BOOKS 2 READ

Connecting independent readers to independent writers.

Did you love *A Lingering Shadow*? Then you should read *A Lethal Arrogance*[1] by D.S. Lang!

After returning home from her service as a United States Army Signal Corps operator in the Great War, Arabella Stewart's goal, to save her family's resort, seems within reach as the summer season progresses. She and her business partner, look forward to re-establishing a successful championship golf tournament, once the signature event of the resort's year. Problems arise when one of the contestants clashes with more than one person. When he is found dead, the victim of a suspicious automobile crash, Bella once again

---

1. https://books2read.com/u/3JZ6nX

2. https://books2read.com/u/3JZ6nX

helps Jax Hastings, the town constable and her childhood friend, investigate. As they pursue answers, Bella and Jax find several suspects who might have wanted to make the victim suffer for his lethal arrogance.

Read more at https://www.dslangbooks.com.

Also by D.S. Lang

Arabella Stewart Historical Mysteries
A Precarious Homecoming
A Lingering Shadow
A Lethal Arrogance
A Baffling Absence
A Fatal Reunion
A Surreptitious Undertaking
A Treacherous Accusation
An Uncertain Ceremony
Arabella Stewart Historical Mysteries Boxed Set 1
Arabella Stewart Historical Mysteries-Books 5-8

Doro Banyon Historical Mysteries
The Catalogued Corpse

Watch for more at https://www.dslangbooks.com.

About the Author

D.S. Lang started making up stories to entertain herself as an only child, and she is still making them up. Now, she puts them in writing!

After obtaining Bachelor's and Master's degrees in Education, D.S. worked as a golf shop manager, teacher (junior high, high school and college), program manager, tutor and mentor. She has a lifelong love of history and often gets sidetracked on research when she should be writing.

When she is away from the computer, D.S. enjoys reading, swimming, spending time with family and friends, and walking her dog Izzy.

Read more at https://www.dslangbooks.com.